THE MADAME

Power. Control. Survival.

B.C. JONES

A Dark Romance Novel

Content Advisory

This book contains themes and scenes that may be distressing to some readers.

Topics include, but are not limited to:

- Human trafficking
- Sexual abuse (graphic references)
- Violence and physical assault
- Sexual Violence
- BDSM/ Kink
- Forced Proximity/Captivity
- Substance abuse-Drugging without Consent
- Danger to Children
- Sexual assault of a minor
- Psychological trauma and PTSD
- Emotional manipulation
- Dark romantic themes and morally complex characters

Reader discretion is advised.

If any of these topics may be triggering for you, please proceed with care.

Content Warning: This book contains themes that may be distressing to some readers, including references to violence, trauma, and abuse. Reader discretion is advised.

First Edition

Cover design by B.C. Jones
Interior formatting by B.C. Jones

ISBN: 979-8-9954082-0-8

Published by B.C. Jones

Table of Contents

Prologue

Cosette

I don't remember running out of that door. I don't remember when I started running.

I just remember that I didn't stop. Someone left the door open for me. Told me what to do. So I did exactly that.

My lungs burn. My legs ache. Every breath feels like it's scraping my throat raw, but I keep moving anyway—bare feet slamming against pavement, then dirt, then something uneven scrapes against my foot that nearly sends me down.

I don't fall. I don't dare.

I can't.

There are voices behind me. Dogs barking.

Distant.

Closer than I want them to be.

"Find her you fucking idiots!"

My chest tightens.

Not from exhaustion.

From recognition. I hear his voice. The one that will haunt me forever.

I don't look back.

I learned that early.

Looking back slows you down.

Looking back gets you caught. Gets you punished. Not again! Not ever!

The air is cold against my skin. Too cold. I didn't have time to grab anything—no shoes, no jacket, nothing but the thin see-through fabric clinging to me that those disgusting men made me wear and the sound of my own pulse pounding in my ears.

I focus on that instead.

The rhythm.

The movement.

Forward.

Always forward.

Seventeen.

That's what I am. I hope I didn't skip a birthday year. It was hard to keep track when I wasn't given access to a clock or calendar.

Old enough to know better.

Young enough that they thought I wouldn't make it far.

They were wrong.

A branch snaps somewhere behind me.

Too close. Shit!

I push harder.

My foot slips on the blood—gravel shifting beneath me, but I catch myself, barely, palms scraping against the ground before I force myself upright again.

Pain shoots up my arm.

I ignore it.

Pain means nothing right now.

There's a road ahead.

I can see it now.

Faint reflectors.

Empty.

Lit just enough by a flickering streetlight that hums like it's barely holding on.

Freedom doesn't look like I thought it would.

It looks… quiet.

Uncertain.

I don't know what I was expecting. Maybe a nearby gas station or something.

I reach it anyway.

My legs almost give out the second I step onto the pavement.

Almost.

I stagger forward, scanning—left, right, nothing but darkness stretching in both directions.

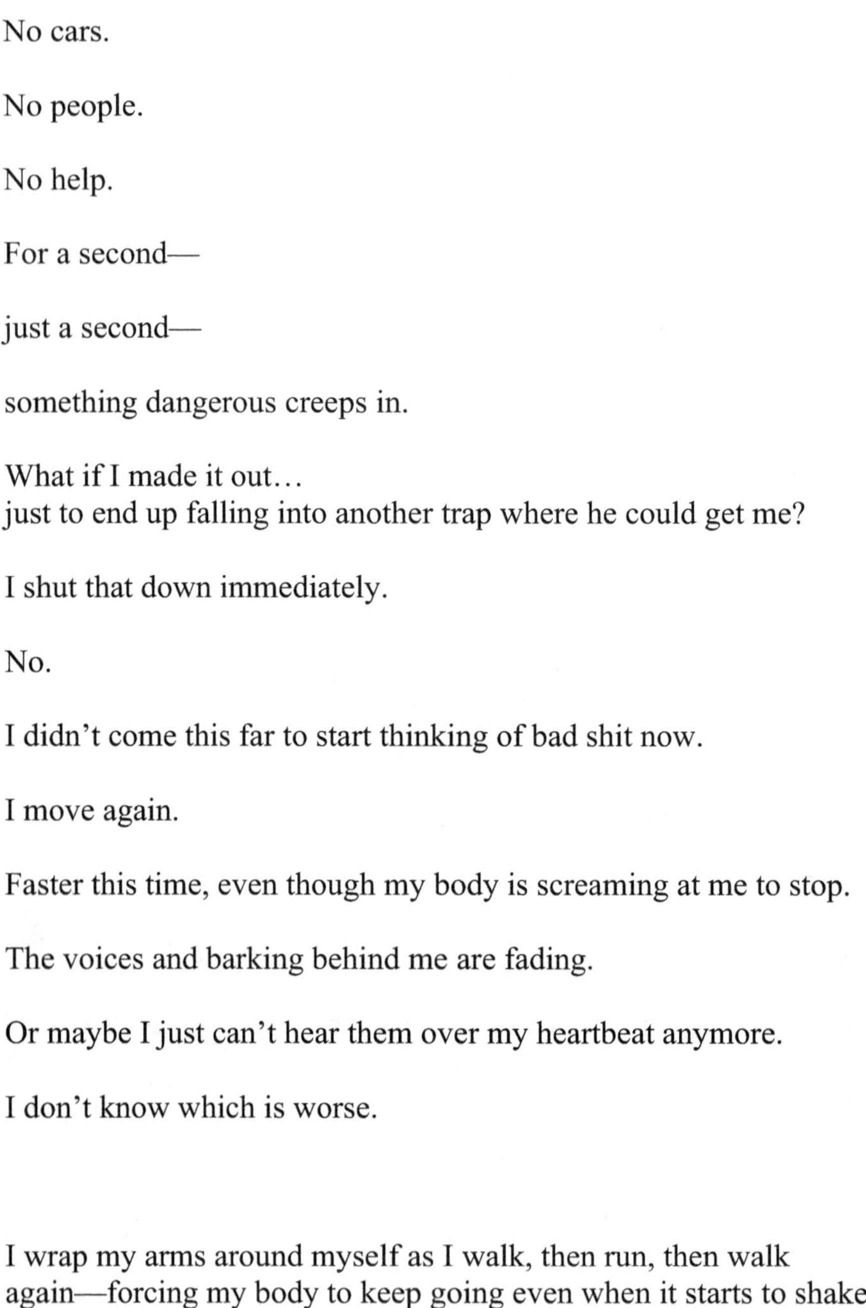

No cars.

No people.

No help.

For a second—

just a second—

something dangerous creeps in.

What if I made it out…
just to end up falling into another trap where he could get me?

I shut that down immediately.

No.

I didn’t come this far to start thinking of bad shit now.

I move again.

Faster this time, even though my body is screaming at me to stop.

The voices and barking behind me are fading.

Or maybe I just can’t hear them over my heartbeat anymore.

I don’t know which is worse.

I wrap my arms around myself as I walk, then run, then walk again—forcing my body to keep going even when it starts to shake.

I don’t know where I’m going.

I don't know who I can trust.

I don't know what happens next.

But I know one thing.

I'm not going back.

Not to him.

Not to that place.

The streetlight flickers again as I pass beneath it, casting my shadow long and thin across the pavement.

For a second, it doesn't look like me.

Good.

Because the girl they took—

the one who didn't know how to fight, how to think, how to endure—

She doesn't exist anymore. That girl is dead, along with her innocence. That existence will do it to you.

I slow just enough to catch my breath, pressing my hand against my chest as I look out into the darkness ahead. I stick close to the shadows. I hope my bloodied feet aren't leaving a trail. If they are, I don't know what else to do.

The darkness. It's wide.

Endless.

Terrifying.

And for the first time—

I realize something that almost feels like relief.

No one is coming to save me.

Good.

I don't need them to.

I take one more breath, then I keep moving.

Because whatever happens next—

Whatever I have to become to survive it—I will.

Chapter One

Cosette

By midnight, The Dungeon is full.

Not crowded. Never crowded.

There's a difference.

Crowded is sloppy. Cheap. Unmanaged.

Full means every table is booked, every room is spoken for, and every person inside knows they're exactly where they begged to be.

I stand on the upper level with one hand resting against the railing, looking down at the floor I built from the ground up—or maybe from the wreckage up. Depends on the day.

From up here, the place looks the way I intended it to.

Low light. Velvet. Gold. Deep shadows that soften everything just enough to make people feel braver than they are anywhere else. The music is loud enough to drown out erotic noises but not so loud that you can't flirt with the person next to you. Bodies melding together in sensual movements. Men and women are being walked over to various parts of the club for more "personal" time.

The Dungeon isn't a free-for-all, despite what people assume when they hear the name. It's curated. Structured. Safe.

That last part matters most.

People come here because they want freedom. Freedom to choose. Freedom to explore all of their naughty desires. Freedom from judgmental eyes. They stay because I make sure freedom doesn't come at the expense of dignity. Unless they want it to. But again, that's freedom of choice.

Below me, laughter rises from one of the private lounge sections. At the bar, glasses catch the light in soft flashes. Near the stage, one of the dancers glides to a seated couple with the kind of sexy confidence that can't be faked. She walks over, naked, with rhinestones glued to certain parts of her body that accentuate her curves. She bends over and starts twerking. Smacking her ass and looking over her shoulder. Oh, she's drawing them in. Everyone is watching. The dancer, Hazel, knows her audience, and she doesn't disappoint. She turns her body around and walks over to the woman who is in her pantsuit with the shirt unbuttoned, revealing her luscious breasts. She must have come over straight from work. The woman is panting like she wants to reach out and touch Hazel. The man begins to touch his already rock-hard dick through his pants. He knows that no nudity is allowed on the main floor except in the private rooms for playtime. He's watching intently as Hazel props one leg on the woman's shoulder and proceeds to roll her hips up and down, giving the woman a nice view of her pussy.

The woman brings out her phone. At first glance, it looks as if she's texting someone. But here at The Dungeon, cash isn't thrown at the dancers and performers as if they're performing monkeys. Money is transferred. That way, the funds get put into an account in which the dancer gets paid for the time they danced or put on a special performance for the members. Hazel finishes with the couple and winks at them as she walks back to the stage. I notice the man pulling the woman into one of the private rooms. She goes willingly. No doubt, they both need a release.

The club is alive, but never chaotic.

Exactly how I like it.

"Tell me you're admiring your kingdom and not dissociating."

Antoinette's voice slides in beside me, dry and familiar.

I glance over. "You could kill a wet dream, you know that?"

She smiles, completely unbothered. "I could create some, too. It's one of my better qualities."

Antoinette is wearing a black sleek dress with a white bralette peeping through, sharp heels, hair in a perfect bun with a red lip. She looks like she belongs in a boardroom and a bad decision at the same time, which is probably why people underestimate her. She's known as 'Kitty' here at the Dungeon. But to me, she's my best friend.

I learned better than to underestimate her years ago.

She hands me a tablet. "Quarterly membership renewals are up twelve percent. VIP applications are getting ridiculous. One man sent a handwritten letter and a bottle of eighteen-year Scotch."

I take the tablet, scanning the numbers. "Did you keep the Scotch?"

"Please. I'm not above a bribe, just selective about it."

A smile tugs at my mouth before I can stop it. "And the letter?"

"He used the phrase *sensual sanctuary* twice."

I hand the tablet back. "Reject him on principle."

"Already did."

"That's why I keep you."

She touches a hand to her chest. "Is that affection?"

"Don't get emotional. It's ugly on you."

Her laugh is quiet, but real. That's the thing about Antoinette, or Nette, as I sometimes call her—she knows when to keep things light and when to read the room before I do. She's my assistant on paper, but that's never been the whole truth. She's my bestie, my second set of eyes, and occasionally the only person in the building willing to tell me when I'm being a bitch.

An important role. A dangerous one, but so necessary.

Her gaze shifts to the floor below. "Everything's smooth so far. Security's done a full sweep. The west lounge requested another bottle of champagne, and one of the new members tried to ask Sasha if 'respect' was a flexible guideline."

I sigh. "And?"

Antoinette's expression turns bland. "And now he's outside."

"Good."

Respect isn't optional here. None of the rules are.

People assume an exclusive club like mine runs on temptation. It doesn't. It runs on boundaries.

Staff do not fraternize with members. No exceptions.

Respect is non-negotiable.

Protection is required during all play.

And if anyone decides those rules don't apply to them, they lose access to this place immediately.

Simple. Clean. Effective.

That's how people stay safe. That's how trust is built.

And trust, I've learned, is a far more valuable currency than desire.

I look back down at the main floor. One of the attendants passes through the crowd with a tray of drinks, unhurried and composed. Near the far wall, a pair of members is being escorted toward one of the private rooms after a quiet check-in with floor staff.

No fear. No pressure. No spectacle.

Just consent, privacy, freedom, and discretion.

The way it should be.

“Do you ever think about taking a night off?” Antoinette asks.

I turn to her slowly. “Do you ever think about minding your business?”

“Constantly. I just choose not to.”

“That tracks.”

She leans against the railing beside me. “I’m serious, Cosette. You’ve been here every night this week.”

“This is my business.”

“You say that like the place catches fire the second you leave.”

“It might.”

She gives me a look. “You’re not that irreplaceable.”

I lift a brow. “That sounded rude.”

“It was meant to be reassuring.”

“Interesting strategy.”

She shrugs. “I work with what I have.”

I should tell her she's annoying. I usually do.

Instead, I let my gaze drift back over the club, soaking in the familiar rhythm of it. For most people, this place is indulgence wrapped in secrecy. For me, it's something simpler.

Proof.

Proof that what happened to me didn't get the last word.

Proof that I can build something beautiful without letting it become dangerous.

Proof that there are parts of desire that don't have to come with fear attached to them.

Most nights, that's enough.

Tonight, though—

A sharp burst of laughter from the floor below cuts through my thoughts, and something inside me tightens before I can stop it.

Not because of the sound itself.

Because for half a second, my body doesn't know where I am.

A locked room.
A laugh outside the door.
The scrape of a chair against concrete.

I go still.

It's brief. So brief that no one watching me from across the room would catch it.

But Antoinette isn't across the room.

"You with me?" she asks, quieter now.

I exhale once through my nose. "Unfortunately."

Her expression softens, though not enough to pity me. She knows better than that, too. Antoinette knows some of my story. She had a relative who went through a similar experience but never made it out unscathed. I guess we all have scars to bear.

"You want to step into your office for a minute?"

"No."

Too fast.

I soften it a second later. "I'm fine."

Antoinette says nothing, which is usually how I know she thinks I'm lying.

I appreciate that she doesn't push. It's one of the reasons she's still here.

Below us, one of the staff members says something that makes a group near the bar laugh again, and this time it lands where it should. Present. Harmless. Real.

I straighten slightly.

"Any issues with the new security rotation?" I ask.

She studies me for a beat before answering. "No. Hulk's been all over it."

Of course he has.

As if summoned by name alone, Hulk appears at the edge of the lower level, broad shoulders cutting through the crowd without effort. At six foot eight, he's hard to miss. At his size, people tend to assume intimidation is the point.

It isn't.

Not entirely.

What makes him good at his job isn't the muscle. It's the patience. The restraint. The way he can scan a room in three seconds and know who belongs, who's nervous, and who's about to become a problem.

He glances up, catches my eye, and gives one short nod.

Everything secure.

I nod back once.

Message received.

Antoinette follows my line of sight. "He scared two applicants just by opening the front door earlier."

"That saved us time."

She smirks. "You're impossible."

"And yet."

"And yet I'm still here."

"There's still time to make better choices."

She laughs again, then checks something on her tablet. "Speaking of choices, I approved the final interviews for the new bar hire."

I look at her. "You did what?"

Her mouth curves. “Relax.”

“Never.”

“The last head bartender left, remember? Voluntarily. Because apparently ‘I don’t like being watched by rich people with unusual hobbies’ is now a career boundary.”

“That sounds fair, actually.”

“I know. I wished him well.”

I fold my arms. “And you hired someone without running it by me first?”

“Interviewed,” she corrects. “Not hired.”

“That’s a very important distinction to you right now, isn’t it?”

“Extremely.”

I stare at her until she smiles wider.

Then I sigh. “Tell me.”

“He’s experienced. Quiet. Doesn’t seem easily rattled.”

“That describes half the people who lie well.”

“True,” she says. “But this one’s interesting.”

I narrow my eyes slightly. “Interesting is not a hiring qualification.”

“It is when the bar has been boring me.”

I laugh once, low and brief. “That sounds like a you problem.”

“It usually is.”

She taps her tablet, then turns it so I can see the profile. Minimal employment history. Enough experience to be credible. Not enough to say much. I don't love that.

I love the headshot even less.

Not just because he's attractive, though he is in an annoyingly deliberate kind of way.

Because something about his face unsettles me immediately.

Not familiarity.

Something sharper than that.

Instinct.

"Name?" I ask.

"Antonio. Goes by Angel."

I look at the photo again.

Blue eyes. Dimples. Shaved head. Tattoo sleeve on one arm. Tall as hell and muscular, but not overly so. Steady expression. The kind of face that doesn't give anything away unless it wants to.

"No last name?"

"Not one he felt like advertising, apparently."

"How charming."

Antoinette tips the tablet back toward herself. "I can keep looking if you want."

"No," I say, still staring at the floor below, even though I'm not really seeing it now. "Schedule the interview."

Her brow lifts slightly. "Tonight?"

"If he's serious, he'll be available."

That earns me a knowing look. "And if he isn't?"

"Then he's not a fit."

Antoinette taps a note into the tablet. "Done."

The music shifts below us, smooth and low, and the room seems to exhale with it. For a moment, everything settles back into place—the glow, the movement, the soft weight of a hundred private desires contained neatly inside the walls I built to hold them.

I should feel satisfied.

I usually do.

Instead, there's a strange little prickle at the base of my neck. The kind that tells me the night is about to tip in some direction I didn't plan for.

I hate that feeling.

Mostly because it's rarely wrong.

Antoinette glances at me again. "You're doing that thing."

"What thing?"

"The one where you pretend your instincts aren't already three steps ahead of everyone else's."

"That's not a thing."

"It absolutely is."

I tilt my head. “Do you ever get tired of narrating me back to myself?”

“Not once.”

“Disturbing.”

She grins. “You love me.”

I give her a flat look. “Careful. That sounded sincere.”

“Fine,” she says. “You tolerate me in a way that borders on emotional dependency.”

“That’s more accurate.”

“Much.”

Her smile fades just enough for me to know she’s about to ask a real question.

“You okay for tonight?”

I could lie.

I almost do.

Then I look out over The Dungeon again—the warm haze over the velvet seating, the attentive staff, the steady movement of a place that works because every person inside it understands the line between freedom and carelessness.

This place is many things.

But it is never unsafe.

And for tonight, that has to be enough.

“I’m good,” I tell her.

This time, it’s close enough to the truth that she lets it go.

“Great,” she says lightly. “Then try not to terrify the new bartender.”

“No promises.”

“That’s my girl.”

I roll my eyes, but she’s already walking away, tablet in hand, heels clicking softly as she disappears into the private corridor.

Below me, the club keeps breathing.

Somewhere near the far end of the room, a member laughs again. Someone at the bar raises a glass. A performer slips past in a shimmer of dark silk and confidence.

And I stand there for one more moment, looking down at the life I made out of everything that should have destroyed me.

Then I turn and head for my office.

If Antonio wants to work in my club, he can come explain himself to me directly.

And if the feeling in my gut means anything at all—

This interview is going to be a problem.

Chapter Two

Antonio

I notice her before anyone says her name.

That's the first problem.

I've worked in places that pretend to be exclusive.

This isn't one of them.

You can tell within seconds whether a space runs on illusion or intention. Most lean on illusion—dim lighting, overpriced bottles, the suggestion of sex and desire without any real control behind it.

This place is different.

Everything here is deliberate.

The way people move. The way staff circulate without hovering. The way no one crosses a line they can't see—but somehow understands.

That doesn't happen by accident.

That comes from one person.

Her.

She's above it all—literally.

Upper level. One hand resting against the railing, looking down at the room like she's reading it, not admiring it. No theatrics.

No need.

She doesn't belong to the space. She defines it.

I keep my hands moving behind the bar—polishing, aligning, adjusting bottles that don't need adjusting, per Kitty's instructions. Keeps me grounded. Keeps me from staring.

Doesn't stop me from watching. I see it all. The couple to the left kissing. The couple to the right getting a lap dance from a dancer who's grinding her naked pussy in front of them.

She doesn't look at anyone for long, but I can tell she sees everything.

Nothing slips past her. Good thing she can't see me looking up at her from my viewpoint. And what a sight she makes.

That's the second problem.

"Try not to make it obvious."

The voice comes from my left. One of the bar staff, already comfortable enough to offer commentary I didn't ask for.

I sigh. I don't need some piece of shit clocking my every move. "And you are?"

"Myles. But my club name is Mouse".

I laugh at that. But 'Mouse' doesn't look amused.

"Did you choose it or was it given to you?"

"It was a name given to me in high school before working out became my obsession."

Yeah, no shit, because this guy was all lean muscle. I didn't do too badly myself, either. But my physique comes from a mix of old-world Italian genes and my past life. You tend to bulk up by eating good food and using your body for various jobs. I guess it helped looking this way when our club uniform was black dress pants, a belt, and black dress shoes. No shirts allowed, especially for the bartenders. We could wear a tie, but it was optional.

I turn away from him. Enough chit chat. "I'm working."

"Sure," he says. "Just remember where you are."

I glance at him now. "And where's that?"

He nods upward, subtle but intentional. "Her house."

Right.

"And the rules?" he adds. "They're not suggestions."

"I don't deal in suggestions," I say.

He studies me for a second. There's something off about him, but I can't quite put my finger on it. I don't have time for this shit. This job is supposed to be simple. Watch operations and walk away.

He gives a short nod, like that answer was acceptable enough, before moving on.

I go back to the bar.

But I'm already cataloging what matters.

Staff doesn't cross lines with members or her.

Respect isn't optional.

Protection is mandatory.

And anything outside of that?

Handled immediately.

Clean system.

No gray areas.

I respect that.

I glance up again.

She's still there—but now she's talking to someone.

The woman beside her. The one I did my pre-employment screening with—sharp, composed, watching the room while holding a tablet—is close enough to stand beside her without hesitation. No, No. That won't do. I want her to talk to me. But how would that even be possible? Follow the rules, Antonio. I have to keep things simple. Seamless. What the fuck is wrong with me? She's just a woman. A beautiful one. But nothing more.

The woman beside her is trusted. Important. I need to stay on her good side.

She says something that makes Madame's mouth curve slightly.

Not a full smile.

But enough.

That's the third problem. Damn. She's fucking gorgeous. That smile, even a slight one, is enough to make my mouth water. Those lips would look pretty wrapped around my… Fuck! I'm not going to finish that thought.

She's just not what I expected.

"Angel."

The name lands in my direction.

I turn slightly.

Another staff member—this one younger—nods toward a waiting guest. "They're asking for you."

Right.

I step forward, slipping into the role without thinking.

"Evening," I say, voice smooth, neutral.

The guest smiles, already at ease. "I heard you're the one to ask for something… specific."

"I can make most things happen," I reply.

Keep it professional.

Keep it clean.

Keep it separate.

That's how this works.

I mix the drink, precise and efficient, sliding it across to them without unnecessary conversation.

No lingering.

No blur.

But even as I step back—

My attention shifts again.

She's looking at me.

Not casually.

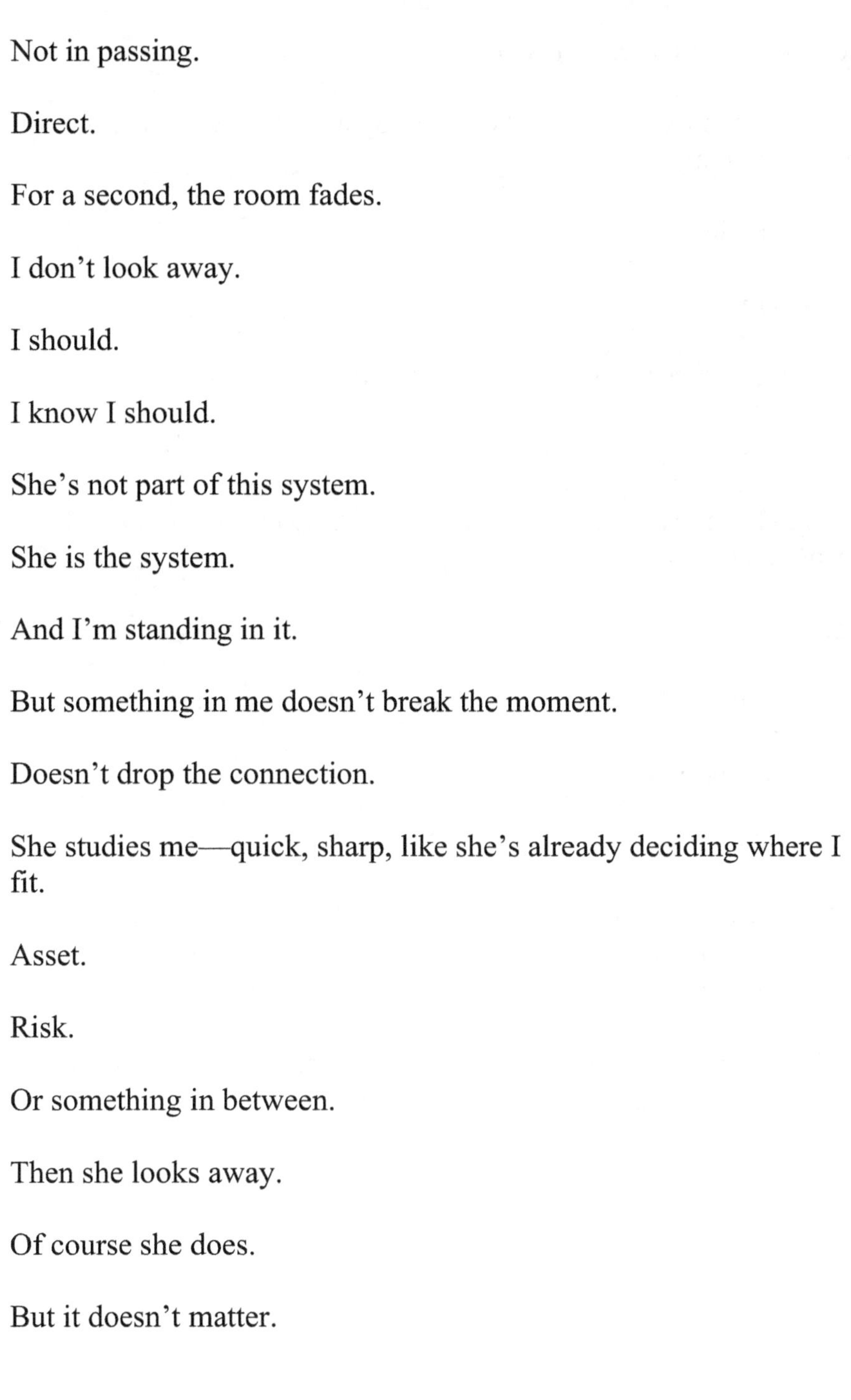

Not in passing.

Direct.

For a second, the room fades.

I don’t look away.

I should.

I know I should.

She’s not part of this system.

She is the system.

And I’m standing in it.

But something in me doesn’t break the moment.

Doesn’t drop the connection.

She studies me—quick, sharp, like she’s already deciding where I fit.

Asset.

Risk.

Or something in between.

Then she looks away.

Of course she does.

But it doesn’t matter.

The moment has already happened.

“Careful,” Mouse mutters as he passes again. “That’s Madame you’re watching.”

I almost smile.

“I’m aware.”

I reach for another bottle, more for something to do than necessity.

This isn’t supposed to happen.

I need to keep my head down. Do the job. Stay out of anything that doesn’t concern me.

That’s how you move forward.

That’s how you don’t get pulled back into things you left behind.

But the second I walked in here—

something shifted.

And now I’m standing behind a bar, watching a woman I shouldn’t be watching, already calculating how close I can get without crossing a line.

That’s not simple. I always cross the line. Lines don’t exist to me. They’re invitations.

That’s a problem.

“Angel.”

Different voice this time.

Female.

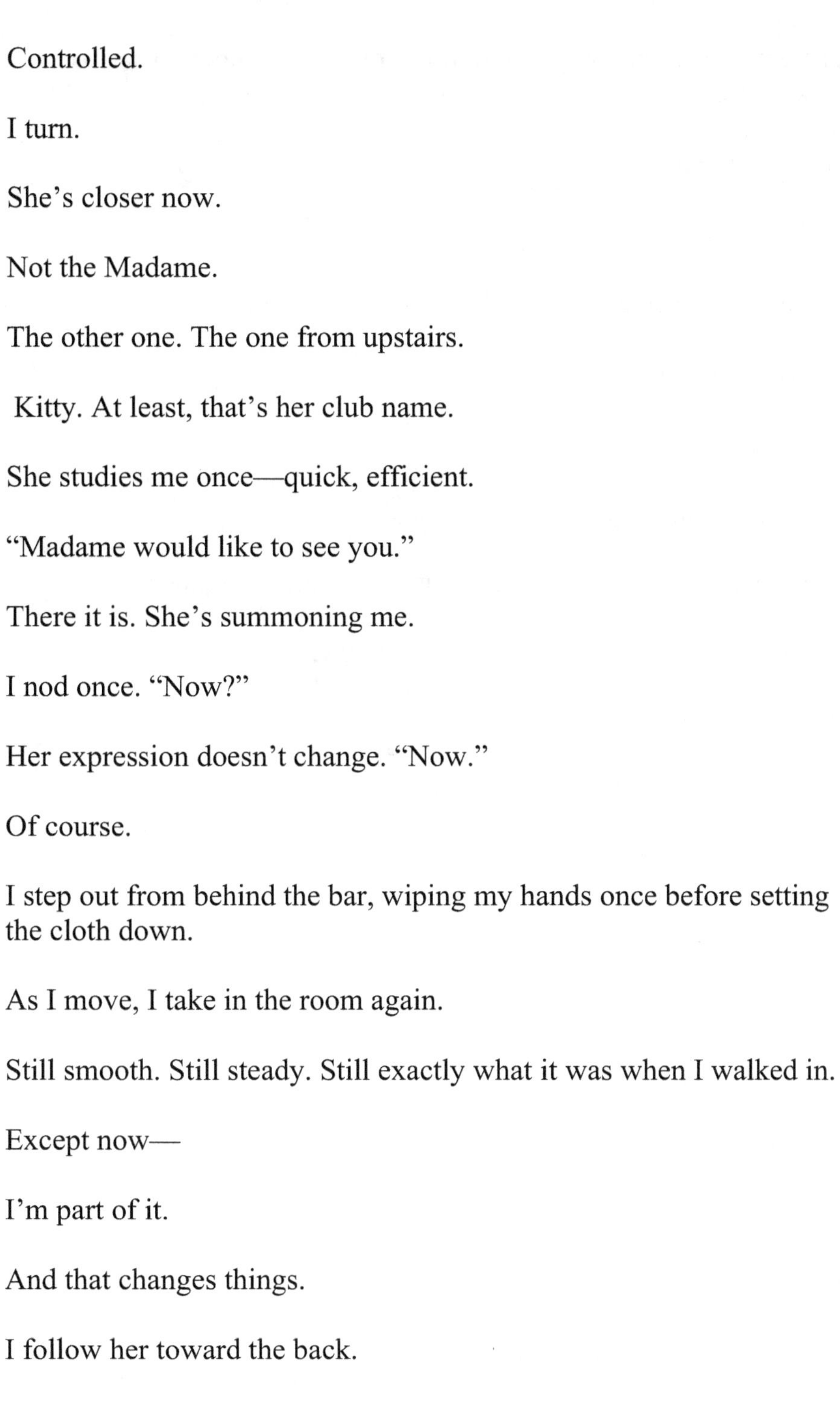

Controlled.

I turn.

She's closer now.

Not the Madame.

The other one. The one from upstairs.

Kitty. At least, that's her club name.

She studies me once—quick, efficient.

"Madame would like to see you."

There it is. She's summoning me.

I nod once. "Now?"

Her expression doesn't change. "Now."

Of course.

I step out from behind the bar, wiping my hands once before setting the cloth down.

As I move, I take in the room again.

Still smooth. Still steady. Still exactly what it was when I walked in.

Except now—

I'm part of it.

And that changes things.

I follow her toward the back.

The entrance is subtle—easy to miss if you don't know what you're looking for.

Hidden in plain sight.

Makes sense.

As soon as we step through, the atmosphere shifts.

Less performance.

More purpose.

"Try not to stare," she says over her shoulder.

I let out a quiet breath. "That seems to be a recurring theme."

She almost smiles. "You'll understand why."

We stop at a door.

She knocks once, then opens it without waiting.

"Madame," she says.

And steps aside.

I walk in.

No distance this time.

No shadows to soften anything.

Just her.

She doesn't greet me.

Doesn't offer anything unnecessary.

Just watches.

I return the favor.

She's sharper up close.

More precise. Even more beautiful. Definitely not wearing a bra in that red pantsuit.

Like every detail about her is intentional—even the things that look effortless.

"Angel," she says.

My club name sounds different coming from her.

More… deliberate.

I incline my head slightly. "Madame."

A pause.

Then, she steps forward just enough to close the space between us by half.

"Let's be clear about something," she says.

Straight to it. I respect that.

"You work here," she continues, "which means you follow my rules."

There it is.

"Of course," I say.

Her gaze doesn't move.

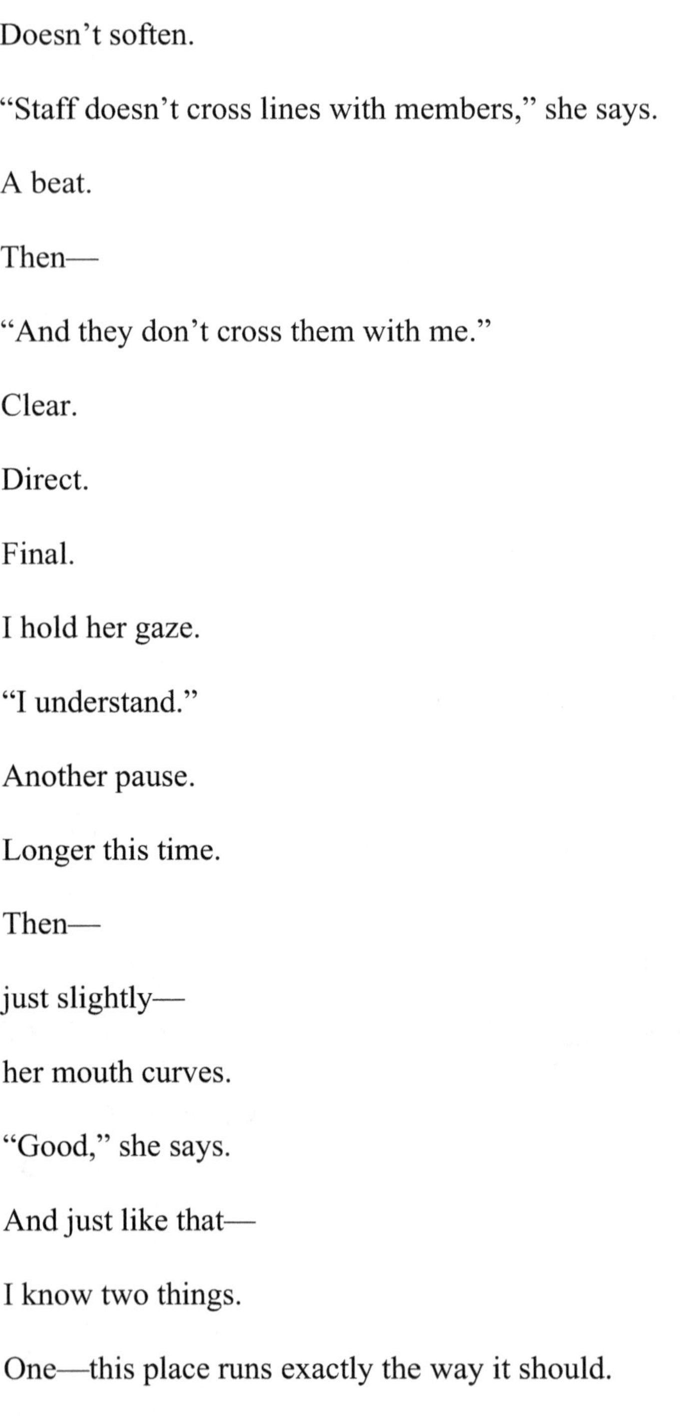

Doesn’t soften.

“Staff doesn’t cross lines with members,” she says.

A beat.

Then—

“And they don’t cross them with me.”

Clear.

Direct.

Final.

I hold her gaze.

“I understand.”

Another pause.

Longer this time.

Then—

just slightly—

her mouth curves.

“Good,” she says.

And just like that—

I know two things.

One—this place runs exactly the way it should.

And two—she's going to be the problem.

Not the job. Not the rules.

Her.

And the fact that, for the first time in a long time—

I don't mind.

Chapter Three

Cosette

I don't rush interviews.

People usually expect that.

Nerves. Pressure. The need to prove something quickly.

I prefer the opposite.

Silence does more work than questions ever will.

Angel stands across from my desk like he belongs there.

Not comfortably.

But not out of place either.

That's… interesting.

Most people shift under this kind of attention. They fill the space with unnecessary words, over-explain, and try to read me before they understand who they're dealing with.

He doesn't.

He waits.

That alone earns him a few points. He's not trying to get off on his good looks. And he does look good. I must admit.

I lean back slightly in my chair, crossing one leg over the other, letting the quiet stretch just long enough to see what he does with it.

Nothing.

Not a single fidget.

Not even a glance toward my breasts or any other part of my body. That's new. Who is this guy?

"Do you always walk into new environments as if you've already decided you belong there?" I ask.

A beat.

His mouth curves just slightly. Those fucking dimples. I refuse to look at them…or his lips.

"Only when I'm sure I can do the job."

Confident.

Not arrogant.

There's a difference. Nice touch.

"And you're sure?" I ask.

"Yes."

No hesitation.

No elaboration.

I study him for another moment.

"Experience?"

"Enough."

That almost makes me smile.

"'Enough' isn't an answer," I say.

"It usually is," he replies.

There it is.

A small spark of something—sharp, controlled. He's not new to this. He's true to it.

I tap my fingers once against the desk, slow, deliberate.

"Tell me why you want to work here."

This is where most people fail.

They talk about money. Atmosphere. Curiosity.

They say what they think I want to hear.

He doesn't rush it.

Of course he doesn't.

"I prefer places that know what they are," he says finally.

I tilt my head slightly.

"Meaning?"

"Meaning this place doesn't pretend," he says. "There are rules. People follow them. And the ones who don't… don't stay."

Accurate.

He continues, voice steady.

"Most places like this lose control because they try to cater to everyone. This one doesn't. You intentionally cater to the needs of your members. Not the general public."

I watch him carefully now.

Not just what he's saying—

how he's saying it. Is that a slight accent I hear?

"And that appeals to you?" I ask.

"It makes sense," he says.

I let the silence settle again, then stand.

He tracks the movement without turning his head too quickly.

Again—

controlled. Very Impressive.

I walk around the desk slowly, stopping a few feet in front of him. Cleavage on full display.

Close enough to shift the dynamic.

Not close enough to blur it, no matter how badly I would love to.

Where the hell did that come from?

"You understand what kind of place this is?" I ask.

His gaze holds mine.

"Yes."

"Say it."

A flicker of something crosses his expression.

"This is a space where people come to explore their needs and desires without being exploited, without being judged," he says. "Where boundaries are enforced, not suggested. Yet there is freedom in a way that most people have not experienced."

Good.

"And your role?" I press.

"To provide a service," he says. "Nothing more."

There's a slight emphasis on the last part.

Intentional.

I let my gaze sweep over him once, slow and assessing. Yes, I'm shamelessly looking him over. He's sexy. But those damn blue eyes… I could get lost in them. He's well over six feet tall. Broad shoulders and lickable abs. There's no time for that. I need to focus. If I don't, he's going to be a serious distraction.

He doesn't shift under my gaze.

Doesn't flinch.

"Staff doesn't cross lines with members," I say.

"I'm aware."

"And they don't cross them with me."

A pause.

"I understand, Madame."

The way he says it—

Seductive. Like a caress.

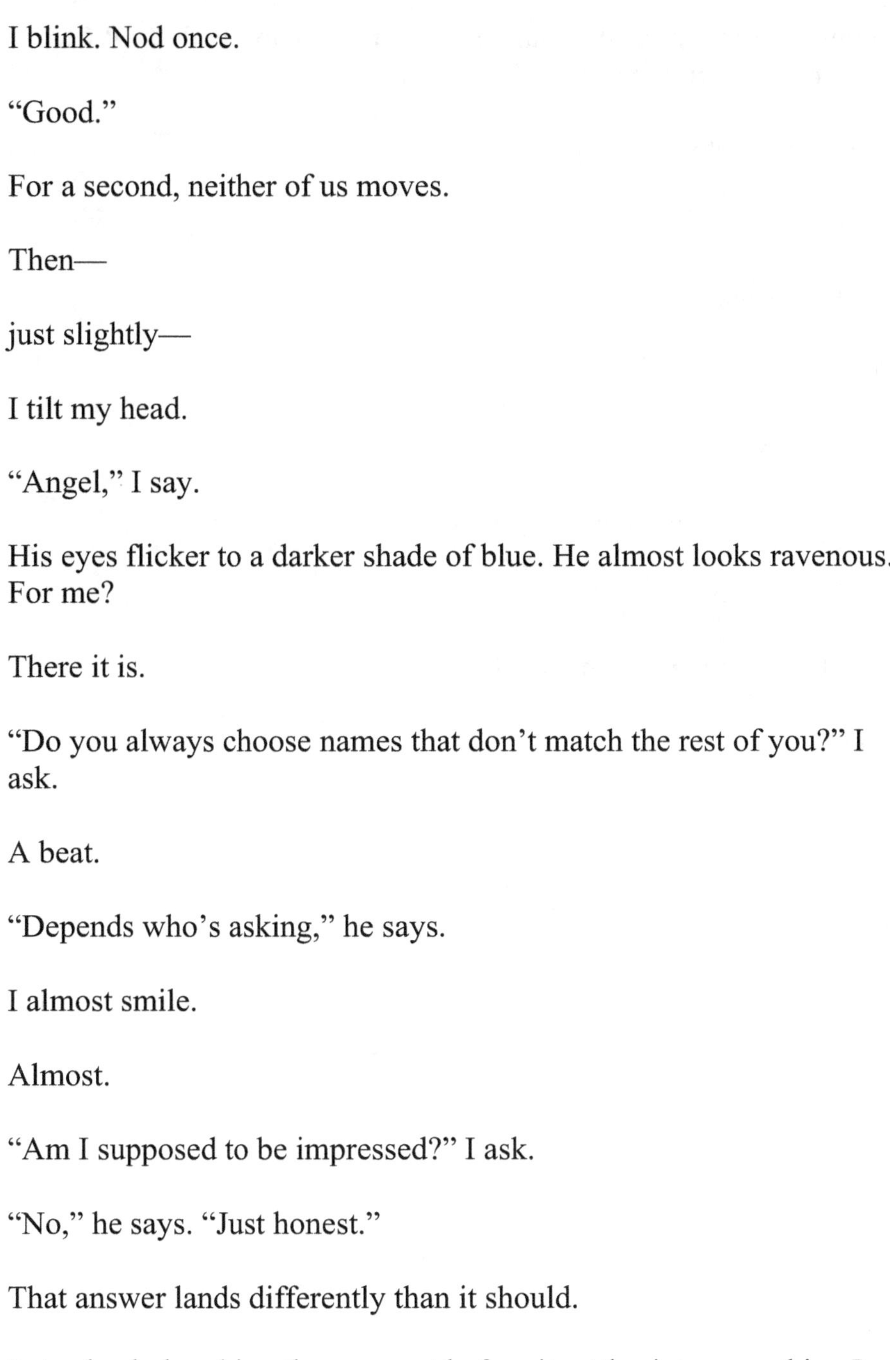

I blink. Nod once.

“Good.”

For a second, neither of us moves.

Then—

just slightly—

I tilt my head.

“Angel,” I say.

His eyes flicker to a darker shade of blue. He almost looks ravenous. For me?

There it is.

“Do you always choose names that don’t match the rest of you?” I ask.

A beat.

“Depends who’s asking,” he says.

I almost smile.

Almost.

“Am I supposed to be impressed?” I ask.

“No,” he says. “Just honest.”

That answer lands differently than it should.

I step back, breaking the moment before it settles into something I don’t want to name yet.

“Your references are minimal,” I say, returning to my desk. Where it’s safe. My body feels warmer than it should.

“I prefer it that way.”

“I don’t.”

Another pause.

Then—

“I can give you a trial shift,” I say.

Antoinette is going to have opinions about that.

She always does.

Angel doesn’t react immediately.

Good.

“Understood,” he says.

“You’ll follow the structure already in place,” I continue. “You’ll take direction from senior staff. And you will not improvise outside of your role.”

“Yes, Madame.”

His tone doesn’t change.

Not submissive.

Not challenging.

Balanced.

I pick up a file, mostly for something to do with my hands. Don't want to walk back over and touch him. I can't go around breaking my own rules.

"Kitty will finalize your schedule."

He nods once.

And then—

He doesn't leave.

I glance up.

"You're still here," I say.

A slight shift in his expression.

Almost amused.

"You didn't dismiss me," he replies.

That—

That gets a real reaction.

A small, unexpected laugh slips out before I can stop it.

I shake my head once. "You're observant."

"I try to be, Madame."

Again. It's the way he says it. Like he wants to kiss me or something. God, I hope he doesn't. The way I'm feeling, I don't know what I'd do if he tried. What the hell is wrong with me? I see nice-looking men all the time. But Angel is making me feel feral. He needs to get the fuck out of my office. Now!

I study him for another second, then nod toward the door.

“You’re dismissed, Angel.”

This time, he moves.

But before he reaches the door—

He pauses.

Just briefly.

Then he looks back.

Deliberate.

“Madame.”

I meet his gaze.

“If I cross a line,” he says, “you’ll tell me.”

Not a question.

I lean back slightly in my chair.

“Yes,” I say.

A beat.

“And you won’t get the chance to do it twice.” Something in his expression sharpens. Something closer to respect.

“Understood.”

Then he leaves. The door closes softly behind him. And just like that—the room feels different.

I exhale slowly, staring at the space he just occupied.

"That was interesting."

I don't turn.

"Eavesdropping is a bad habit," I say.

Antoinette steps fully into the room anyway, completely unbothered.

"It's not eavesdropping if I work here."

"Debatable."

She leans against the wall, arms crossed, watching me with that look I know too well.

The one that says she's already ten steps ahead of whatever I'm about to say.

"Well?" she asks.

"Well, what?"

"Don't do that," she says. "You know exactly what."

I glance back down at the file in front of me, flipping it closed.

"He's competent."

She stares at me.

"That's what we're going with?" she asks.

"It's accurate."

"It's boring."

“I don’t hire for entertainment.”

She pushes off the wall, walking closer.

“No,” she says, “but you do notice when someone isn’t.”

I lift a brow. “Are you analyzing me now?”

“Always.”

I sigh, leaning back in my chair.

“He’s different,” I admit.

“There it is,” she says, satisfied.

“That doesn’t mean anything.”

“It means you noticed.”

I look at her.

“I notice everything.”

She smiles slightly. “Not like that.”

I don’t respond to that because I don’t need to. Instead, I stand, smoothing my hands over the front of my suit.

“We’ll see how he performs,” I say.

Professional. Neutral.

Antoinette watches me for another second, then nods.

“Of course,” she says lightly.

But the look she gives me before she turns away says she knows I'm full of shit.

And the worst part?

I know Angel affected me more than I dare to admit. I need a drink.

Chapter Four

Antonio

Oh, she's asking for it. Begging for it. Damn, I'm in trouble.

I've worked under people who demanded respect.

Loudly. Constantly. Like if they didn't remind you every five minutes, it might disappear.

She doesn't.

That's the first thing that stays with me after I leave her office.

Not what she said. Not even how she said it. It's the fact that she didn't have to try. I actually want to respect her.

I step back behind the bar, sliding into place like I never left. The rhythm of the room hasn't changed. Orders come in. Glasses move. Conversations blur into background noise.

Everything flows.

But I'm not seeing it the same way anymore.

Because now I know who's behind it.

Madame. I glance up without meaning to.

Upper level.

She's back where I first saw her, like she never left.

Of course she is.

Only now, I'm noticing more.

The suit, for one.

Red. Tailored so precisely it doesn't just fit—it defines. Clean lines. Sharp edges. Structured without being stiff. The way she crossed her legs behind that desk. If she'd been wearing a dress, my composure would have slipped.

I should be cold towards her. But I can't. She has no clue who I am, and I'm almost sad that she doesn't. But it's for her own good. For now.

I already made it up in my mind that she will be mine. Not sure how it will happen. Shit! I just met her. It should concern me.

It doesn't.

Because underneath, the animal within me is hungry. And it wants her.

Mmm. Just barely visible when she shifts is a hint of nipple.

Ready for me to nip at.

That detail shouldn't matter. But it does. And that fucking suit. A suit should not be sexy. Does she not know that red is my favorite color? The color of blood. The color of her ass when I'm done having my way with her. It makes me want to growl at the thought.

My jaw tightens slightly as I reach for a glass.

Focus.

Her hair falls in long, dark curls down her back—looser than I expected. Not overly styled. Not rigid. It softens the rest of her without taking anything away from it. Enough to yank on while she begs me to dig into her pussy.

If anything, it makes the contrast sharper.

And her skin—

Mahogany. Smooth. Warm against the low lighting of the room, catching just enough of it to stand out without ever looking like she's trying to.

It's… distracting. Fuck! Everything about her is distracting. Almost painfully so.

I don't like that.

Her eyes find mine again.

Chocolate.

Deep enough that they don't reflect much back.

They take things in instead.

There's a difference between looking at a room and reading it.

She reads everything.

Including me. I know she sees something dangerous in me. Good. She needs to be wary of me.

I hold her gaze for a second.

Then break it.

Not because I have to.

Because I choose to. If I don't….

"Angel."

I turn slightly, already reaching for the next order.

“Two bourbons,” the guest says.

“Of course.”

Routine.

Movement.

Precision.

But my attention keeps splitting.

Back to her.

It’s not just how she looks. It’s what she’s built. Places like this don’t run smoothly by accident. Not at this level. Not with this kind of clientele. There are too many variables. Too many personalities. So much money.

Too many ways things can go wrong.

And yet—nothing here feels unstable.

That’s her.

Every detail.

Years ago, I would have killed for a woman like her. To help run my empire. Bare my children. I don’t even like children like that. My own mother abandoned me. My father was murdered while working for his brother. As an only child growing up in The Life, you only have a few options: Join or die. I have no plans of dying early, even though I’ve come close. Women are a distraction. Pretty ones, but distractions nonetheless. Fuck them, then leave them.

I haven’t forgotten the familiarity I feel every time she’s near. Like I’ve seen her before, but I can’t place her.

She has boundaries for a reason, and they work for her. But for me, it's not the boundaries. It's what I won't do to get close to her. She may want to shoot my dick off if I tried, but once I have her panties in my teeth, she'll come to see that I don't like to play with my food. I will devour every part of her being. Or die trying. Shit! The thought makes my dick rock hard.

This job is going to have to be short-term. I would have loved to try to start my life over here, but with her around, it won't be possible.

Or will it? I could keep a closer eye on her. Not just because I know she's hiding something. It would allow me to make sure no one else is trying to claim her. What's mine is mine. I don't share. Those who touch what is mine won't make it to see their next birthday.

I've seen what happens when people try to control a room through force. It cracks. Always. My uncle has a knack for cracking things. Beautiful things. Young things. The thought makes me see red. No way did I ever think someone would be so depraved that they would do things of that nature. I can't ever go back to that. The Life gives you plenty of jobs that get your hands dirty. But the underground business my uncle runs is beyond anything I could ever think of.

And for a moment, I'm transported back in time.

Dark room. A young girl is chained up to a wall. Blood running down from between her thighs. She has bruises on her face and a gash on her head. A vibrator is connected to her private parts. Her nipples have clamps on them, and she's completely naked. She can't be more than 15 years old. I came upon the room by accident. As soon as one of the guards came in, he looked at me. Recognized who I was.

"Did your uncle send for you?"

"No", I managed to get out. "Who is she?"

"If your uncle didn't send for you, get the fuck out. I have some unfinished business here."

As bile rose in my throat, I walked out of the room without a second glance at the young girl.

That's when I knew. This life wasn't for me. There are lines even I won't cross. Never harm someone who can't defend themselves. An animal. The elderly. Children.

I shake my head from the memory.

I'll never go back to that.

But this?

This is something else.

She's not controlling it.

She understands it.

That's harder.

And—

if I'm being honest—

it's… annoyingly attractive.

I set a glass down a little harder than necessary.

Annoying because I don't need distractions.

Attractive because I recognize what it takes to build something like this.

Discipline.

Awareness.

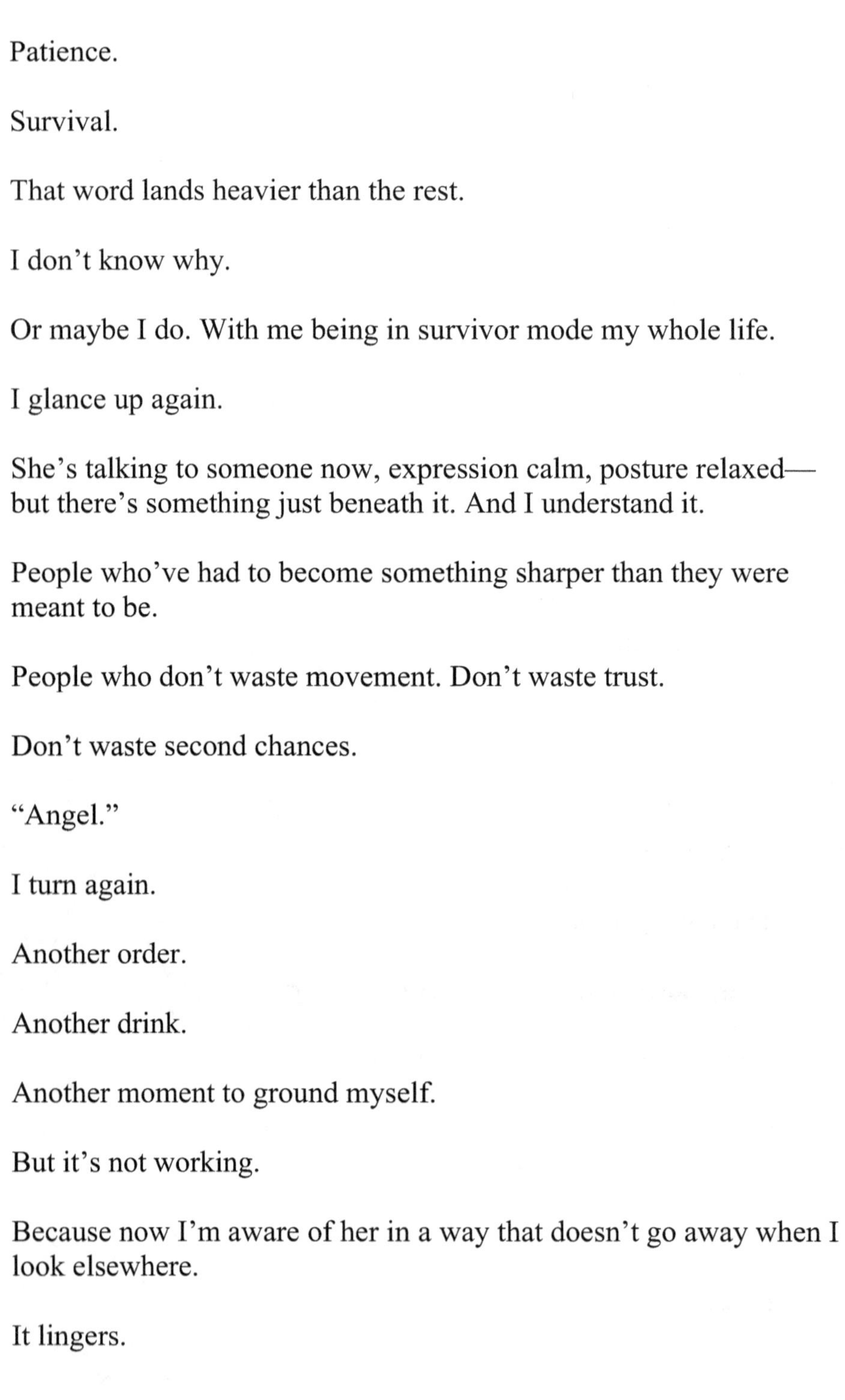

Patience.

Survival.

That word lands heavier than the rest.

I don't know why.

Or maybe I do. With me being in survivor mode my whole life.

I glance up again.

She's talking to someone now, expression calm, posture relaxed—but there's something just beneath it. And I understand it.

People who've had to become something sharper than they were meant to be.

People who don't waste movement. Don't waste trust.

Don't waste second chances.

"Angel."

I turn again.

Another order.

Another drink.

Another moment to ground myself.

But it's not working.

Because now I'm aware of her in a way that doesn't go away when I look elsewhere.

It lingers.

And that’s dangerous. I don’t mix work with anything personal.

I don’t blur lines or make the same mistake twice.

And yet—I’ studying everything about her.

I can already see how this goes wrong.

Not because she’ll let it.

But because I might. I’m already staring at her like a damn idiot.

I exhale slowly, rolling my shoulders once before reaching for the next bottle.

Get through the shift.

Do the job. Watch operations.

Stay where you’re supposed to be.

Simple.

Except—nothing about her feels simple.

And somehow, it makes her even harder to ignore her.

Chapter Five

Cosette

I don't usually watch new hires during their first shift.

That's what management is for.

Structure exists, so I don't have to hover over every detail.

Tonight—

I make an exception.

I take my usual position on the upper level, one hand resting lightly against the railing as I look down over the floor.

Everything is running the way it should.

Measured.

Smooth.

Contained without feeling restricted.

Exactly as designed.

But my attention keeps drifting.

Back to the bar.

To him.

Angel moves like he's done this a hundred times.

Not just the mechanics of it—the pouring, the timing, the way he reads orders before they're fully spoken.

That part can be taught.

It's everything else.

The way he doesn't lean too far into conversation, but doesn't shut it down either.

Balanced.

Intentional.

Annoying.

"You're doing it again."

Antoinette's voice appears beside me like it always does—uninvited and perfectly timed.

"Damn. You must have a tracker on me," I say as I glance at her. "I don't know what you're talking about," I say, turning back around.

"Of course you don't."

She follows my line of sight without asking.

Takes about two seconds to figure it out.

"Mm," she hums. "The new one."

"He's working," I say.

"So are you," she replies.

"I'm observing."

She smiles slightly. "You've been observing him specifically for the last seven minutes."

"I'm thorough."

"You're predictable."

That gets another glance.

"Bitch, please. I'm never predictable."

She lifts a brow. "You hired him on a trial shift after one interview."

"That's not unpredictable. That's efficient."

"That's you being curious."

I don't respond to that.

Because she's not entirely wrong.

Below us, Angel slides a drink across the bar, saying something low enough that I can't hear it—but it earns a small laugh from the woman across from him. His charm knows no bounds. It's effortless.

Not flirtation.

Not performance.

Ease.

That's harder to fake than people think.

"He's good," Antoinette says quietly.

"I know."

"That's not what I meant."

Of course it isn't.

I shift my weight slightly, resting my elbow against the railing now.

"His boundaries are intact," I say. "That's what matters."

"For now."

I glance at her again.

"You're assuming they won't be."

"I'm assuming you'll test them."

I almost smile.

"I don't test employees," I say.

She gives me a look.

"You absolutely do."

"That's different."

"How?"

I pause.

"It's structured," I say finally.

She laughs softly. "Right."

Below us, something shifts near the far end of the bar.

Subtle.

Most people wouldn't notice.

I do.

One of the newer members—early thirties, too comfortable too quickly—leans in closer to one of the staff.

Too close.

The staff member shifts back slightly, polite but firm.

He doesn't take the hint.

I straighten.

"Excuse me," I say, already moving.

Antoinette doesn't follow.

She doesn't need to.

By the time I reach the bar, Hulk is already repositioning, watching the interaction from the side.

Good.

I step in before it escalates.

"Is there a problem?" I ask.

My voice isn't raised.

It doesn't need to be.

The member turns, smile already halfway formed.

"Not at all," he says. "We were just—"

"You were just standing too close to my staff member," I finish.

The smile falters.

"I didn't realize—"

"You don't need to realize," I say calmly. "You need to respect this establishment."

A pause.

The staff member beside him relaxes slightly.

Good.

"I apologize," he says quickly. "I didn't mean—"

"I know," I say.

I hold his gaze just long enough for it to settle.

"But you will correct it."

"Yes, Madame."

He steps back immediately.

Hulk doesn't move.

But he doesn't need to.

I give a single nod, then turn away like the situation no longer exists.

Because it doesn't.

Handled.

As I move back toward the stairs, I feel it before I see it.

His attention.

Angel.

I glance toward the bar.

He’s watching.

Not obviously.

Not in a way anyone else would catch.

But I do.

Of course I do.

I slow slightly as I approach, stopping just short of the bar counter.

“Everything running smoothly?” I ask.

It’s a general question.

His Blue-eyed gaze meets mine.

Steady.

“Yes, Madame.”

Seductive.

I rest my fingers lightly against the edge of the bar.

“Your timing is consistent,” I say. “You’re not over-engaging.”

A pause.

“Is that a compliment?” he asks.

I tilt my head slightly.

“It’s an observation.”

His mouth curves.

"I'll take it," he says.

I shouldn't stay.

I know that.

Instead—

I let my gaze flick briefly to the glass in front of him.

"Make me something," I say.

That gets a reaction.

Subtle.

"Anything specific?" he asks.

"No," I say. "Surprise me."

Antoinette is going to have something to say about this.

I ignore that.

Angel turns, already reaching for a bottle.

I watch him this time.

The way his hands move.

Strong. Precise. Controlled. The way he doesn't rush. Doesn't try to impress. Those big ass biceps.

He finishes, sliding the glass toward me.

Our fingers don't touch.

But they come close enough that I notice.

I lift the glass, taking a small sip.

It's good. Not too strong. Intentional.

I lower it slightly.

"Well?" he asks.

I meet his gaze.

"What's the name of it?"

"Yummy Pussy".

I just blink at him. Caught completely off guard.

"Is that part of the menu?"

"No. It's something I learned around the way."

"Interesting."

"It has just enough Tequila infused with some fruit juices, creating a pretty internal pink color. I thought it might suit your palate."

"You're observant," I say, taking another swallow.

A beat.

"So are you," he replies.

That lingers for a second too long.

I set the glass down.

"Careful, Angel," I say lightly. "Confidence can be mistaken for something else."

His expression doesn't change.

"What would that be?" he asks.

I hold his gaze.

"Assumption."

A pause.

Then—

"I don't assume," he says.

Of course he doesn't.

That's part of the problem. It's like he knows something I don't dare give a voice to.

I straighten slightly, stepping back.

"Good," I say.

A beat.

"Keep it that way."

I turn before the moment can settle into something else.

Because I recognize it.

That shift.

That pull.

And I don’t indulge things that complicate my structure. It’s all I have to keep things, and myself, from falling apart.

As I make my way back toward the stairs, I can feel Antoinette watching me already.

Of course she is.

I don’t look at her until I reach the upper level.

“Well?” she asks.

I pick up my glass again, taking another sip.

“He follows direction,” I say.

She stares at me.

“That’s what we’re calling that?”

I don’t answer.

Because this time—I’m not entirely sure what to call it.

Chapter Six

Antonio

I had her right where I wanted her. I came up with that drink name right on the spot. But the actual mix was on the menu. I laugh at myself.

The way she stood at the bar.

The way she said *surprise me* like it wasn't a challenge—but it was.

Madame doesn't linger. I had to make it count.

She moves. Observes. Corrects. Leaves.

She doesn't stay.

But she did. For me.

I tighten my grip slightly around the glass in my hand, forcing myself to focus on the next order.

Pour.

Slide.

Move.

Routine.

Except my attention keeps pulling back to the same place.

Her.

She's on the lower level tonight. Not above, not removed. Present.

This is my 3rd week on the job. But seeing her every night makes it worth it.

That alone makes the job worthwhile.

People are more aware.

Staff is sharper. Mouse stares at me from afar like he knows what's up. He needs to mind his fucking business before his eyes go missing.

The energy tightens just slightly—not in fear.

In respect.

There she is. In all her glory.

I catch her eye again.

This time—

She doesn't look away.

She walks toward me.

Slow and deliberate.

Hips swaying.

Not for show. Never for show.

My pulse shifts.

Just slightly.

"Angel."

My name again. Like a fucking caress.

That alias. Chosen when I was a teen. Perfect for a man with a black heart.

I lean forward just enough to meet her halfway.

“Madame.”

There’s a pause.

“You’re settling in,” she says.

“I’m doing my job.”

Her gaze sharpens slightly.

“Is that all you’re doing?”

I hold her eyes.

“That depends.”

“On what?”

I let the silence sit for a second.

“On what you’re looking for.”

A flicker.

Not visible to anyone else.

But I catch it.

She steps closer.

Not enough to cross a line.

But close enough to blur it. She's close enough for me to see those chocolate mounds in her suit jacket. She's doing this shit on purpose by now. I catch the scent of her perfume. Something floral, simple yet mouthwatering.

"You should be careful with answers like that," she says quietly.

"I am," I say.

She studies me for a long second.

Then—

"Come with me."

Not a suggestion.

I don't hesitate.

I step out from behind the bar, already aware of the shift in the room as I move.

Mouse and Hulk notice.

Of course they do.

But no one says anything.

Because she gave the order.

I follow her through the floor, past the velvet and low lighting, through the hidden entrance most people never notice.

The moment we cross into the hallway—

everything changes.

Quieter.

More intimate.

She doesn't look back to see if I'm following.

She already knows.

We stop outside a door—a private VIP room.

She opens it without knocking.

Her private space.

I step inside.

The door closes behind me with a soft click.

And for the first time since I walked into this place—

there's no one else watching.

No room to perform.

No reason to pretend.

Just her.

She turns slowly.

No distance now.

No bar between us.

No crowd.

"Do you always follow orders this easily?" she asks.

Her tone is light.

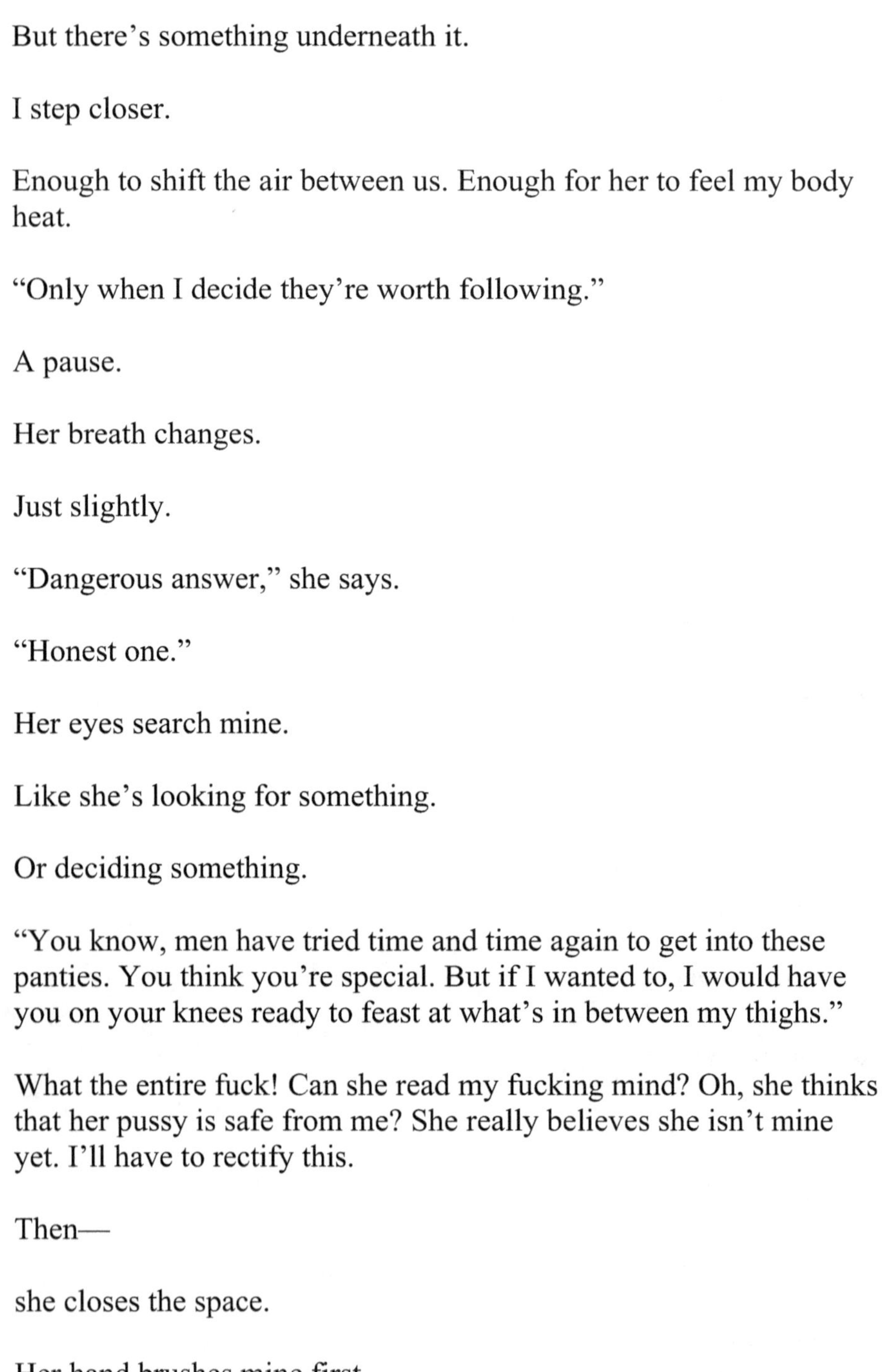

But there's something underneath it.

I step closer.

Enough to shift the air between us. Enough for her to feel my body heat.

"Only when I decide they're worth following."

A pause.

Her breath changes.

Just slightly.

"Dangerous answer," she says.

"Honest one."

Her eyes search mine.

Like she's looking for something.

Or deciding something.

"You know, men have tried time and time again to get into these panties. You think you're special. But if I wanted to, I would have you on your knees ready to feast at what's in between my thighs."

What the entire fuck! Can she read my fucking mind? Oh, she thinks that her pussy is safe from me? She really believes she isn't mine yet. I'll have to rectify this.

Then—

she closes the space.

Her hand brushes mine first.

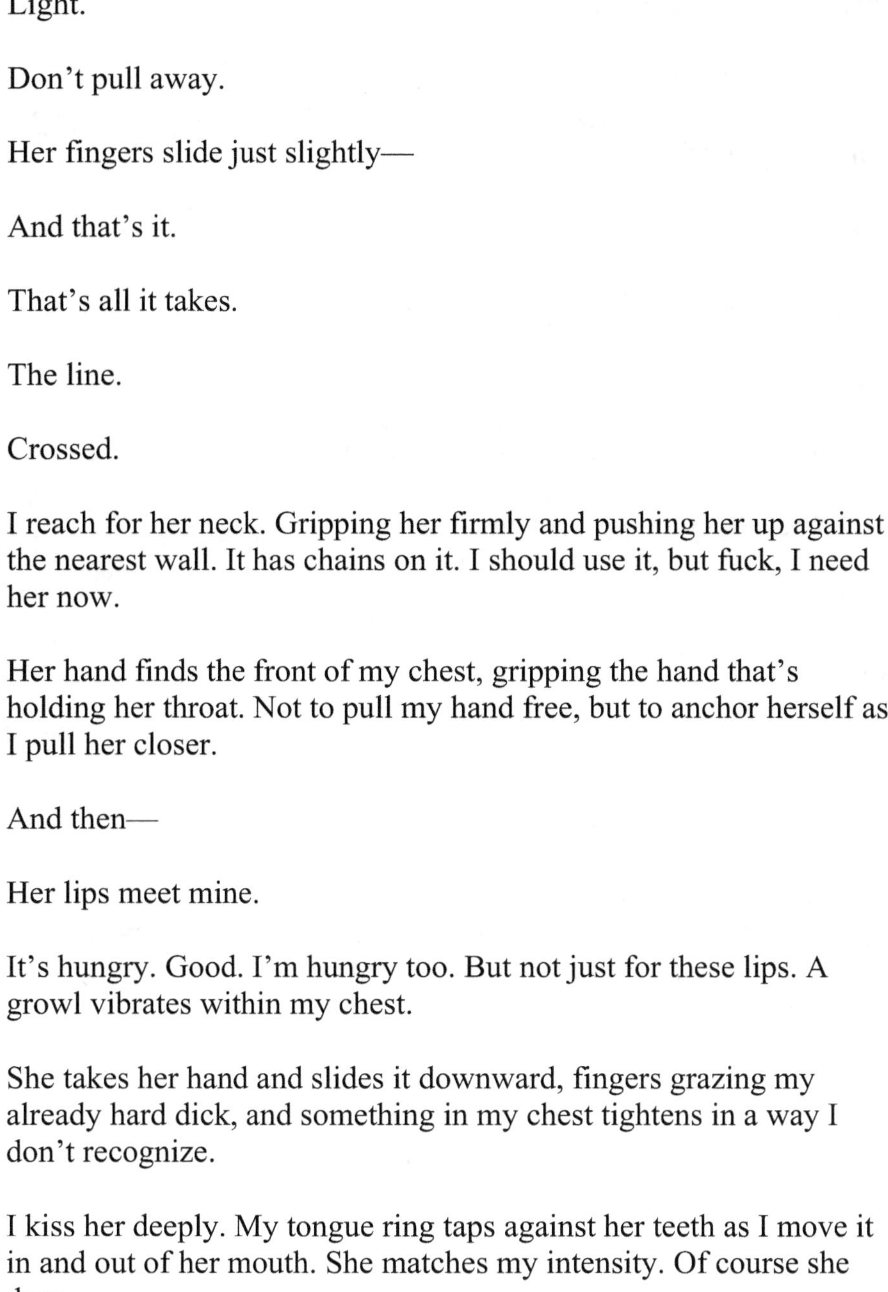

Light.

Don't pull away.

Her fingers slide just slightly—

And that's it.

That's all it takes.

The line.

Crossed.

I reach for her neck. Gripping her firmly and pushing her up against the nearest wall. It has chains on it. I should use it, but fuck, I need her now.

Her hand finds the front of my chest, gripping the hand that's holding her throat. Not to pull my hand free, but to anchor herself as I pull her closer.

And then—

Her lips meet mine.

It's hungry. Good. I'm hungry too. But not just for these lips. A growl vibrates within my chest.

She takes her hand and slides it downward, fingers grazing my already hard dick, and something in my chest tightens in a way I don't recognize.

I kiss her deeply. My tongue ring taps against her teeth as I move it in and out of her mouth. She matches my intensity. Of course she does.

This isn't casual.

This isn't just attraction.

This is something else.

Something that feels—

dangerous.

She pulls back first. As much as she can, anyway.

Just enough.

Just enough that I can feel the absence of her.

Her forehead rests briefly against mine.

A pause.

A breath.

Then—

"I need more," she whispers.

I release her neck just in time to pick her up by the waist. She grips my face and kisses me again. My hand easily supports her weight as she wraps her legs around my waist. I grip her ass as I make my way over to a velvet-covered couch.

Fuck the rules. All of it.

As I lay her down, there's an expression in her eyes. Is that fear? Or excitement?

"I will have all of you. I can have you now or later. Won't make a difference to me. Tell me you want this?" I all but growl at her.

Her expression quickly changes from what I saw earlier to desire. She grips my face.

"Make it count. Because you'll never touch me again after this."

I scoff. But now is not the time to go off the rails…yet.

"Get naked. Now."

"Giving orders, I see."

"I'm not a patient man. When I tell you something, you do it."

The fearful look appears for a quick moment before she schools her face again into one that shows she wants this too.

She starts to undress. "When you bark orders at me, it makes me want to peel that smirk right off your face with battery acid. Don't forget, I'm allowing you to have me."

"Mmhmm," I say as I devour her with my eyes. Her threats mean shit to me.

I'll let her think she's in charge again once we're done in this room.

Her heels and pants are off in no time. Then come her jacket and lace bra. I see scars on her shoulders and near her nipples. What the hell? Who did this to her? I catalogue that away to question at another time. I don't want to get distracted from the current task at hand.

But her eyes—the way she's looking at me. Like she needs this as much as I do.

Once she's completely naked, I just take her in. Memorizing all of her. "You're mine."

She chuckles at that.

“Careful, Angel,” she says quietly.

Her voice is steady. Lustful.

“Get on your hands and knees,” I tell her, pointing to the couch.

I keep my voice steady, even though I’m ready to fuck her senseless.

She bares her juicy ass before me when she leans over. Her pussy lips juicy just beneath it. She’s ready for me.

I kneel down and drive my nose up and down her slit from behind.

Fucking heaven. Her scent forever embedded in my memory.

She starts to whimper. Oh no, you don’t. I haven’t even begun. I’m going to make sure she yields to my touch, my dick, my teeth, my every fucking command. She may be The Madame, but I’m her fucking Commander in here.

My tongue joins my nose in smelling and tasting her pussy. “Mmm. Your pussy smells amazing.”

My tongue dives deeper into her pussy. I take my time. I stick my tongue in her tight hole and swirl it around. I remove my tongue and lick my fingers. As I dive into her folds again, I begin to play with her asshole.

“Angel”, she pants, “Please don’t play with my asshole like that. I don’t want to be in pain.”

Fuck. I want to make her scream. A little pain never hurt. Will she bleed? Will I be the one to take her anal virginity?

“I got you, baby. But I’m a big man. You’ll feel pain regardless. Now shut the fuck up and be a good girl for me.”

She moans at that. She sounds so fucking good, I'm about to bust in my pants. But I won't give her the satisfaction of that.

I take some of the wetness from her pussy while I play with her clit. I spit on her ass hole. She arches her back. "Yeah, baby. That's my good girl. Arch that fucking back for me."

She takes direction so well.

I slowly press my finger into her ass as I'm tongue fucking her tight little hole. She cries out my name.

"Angel!"

Fuuuck! All her holes are tight. She can't be a virgin. I'll just have to push a little harder. Her pussy clenches around my tongue. The fact that her body is so responsive lets me know she wants this as much as I do.

I'm used to just taking, but this time, I want to make this moment worth it.

I press my finger in her ass until it's fully inside. "Angel, my body can't take it. You have to stop."

I purr. "Do you really want Daddy to stop, baby?"

She whimpers in response. Good. I didn't think so. I spit on her asshole again. Moving my finger slowly in and out while my thumb fucks her pussy. Yeah. This is going to be fun.

Her pants get shorter and more frequent. She's close. "Oh no, you don't. We're not done here."

"W-w-what? No! Don't stop. I'm so close", she moans.

"I know, baby. But I need you on my face." She turns around to look at me. "You heard me. Assume the position, *Madame*." I used her club name on purpose. That's the next thing I'm going to learn. Her goddamn name. There's nothing about her that will remain a secret from me for long.

She stands up, beautifully naked. Her hair and makeup still intact. I go to lie down on the couch. Pants still on. My dick hurts so bad from the restraint. I know blue balls are in my future. But right now, she's all that matters.

She climbs over my face. Looking up at her, I see the hunger in her eyes. I know she sees the hunger in mine. She's so beautiful in this moment. Not that she's not beautiful in any moment. But her wet pussy is staring at me. She needs a piercing right on her clit so I can pull it with my teeth. But that's a discussion for another time.

I place my hands on her hips as she slowly lowers herself to my waiting mouth. Moving one hand to her pussy, I spread it to reveal what I really want. Her clit and that tight hole. My face dives in, like I haven't eaten in weeks. I flick, lick, suck, nudge. She starts rocking her hips. My tongue darts inside her pussy again. Yes, baby. Let me feel your walls contract.

She's gripping the arm of the chair to anchor herself. I keep fucking her with my tongue, nipping at her clit occasionally. I reach up to search for her breast, only for her to grab one of my hands and start licking my fingers. She takes that same hand and moves it to her left nipple. I take her cue and start rubbing and slapping at her breast. She arches each time she feels the slap on her nipples. Oh, she likes it rough. I got her. Fuck! Between the slaps and pinches, and slurping sounds I'm making against her pussy, I'm about to bust in my pants for sure.

She screams, "Oh fuck Angel. I'm about to cum!"

I growl in response. Cum for me, baby. Let daddy drink you up. Her release comes in a rush. Dripping down my face, I drink up every drop. I wipe my face and lick my fingers. Then I wipe at her pussy and lift my hand to her lips. She gets the hint and licks her juices off my fingers, too. Yeah. That's my dirty girl.

After a while of her sitting somewhat awkwardly on my chest, I slowly start to see the composure creeping back across her face.

My face darkens. “Don’t you fucking dare.”

Now her mask is firmly back in place. “What do you mean?”

“We just shared an amazing moment. Don’t ruin it.”

“And don’t assume you know me.”

She gets to her feet, a little wobbly. “What we just shared was nice, but definitely a one-time thing. Too bad you didn’t actually fuck me.”

Is she mocking me? I stand up instantly and push her against a nearby wall. Grabbing her hands and lifting them above her head. I glare at her. “Don’t fucking mock me. Yeah, I got a past baby, and I can make this pleasant or not so pleasant. But you are mine. Plain and simple.”

She glares at me. But there is also that damn fearful look in her eyes. Good. She needs to be fearful. I don’t play when it comes to what belongs to me. And she does belong to me.

“Let’s get something straight. I work for you at this club, but by no means does that mean I need this job. You won’t fire me, because you know I bring value to this place. But when it comes to you, I won’t hesitate to do what is necessary. You are mine. Doesn’t mean I’m going to go soft on you either.”

She snatches her arms out of my grasp, and I let her. “You don’t own shit! And be careful. Hulk knows how to handle men like you.”

I laugh. “Tell your guard dog to fuck off.”

She smirks at that. But there’s something beneath it now. I watch her as she gets dressed.

"Don't forget where you are."

I hold her gaze.

"I forget nothing."

A beat.

Something passes between us.

Unspoken.

Then she turns.

Opens the door.

And just like that—

it's over.

For now.

I step back into the hallway, adjusting my dick in my pants. I'm still hard unfortunately, but my erection is starting to go down. Good. No chafing.

But nothing feels the same.

Because now—I know exactly how easy it is to break her rules.

And worse—how much I want to do it again.

Just then, I hear a noise coming from my left, but I think nothing of it. It's a private area of the club, but housekeepers are constantly in and out doing their job. I smile on my way back to the bar. Madame's pussy scent on my lips will carry my mood until the end of my shift.

Chapter Seven

My Dearest Cosette,

I'm so sorry that I haven't been able to find you. I've made so many mistakes, but you're not one of them. I hope when I do find you, you can forgive me. You'll understand why things have happened this way. I don't expect you to forgive me right away. But you know what they say, 'Time heals all wounds. I love you so much, and I can't wait for the day when we are reunited. Until then, stay safe and take care of yourself.

Love,
Mommy

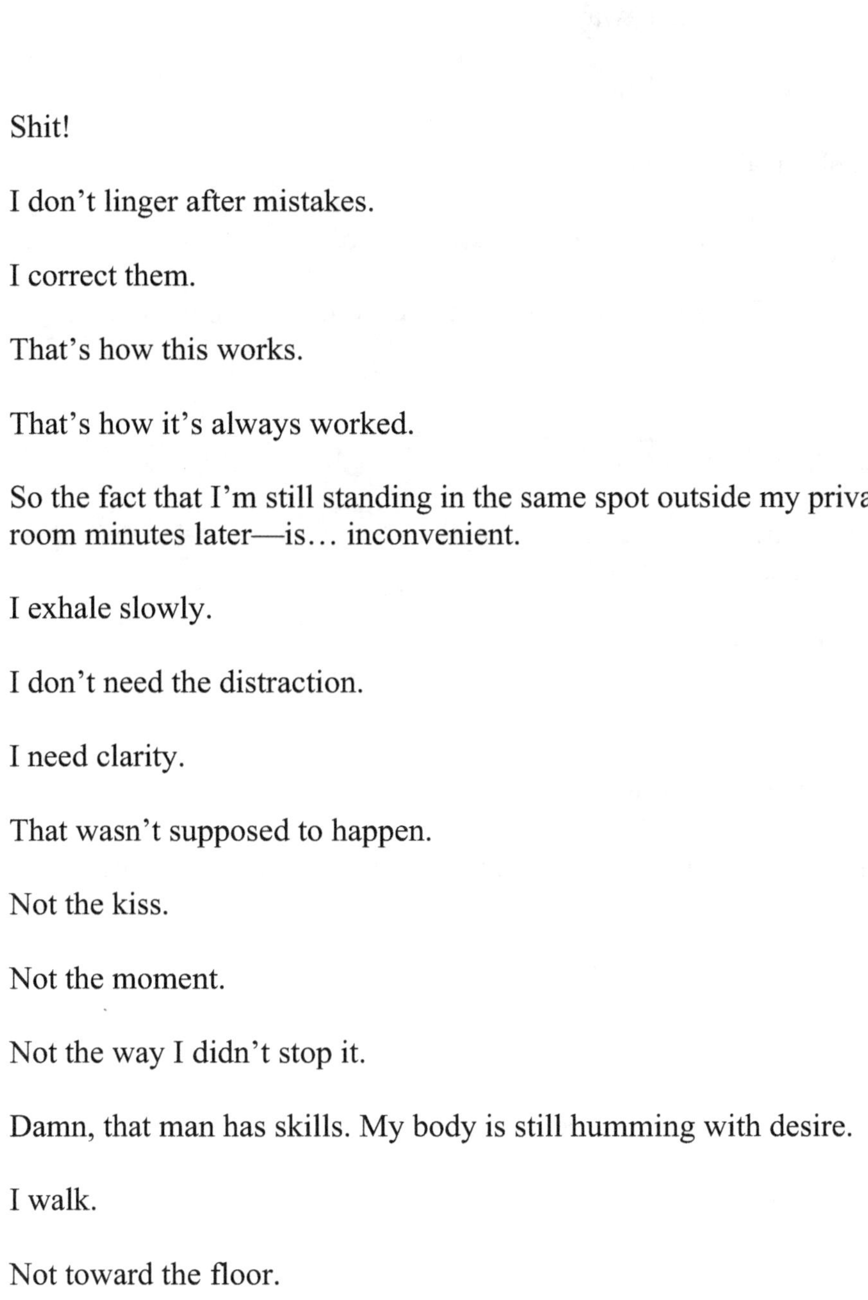

Cosette

Shit!

I don't linger after mistakes.

I correct them.

That's how this works.

That's how it's always worked.

So the fact that I'm still standing in the same spot outside my private room minutes later—is… inconvenient.

I exhale slowly.

I don't need the distraction.

I need clarity.

That wasn't supposed to happen.

Not the kiss.

Not the moment.

Not the way I didn't stop it.

Damn, that man has skills. My body is still humming with desire.

I walk.

Not toward the floor.

Not toward the bar. Hell no.

Away. I need to get away.

The hallway feels different now.

Not physically.

But I'm aware of it in a way I wasn't before.

The quiet. The separation. The distance from everything out there.

It lingers.

I don't.

By the time I step back into my office, I've already started putting things back where they belong.

Thoughts first.

Then reactions.

Then whatever that was.

I close the door behind me, leaning against it for half a second longer than necessary.

Unacceptable.

The problem is—I didn't stop it.

A soft knock doesn't come. Of course it doesn't.

The door opens.

"Cosette."

I don't look up immediately.

"You're early," I say.

Antoinette steps inside anyway, closing the door behind her.

"I was already on my way when you disappeared," she says. "Then I wasn't sure if I should give you a minute…"

She pauses.

"…or ten."

I turn now.

Her expression is neutral.

Too neutral.

"You should mind your business," I say.

"I would," she replies lightly, "if you weren't currently standing in your office like you just made a decision you're about to pretend you didn't."

I walk past her, moving toward my desk instead of engaging directly.

"I interviewed the new hire," I say.

"Mhm."

"I approved his trial shift. He's now a permanent part of the staff. Please see to his paperwork."

"Mhm."

"And I'm assessing his performance."

That earns me a look.

"That's what we're calling it?" she asks.

I pick up a file I don't need, flipping it open without reading it.

"That's exactly what we're calling it."

Antoinette takes a few steps closer.

"You kissed him."

Straight to it of course.

I don't look up.

"You don't know that."

"I know you," she says.

That lands.

I close the file slowly, setting it back down.

"It was a lapse in judgment," I say.

"Mm."

"I corrected it."

"Did you?"

I look at her now.

"Yes."

She studies me for a second.

Long enough that I know she's deciding how far to push.

Then—

"Do you want me to pretend that's true," she asks, "or do you want me to be honest?"

I exhale through my nose.

"That depends," I say. "Which one is less annoying?"

"Definitely not honesty."

I almost smile.

Almost.

"Fine," I say. "Be honest."

She nods once.

"You didn't correct anything," she says. "You interrupted it."

A pause.

"And there's a difference."

I don't respond immediately.

Because she's right.

I hate that she's right. This is not the time for her to be right. My emotions are all over the damn place, and I'm still horny.

"He works for me," I say instead.

"Yes."

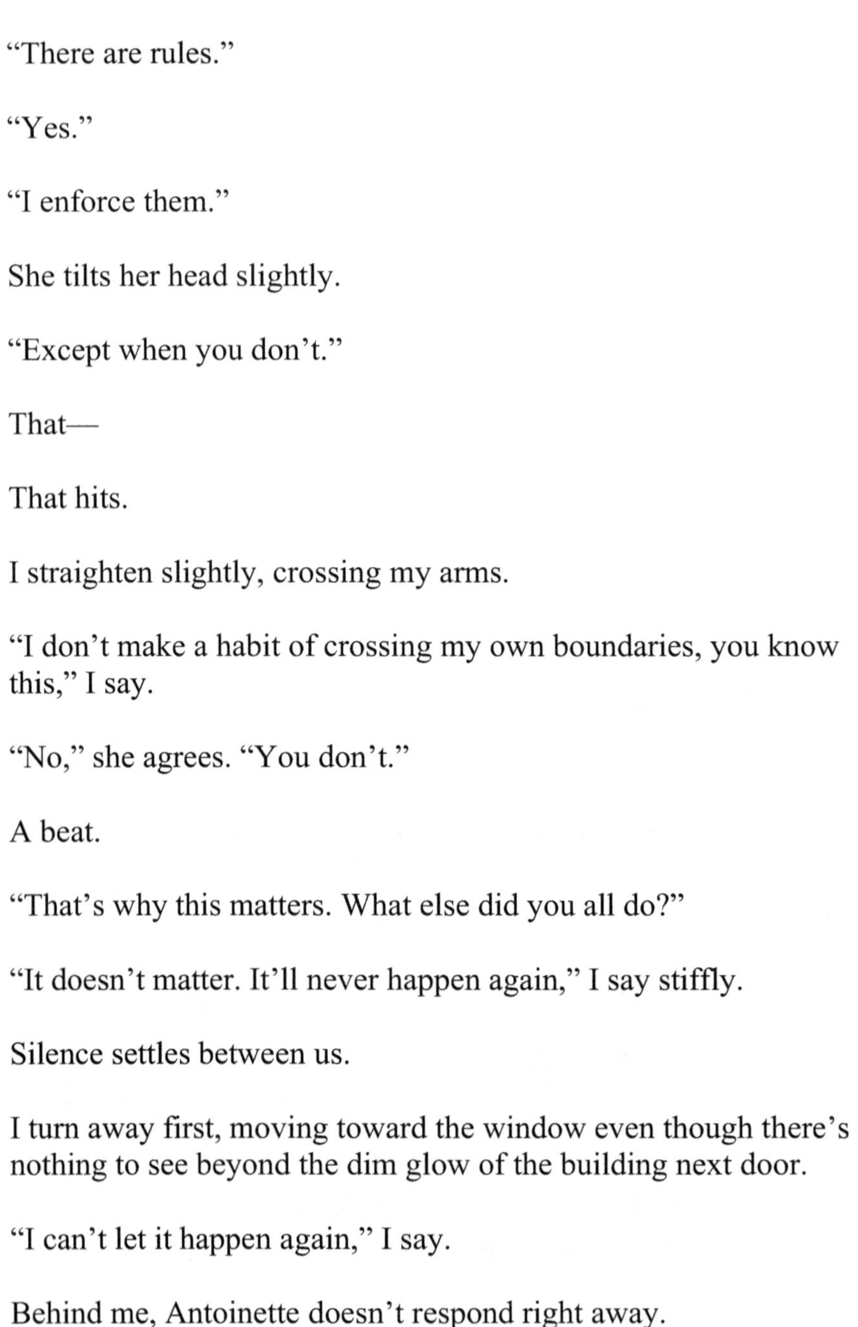

“There are rules.”

“Yes.”

“I enforce them.”

She tilts her head slightly.

“Except when you don’t.”

That—

That hits.

I straighten slightly, crossing my arms.

“I don’t make a habit of crossing my own boundaries, you know this,” I say.

“No,” she agrees. “You don’t.”

A beat.

“That’s why this matters. What else did you all do?”

“It doesn’t matter. It’ll never happen again,” I say stiffly.

Silence settles between us.

I turn away first, moving toward the window even though there’s nothing to see beyond the dim glow of the building next door.

“I can’t let it happen again,” I say.

Behind me, Antoinette doesn’t respond right away.

When she does, her voice is quieter.

“Is that what you want?” she asks.

I close my eyes briefly.

What I want isn’t the point.

It never has been. My choices will never be taken away from me again. That was my own vow to myself so many years ago.

“Yes,” I say.

It sounds steady.

It almost feels true.

Another pause.

Then—

“Okay,” she says.

Simple.

No argument.

No pushback.

That’s how I know she doesn’t believe me.

I turn back around.

“Where is he?” I ask.

Antoinette watches me carefully.

“Back at the bar,” she says. “Doing exactly what you hired him to do.”

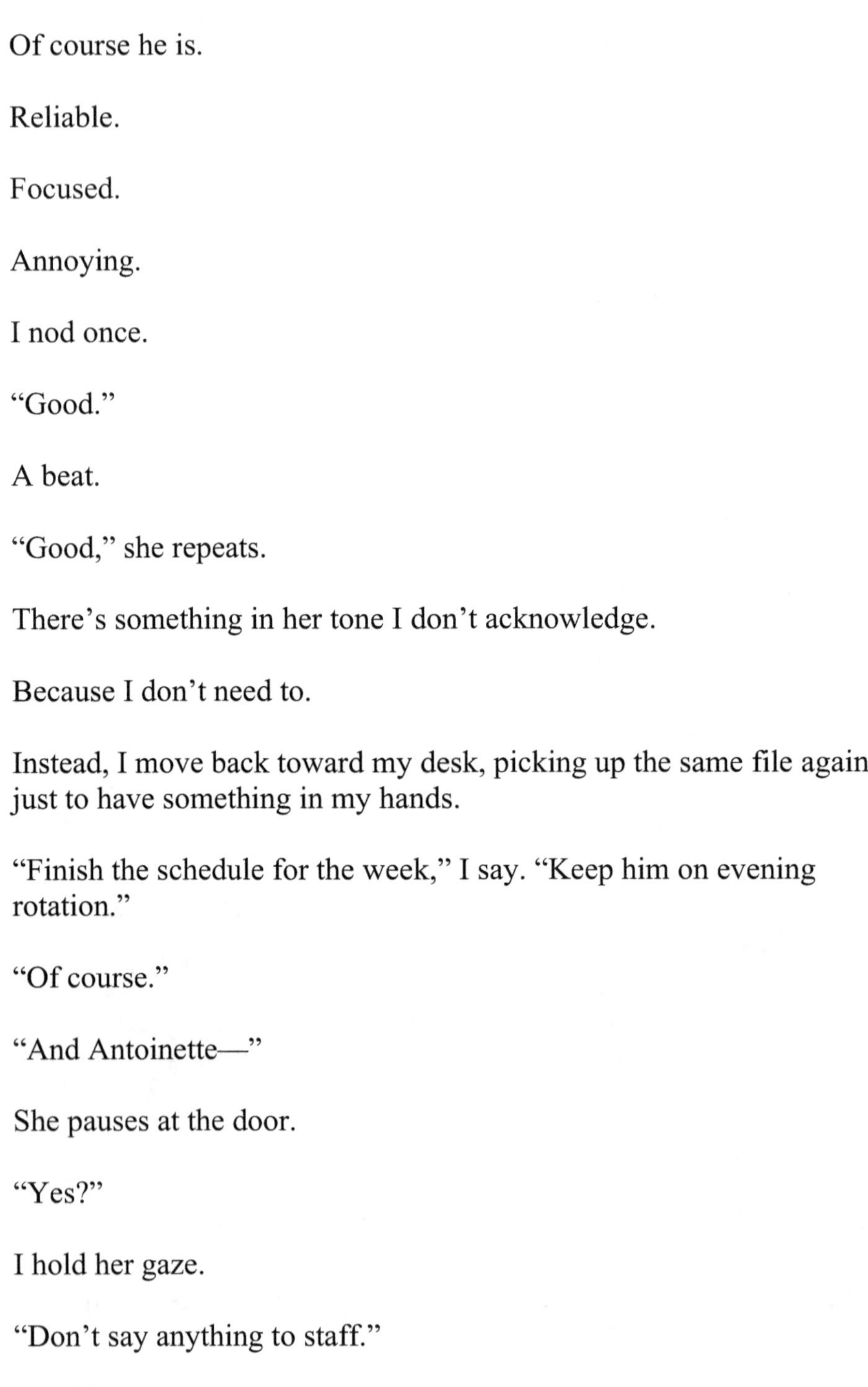

Of course he is.

Reliable.

Focused.

Annoying.

I nod once.

“Good.”

A beat.

“Good,” she repeats.

There’s something in her tone I don’t acknowledge.

Because I don’t need to.

Instead, I move back toward my desk, picking up the same file again just to have something in my hands.

“Finish the schedule for the week,” I say. “Keep him on evening rotation.”

“Of course.”

“And Antoinette—”

She pauses at the door.

“Yes?”

I hold her gaze.

“Don’t say anything to staff.”

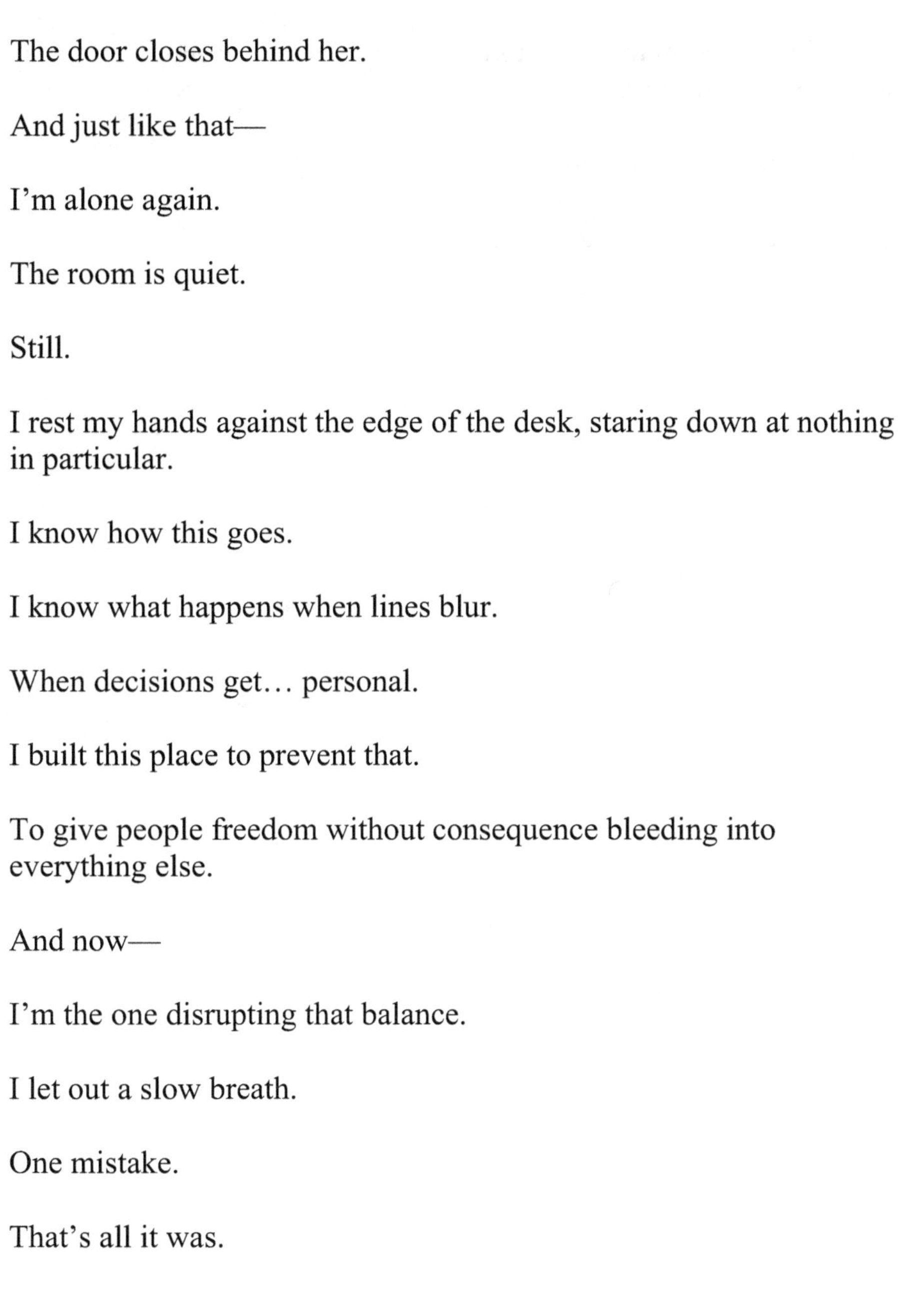

A small smile.

"I never do."

The door closes behind her.

And just like that—

I'm alone again.

The room is quiet.

Still.

I rest my hands against the edge of the desk, staring down at nothing in particular.

I know how this goes.

I know what happens when lines blur.

When decisions get… personal.

I built this place to prevent that.

To give people freedom without consequence bleeding into everything else.

And now—

I'm the one disrupting that balance.

I let out a slow breath.

One mistake.

That's all it was.

It doesn't happen again.

It won't. It can't.

I straighten, smoothing my hands over my sleeves, grounding myself in something familiar.

By the time I step back out onto the floor—

Everything will be exactly where it should be.

Including me.

It has to be.

Chapter Eight

Antonio

I shouldn't be thinking about her.

That's the first thing I tell myself when I step back behind the bar.

The second is that it doesn't matter.

Neither one sticks.

I reach for a bottle, pouring without looking down, muscle memory carrying me through the motion while my mind replays something I should've already filed away.

Her hand.

Light.

Intentional.

The way she didn't hesitate.

That's what stays with me.

Not the kiss.

Not the heat of it.

The certainty.

She didn't.

She decided, then acted.

That's familiar.

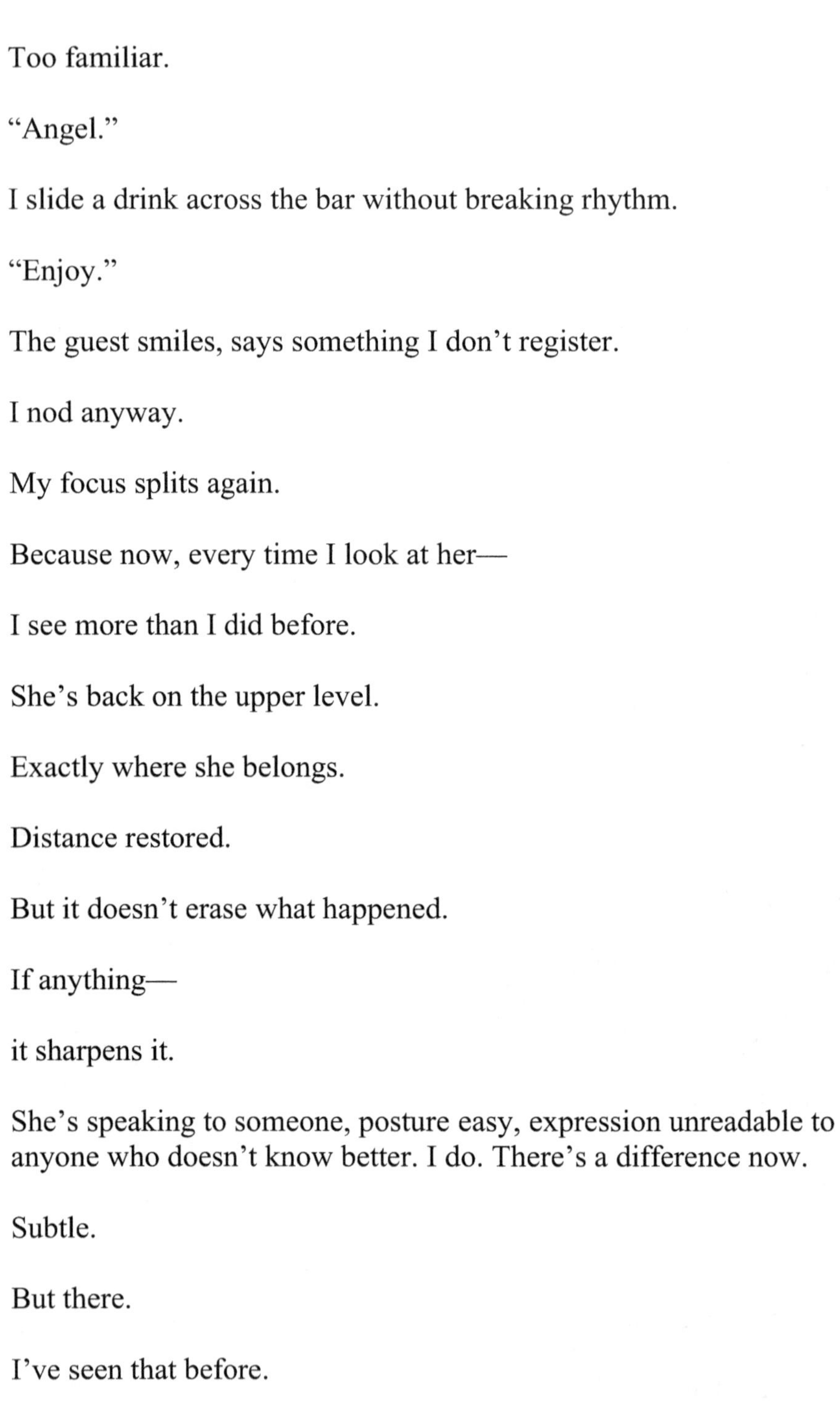

Too familiar.

"Angel."

I slide a drink across the bar without breaking rhythm.

"Enjoy."

The guest smiles, says something I don't register.

I nod anyway.

My focus splits again.

Because now, every time I look at her—

I see more than I did before.

She's back on the upper level.

Exactly where she belongs.

Distance restored.

But it doesn't erase what happened.

If anything—

it sharpens it.

She's speaking to someone, posture easy, expression unreadable to anyone who doesn't know better. I do. There's a difference now.

Subtle.

But there.

I've seen that before.

And just like that—

I'm not here anymore. Not really.

The room fades.

The music dulls.

And I'm somewhere else.

Concrete walls.

No music.

No soft lighting to hide anything. Just a table. A chair. And a Glock lying on the metal table. Someone sitting in the chair across from me with a sack covering their head. The person looks small and frail. Almost childlike, but I can't be sure.

And my uncle standing next to me, like he already knew how the conversation would end.

"You hesitate," he said.

I didn't. I just didn't rush. There's a difference.

"You think too much," he added, circling slowly, the way he always did when he was trying to make a point. He grabbed the victim by the neck. I heard a moan. As if the person was gagged.

I stayed where I was. This wasn't new. Just a change of scenery. I knew what he wanted me to do. I don't kill unless I know what the person did or who they did it to. Did I enjoy it? Sometimes. But only if the person truly deserved it, or if I needed to let off some steam and some asshole was in the wrong place at the wrong time.

I didn't move.

Didn't react.

"Second-guessing like that will have you dead before the top of the hour."

That part was true.

Not thinking gets you killed. I've lost many friends that way. Family too.

Hesitation gets you replaced.

And emotion—Emotion gets you owned.

I remember the way I looked at him then.

Steady. Unmoved. Unimpressed too.

"I'm not you," I said.

He smiled at that.

Not amused. Not proud. Something colder.

"No," he agreed, rolling his cigar around in his fingers.

A pause.

"But you're mine. You'll always be indebted to me," he said, blowing smoke my way.

The words sat between us like a challenge.

A claim. No one owned me. I didn't accept it even when my parents were killed, and I had to go live with him.

"You'll kill this piece of shit, and you'll move on to the next job. You got that, 'wise guy'? I give the orders around here."

I load the gun and place it on my lap. "Remove the head covering. I need to see who this is before I end their life." I was not a request. Either he removes it so I know who's dying, or he can get one of his other guys to do it. Even in the mafia, there's a code of conduct that must be adhered to.

My uncle shrugged and lifted the head covering. My stomach lurched.

It was a young girl. Couldn't be more than 15 years old. Brown skin, long matted hair. She had bruises everywhere. She looked like she had been drugged. My face must have said a few 'What the fucks' because my uncle cleared his throat as he began to speak.

"The family is branching out into a new venture. This girl was meant to be sold to one of my buddies, but she has turned out to be uncooperative. She has lost her value, so she must be dealt with. Be a good nephew and do the honors for me."

My jaw clenched. I hate children, but that didn't mean I go around harming them. Why does my uncle have this young girl here? Then it dawned on me what type of business venture my uncle was involved in. Bile rose in my throat.

"Don't we have enough revenue. Why this?" I tried to sound uninterested, but my face kept morphing into something that reflected disgust.

"Why not more money? More money never hurt anyone. Plus, we can use them for whatever we want. It's a win-win."

"So, we're trafficking children now?"

"Yeah. You could say that."

"Boys and girls?"

"Yeah. I don't discriminate. Black, white, purple. Who cares?" he shrugs.

"What about their parents?"

"Not our concern. They need to keep a closer watch on their kids. Now stop stalling and shoot the little bitch."

I put my gun back in its holster. "Yeah, this isn't a job for me."

"I knew it. You weak fuck!" he roared.

"That's the best you got?" I challenged.

"And you're ungrateful. Just like your father. Fuck his soul."

That did it. I pulled my gun out on him and shot him in the shoulder. "Next bullet will be in your fucking head. Keep my father's name out of your filthy fucking mouth."

He started laughing. "You'll get what's coming to you, Tony. Or should I say 'Angel' since that's what you want to be called."

I turn to walk away. "And when you make good on that threat, I'll be waiting to return the favor."

That was the last conversation we had before I walked away.

Because I knew something he didn't.

I wasn't built for that life. I was born into it. I was trained for it. There's a difference. I learned how to shoot a gun, use various knives, and learn hand-to-hand combat before I could even do my homework.

The memory slips just as quickly as it came.

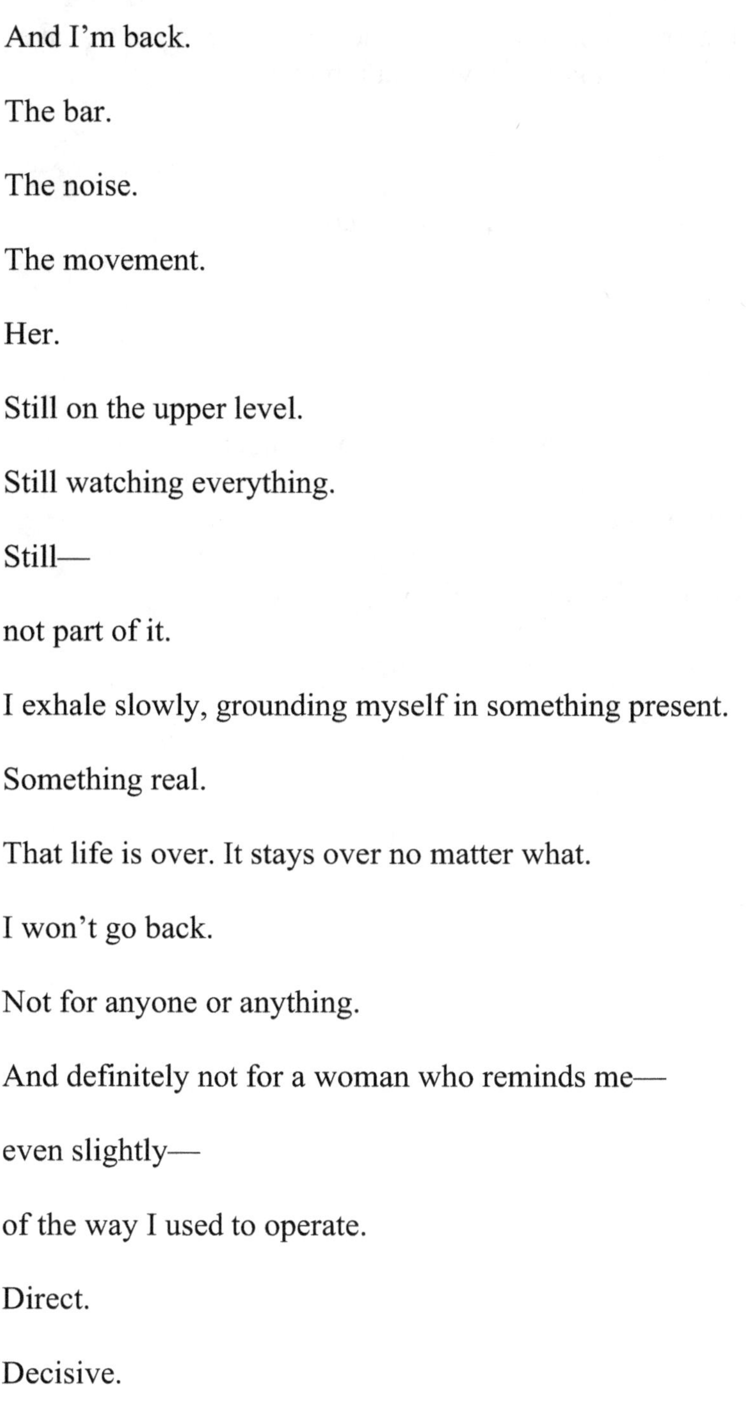

And I'm back.

The bar.

The noise.

The movement.

Her.

Still on the upper level.

Still watching everything.

Still—

not part of it.

I exhale slowly, grounding myself in something present.

Something real.

That life is over. It stays over no matter what.

I won't go back.

Not for anyone or anything.

And definitely not for a woman who reminds me—

even slightly—

of the way I used to operate.

Direct.

Decisive.

Not even of that innocent child. I hope she made it out alive. I shake the thought off. I'm not going down that rabbit hole.

I focus back on her.

She's unafraid to act when she wants something.

That's not a coincidence.

That's experience.

And experience like that doesn't come from nothing.

I don't know her story.

But I know what it takes to move the way she does.

And I know better than to underestimate it.

"Angel."

Her voice.

Not imagined.

Real.

I look up.

She's closer now.

Not at the bar.

But not far from it either.

Watching.

Not the room.

Me.

I wipe my hands once on a clean cloth, stepping forward just enough to close the distance without crossing it.

“Madame.”

There’s a pause.

Short.

But not empty.

“You’re distracted,” she says.

I hold her gaze.

“Am I?”

Her eyes narrow slightly.

Curious.

“Yes,” she says.

A beat.

“You don’t seem like someone who misses details.”

I almost smile.

“I don’t.”

“Then what are you missing right now?”

That’s a better question than it should be.

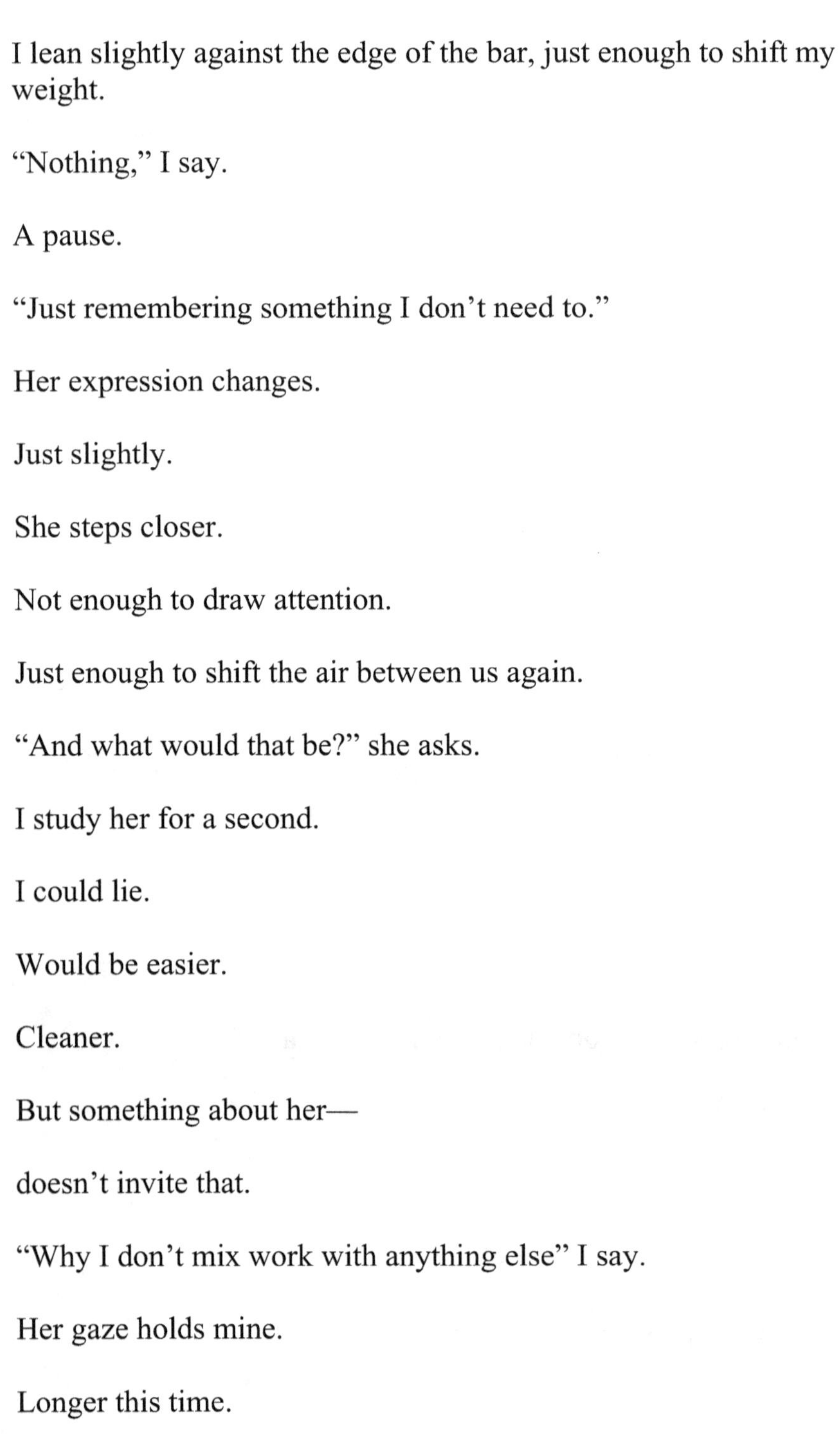

I lean slightly against the edge of the bar, just enough to shift my weight.

"Nothing," I say.

A pause.

"Just remembering something I don't need to."

Her expression changes.

Just slightly.

She steps closer.

Not enough to draw attention.

Just enough to shift the air between us again.

"And what would that be?" she asks.

I study her for a second.

I could lie.

Would be easier.

Cleaner.

But something about her—

doesn't invite that.

"Why I don't mix work with anything else" I say.

Her gaze holds mine.

Longer this time.

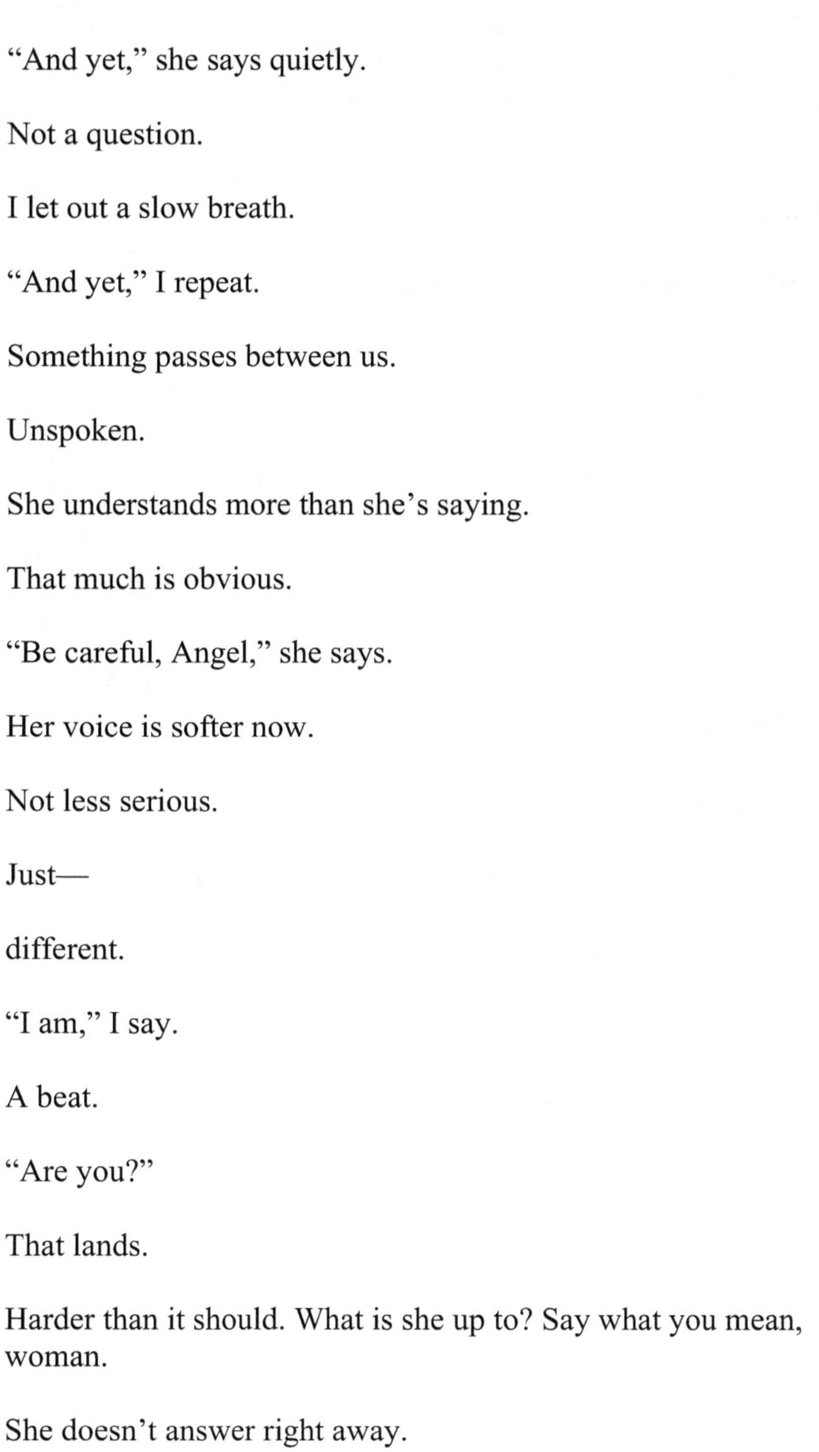

“And yet,” she says quietly.

Not a question.

I let out a slow breath.

“And yet,” I repeat.

Something passes between us.

Unspoken.

She understands more than she’s saying.

That much is obvious.

“Be careful, Angel,” she says.

Her voice is softer now.

Not less serious.

Just—

different.

“I am,” I say.

A beat.

“Are you?”

That lands.

Harder than it should. What is she up to? Say what you mean, woman.

She doesn’t answer right away.

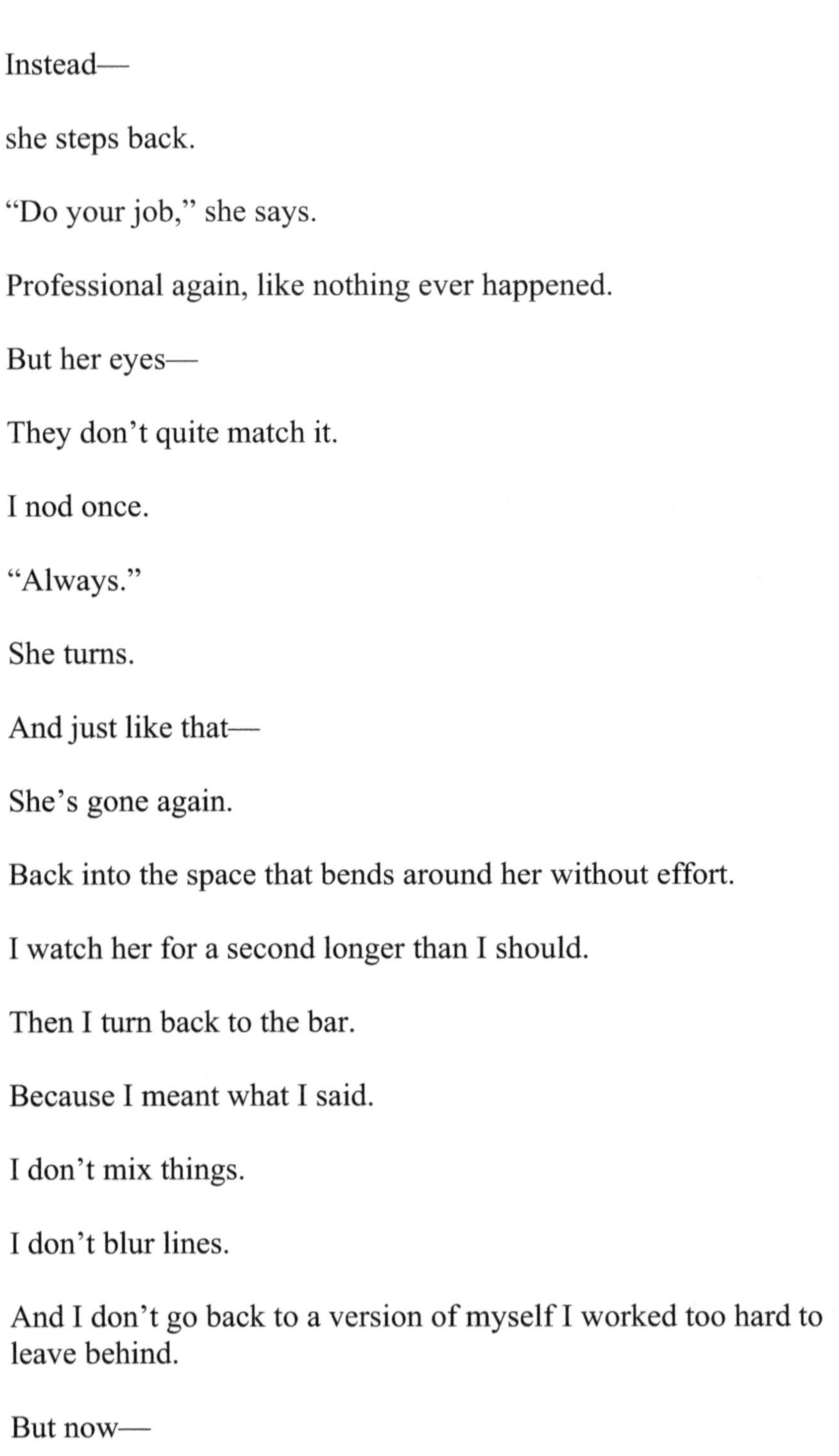

Instead—

she steps back.

"Do your job," she says.

Professional again, like nothing ever happened.

But her eyes—

They don't quite match it.

I nod once.

"Always."

She turns.

And just like that—

She's gone again.

Back into the space that bends around her without effort.

I watch her for a second longer than I should.

Then I turn back to the bar.

Because I meant what I said.

I don't mix things.

I don't blur lines.

And I don't go back to a version of myself I worked too hard to leave behind.

But now—

There's a new problem.

Because she's not part of that past.

She's something else entirely.

And for the first time in a long time—I'm not sure which direction is more dangerous.

Mouse comes up behind me. "I told you to mind the rules, but you didn't listen, did you?"

I ignore him. This little shit is starting to annoy me. "What are you talking about?"

"The Madame. She doesn't break rules for anyone, and yet she broke them for the likes of you."

That got my attention. I stood a little straighter.

My senses on high alert.

Especially when it comes to her. "I don't know what you mean."

"Well, let me enlighten you," he says as I continue to fill orders at the bar. "I have worked here for 3 years, and I have tried repeatedly to get her attention. And you just come in off the street, and her panties are loose around her ankles. What the hell? Tell me your secret."

My jaw ticks. But I moved so fast I didn't have time to think about my actions before I reacted.

I punched and then slammed him into the bar. I then broke a glass and held it up to his eye. "Mention her again, and the eye is gone."

Mouse just smirks at me like this is a fucking joke. To prove to him I wasn't joking, I pushed the broken glass into his cheek, moving it ever so slightly towards his eye. Blood begins to trickle.

Good.

All of a sudden, I feel an arm grip my shoulder. On instinct, I grab and twist, not realizing its Hulk coming to neutralize the situation. He's holding his now broken wrist, and I release Mouse on a huff.

Everyone is staring at me. Members, Mouse, Hulk, and her. Mouse is bleeding, and Hulk is gripping his wrist, which is turned at an odd angle. I storm off outside. Anywhere would be better than being inside with all those stares.

How the fuck could I allow that little piece of shit to get the better of me? I'm supposed to be flying below the radar.

It's her. It's this place. It has my head fucked up.

I hear the back door open. Heels click-clacking towards me. Not hurried, but slow and steady.

"What the fuck was that?"

"My apologies. I know I shouldn't have done that. Hulk startled me."

"And my other bartender? He's going to need stitches."

Her voice doesn't sound upset. But then I don't dare look at her face. "Yeah. I'm not apologizing for what I did to that little bitch."

"Talk to me, Angel. What did he do to you to receive that kind of treatment?"

I'm not one to mince words, so I told her. "He disrespected you. I won't tolerate it."

“I see,” she said simply. “And you think, beating him up and threatening him was the right thing to do?”

“Don’t talk to me like I’m a fucking child!” I bark.

“Lower your tone when you’re speaking to me. I’m not your enemy.”

Taking a deep breath, “You’re right. You don’t deserve my anger.”

I finally look at her. Really look at her. The look on her face is one of…concern? Is it for me or that ‘rat’ Mouse? I walk over to her. “I’m sorry.”

She takes my hand in hers. “It’s not the first time, and it won’t be the last. But you can’t go around beating people up. Especially in front of my members. This place is not one of violence.”

“What’s this incident going to cost me?”

“Well, first, I need to write up an incident report and pay for medical bills.”

“You can dock my pay if you need extra funds to pay for that.”

“As good as that sounds, I got it covered. However, you will be suspended for a week without pay for the incident, as well as Mouse. You both know better than that.”

I nod.

“Let’s go inside so we can get this mess settled. Just make sure this doesn’t happen again.”

I can’t make any promises, but I nod regardless.

She rubs my shoulder. I’m guessing to soothe me in some way.

As we walk back inside, I apologize to Hulk and the rest of the staff, minus Mouse. I'm going to keep an eye on him. He just won't know it. I grab my belongings from my locker and head out on my Harley.

I wasn't lying when I told Madame she could dock my pay for the incident. I'm not hurting for money at all.

Over the years I worked for my uncle, I acquired homes, cars, boats, and everything else under the sun.

Pulling up to my house, I shed my jacket and clothes and hop in the shower. Once I'm dried off, I look at my phone. I see a missed call. I think nothing of it until I get a call from the same number. Maybe it's her.

"Yeah?"

"Is that any way to greet familia nephew?"

Chapter Nine

Cosette

"Keep your legs open, or you'll be punished," The Boss threatens.

I can't do this anymore. He keeps coming back to me. There are other boys and girls here. I don't know why he keeps coming for me. I wish my body would just die. I can't live like this. His penis is disgusting. It smells, and it hurts. I almost forgot he's in the room. I've become good at that while he's inside me. I feel the sting of his slap across my face.

"Pay attention, Cosette," he says.

I can barely keep myself from shaking. He's on top of me now. I feel his breath on my breasts, then he moves down to my 'pussy'. That's what he likes to call my private area.

This man has taken my virginity on my first night as his captive. I hope I'm not pregnant. I would never want to bring a child into this nightmare. I feel him enter me. The Boss gets mad when I don't look like I enjoy it. I make these pretend moaning sounds that I think he wants to hear.

Tomorrow is my 16th birthday, I think. It's hard to keep track of time in a place like this. I wait for him to finish. Sometimes he finishes inside of me. Other times it's in my mouth, on my face or my ass. I forgot that he likes to take me there, too. I bleed so much when he's back there. Why anyone would get pleasure from that, I'll never know.

"You're the best bitch I've had. No doubt about it. The best money I've spent." "If you're a good girl, I'll let some of my buddies have a taste as well."

The tears start now. I can't help it. But I make no sound. I have to get out of here, one way or the other.

I watch as Angel leaves. I have to get this mess cleaned up. Mouse and Hulk are on their way to the emergency room to get their injuries checked out.

Mouse made it very clear on his first day of working at The Dungeon that he wanted me. I shut him down instantly. There's no way that he could know about what Angel and I did. Even if he had an idea, he needs to mind his own damn business. I can sleep with whoever I want. The fact that I even wanted to do something with Angel was somewhat of a miracle. Given my history with any physical sexual encounters, I'm definitely surprised at the fact that I enjoyed being with Angel.

Yes, he has an edge to him that scares the shit out of me. But I know I'm safe with him. If tonight was any indication, he cares about me. Even if it's surface level. Mouse must've really pissed him off. Seeing him enraged liked that over little ol' me, turned me on. I couldn't let the others see it, let alone him.

"Well, that was entertaining," Antoinette says as she approaches the area where the broken glass is.

"Yeah. They're both suspended for a week without pay."

"Good. Is Hulk and Mouse okay?"

"I'm waiting to hear back from them. I sent them to the emergency room to get looked at for their injuries."

"Hmm," she says.

Rolling my eyes, I turn and look at her. "If you have something to say, let's discuss it in my office."

I lead the way. I refuse to discuss anything in front of prying eyes. Angel already caused enough of a spectacle that some of my members left earlier than usual. It's not the first time, and it won't be the last. But I won't add to the cluster fuck by discussing private things in public.

Once we reach my office, Antoinette follows me in and closes the door. "What is truly going on between you and Angel? You didn't want him around before, and now you two can't seem to stay apart for longer than 5 minutes. And let's not mention that you two track each other with your eyes all night. He's only been here a few weeks. Even when you think no one is looking. And Cosi, the team is watching."

By the time Antoinette is finished, I'm rubbing my temples. "Are you done?"

"Not really, but I'll let you get a word in."

"How thoughtful of you." I don't want to give all the details away, but as my bestie, she deserved something. "He and I did share more than a kiss. I mean, he was all over my body. But I did initiate things when I kissed him." The look of shock was apparent on Antoinette's face, but she said nothing, so I kept going. "I can't explain it, Nette. He does something to me. Like I want this man badly. I'm only telling you this because you have been down for me forever. You know you're more than my assistant."

Antoinette holds up her hand. "First of all, I knew it! Secondly, was it good?"

I laugh. "It was so good. But he didn't penetrate me. He only worried about my pleasure. And pleasure me, he did."

"Wait. All of this trouble, and he didn't even stroke the pussy?"

"Oh, he stroked it. With his tongue."

We giggled together at that.

“I am shocked that you kissed him first, Miss ‘I have my boundaries.’”

“I told you; it’s never happening again. I can’t bend the rules for one and not all.”

“But you’re the boss.” That one particular word made Cosette’s skin crawl.

“I’m Madame,” she corrected.

Wincing, Antoinette corrected herself. “Yes, Madame. Which means, you make the rules. Amend whichever rule you want.”

As intriguing as that sounded, I know I could never. Not if I want this place to continue to run like a well-oiled machine.

“No. I’ve made up my mind. It was a one-and-done.”

“Whatever you say. I think this thing with Angel is good for your ego and for the broken parts of you that you think I don’t see.”

“Okay, ‘Iyanla’,” I sigh.

“Well, with him being suspended for the week, will you two link up?”

I should leave him alone.

But I know I won’t. “I honestly don’t know. I won’t say the thought hasn’t crossed my mind.”

She smiles. “Well, think on it and let me know.” And just like that, she’s gone. Thank god. Now I have time to think.

That’s the thought that follows me all evening.

Persistent.

Unhelpful.

And completely ignored.

I don't usually repeat mistakes.

I learn from them.

Adjust.

Move forward.

But this—

This doesn't feel like a mistake.

That's the problem.

Back at the bar, I see another bartender where he should be. Damn. I miss him already. This is madness. I need to finish my night early. Not seeing him is going to drive me crazy.

The bartender spots me. He greets me with a charming smile. It's not the smile I want to see.

"Madame."

"Hello," I reply.

"Can I get you anything?"

"No. I just wanted to make sure everything was in order."

"Yes Madame. I made a list of things for Hulk to order when he gets back."

"Very good. Keep up the good work." I walk away without so much as a sideways glance.

Back in my office, I pull Angel or Antonio's employee file. Staring at his Polaroid picture, he looks so damn yummy. I look to see what he's listed as his number and his address. It's against an employee's privacy to look up their address. But I don't think he'll mind it.

Hmm. That can't be right. That residential area is restricted. Some of the members live in that community. Hell, I almost bought a house in that community. It has to be a mistake. I pay him well, but not that well. Maybe his parents left him some money or some land. Maybe he got it in a divorce settlement. I don't know much about his romantic past. The thought of him running his nose and tongue against anyone but her made her eye twitch. That's a new emotion. Being jealous of women she didn't know from a hole in the wall. I pick up my personal cell phone and dial his number.

"What?"

"Is that how you answer your phone?"

I hear him sigh out loud. "Madame. Are you okay?" He sounds worried.

"I'm fine. Just here in my office. I was checking on you."

"Aww. You were worried about me?"

"In the professional sense."

He laughs. Damn, I missed his voice. "Still lying to yourself."

"Well, what do you want me to say?"

"If we're being honest, I was hoping you were calling because you wanted to see me fully naked."

"Oh really?"

"Definitely." His voice is starting to sound husky.

"Well, this is my personal number. Save it and send me your address."

"Something tells me you already have it. But it's okay. I'll send it anyway. Does this mean you're coming over?"

"It means I'll think about it." I hang up the phone before he can say another word. I can't believe I'm actually considering going over to this man's house.

I feel my phone buzz, letting me know I have a new text message.

It's him.

He shared his address with me and a little winking face. Buzz. Another text comes in. These reads:

Can't wait to taste you again.

Jesus help me! He just gave me butterflies. Ooh, I need to get a grip.

When I step out of my office, I find Hazel, one of the dancers, coming from her dressing room, looking upset.

"Everything okay, Hazel?"

She notices I have my purse and keys in my hands.

"Nothing, Madame. I just needed a moment to collect myself."

"Are you sure?"

"Yes, just personal problems. Nothing I can't take care of."

"Okay. If you need to chat, my office is always open to you. We can discuss whatever you're comfortable discussing."

She nods and walks back towards the main floor.

Walking towards my private exit door, I shoot Nette a text letting her know I'm ending my evening early. She responds instantly with a devilish winking face emoji. I laugh to myself. She already knows what decision I've made. Tonight, Antonio will have me in every which way he wants.

As I walk to my car, I hear noise coming from my left. I freeze. It's 12:25 AM. Who is out here this late? This area doesn't do loiterers.

I take out my taser just in case. My gun is in my car. The next thing I see is a raccoon looking for food in the trash. I take a sigh of relief and quickly get in my car. I'll figure out his address when I get somewhere better lit where I'm not by myself. I should have asked one of the other security guys to walk me out. This back alleyway gives me the chills. I can't stand it. I don't want to think about that time I spent in hell with that man. No ma'am. Not now. Tonight, I'm getting turned every which way but loose. And I don't want to keep him waiting.

I arrive at Angel's gated community and think, 'What does this man do on the side, because he definitely can't afford to live in here with what I pay him. Even with tips, he can't afford this. I promised myself I would keep my opinions about it to myself, but I can't help but gawk. These homes are beautiful. I give the guard at the gate my information, and he waives me through the gate. Angel must have put my name on the guest list. I follow the GPS to his house. It's even more beautiful than I imagined. It's like a mini mansion. 2-stories, black iron gates surrounding, what looks like, a couple of acres of land, with its roundabout driveway. Angel meets me outside. He's wearing a plain white t-shirt and some sweatpants, barefoot. He looks amazing.

He comes to open my door. “I hope you found it okay.”

I give him a look. “You know this place is outside of the salary I give you, right?”

He shrugs and smiles. “I’m really good at saving.”

Yeah right. But I don’t press. He takes my hand and walks me up the few steps and through his front door. Either this man comes from old money, or he was a drug lord in his past life.

“Your silence lets me know you like my house.”

“It’s beautiful.” I can’t deny that. He has artwork up and various musical instruments up as well; guitars, both electric and acoustic. I look at one of the autographed guitars. “Is this who I think it is?”

“Yeah. I was pretty obsessed with blues at one point, and rock. B.B. King was gracious enough to sign one of my guitars.”

“That’s incredible,” I say as he takes my jacket.

“You’re incredible.”

That stopped me right in my tracks. I didn’t know what to say to that. So, I just looked at him and smiled. I hope he doesn’t think he’s going to sweet-talk me out of my panties.

“Would you like some wine?”

I nod.

“Then I can take you on the grand tour.”

I smile as I watch him pour the wine. I don't trust people who want to make me a drink unless I'm watching them or pouring it myself. As we're sipping and he's guiding me through his castle-like house, I wonder how he got it. He must've read my face.

"My last job paid me very well. I saved, and I bought this house a few years ago. The look on your face is priceless." He laughs.

"That was definitely going to be my next question. You must've had a really great job. Why did you leave it?"

Something dark appeared in his features. "You don't have to answer if you don't want to." I could tell he was thinking it over from the silence that fell afterwards.

He took a moment, then said, "I needed a change. Plain and simple. The job that I was working was more of a family business. I moved away from it all, determined to start anew."

I guess that was a good answer, as any. I assume there's more that he's not telling me, but those are his secrets to keep. As long as those secrets don't harm anyone at the club.

After a moment, he moved towards me. He got so close, I could feel the heat coming off his body. "There's another room I want to show you." He took my free hand and led me up the stairs to a room with double doors.

"I'm going to assume this is your own personal Dungeon?"

"In a way. It's my bedroom." He was all business now. There was a sexy edge to his voice that I found irresistible. "Would you like to come inside?"

"Yes, I would." There was no use in pretending anymore. I wanted this man. This very tall, sexy man. I was beginning to believe Angel had many layers, and we barely scratched the surface of one layer.

He opens the doors and allows me to enter before him. Same marble tile throughout the entire house. A black oversized rug underneath his California king-size bed. What the hell does he need all that space for? Was he a pimp? Was that how he made his money? Selling women's bodies and sexual favors? I feel sick all of a sudden. And of course, Mr. Pimp notices.

"What's wrong?"

"Is this where you take your women?"

"Umm, no. What's going through that mind of yours?"

"The fact that you pimp women out for sexual favors and monetary gain. Why do you need so much bed space?"

The grin that spread across his face pissed me off. Why was he so happy all of a sudden? Did he think to add me to his harem? I think-the-fuck-not!

"Jealousy looks amazing on you. You know that?"

I laughed. Jealous? Me? Not likely. Although I did get annoyed thinking about the number of women who could've potentially fucked him. "I'm not jealous. I just need to make sure you're legit."

"I'm not a virgin. Yes, I've had a few women. But my previous job required my complete attention. Women were a distraction."

"I can understand that. What is it that you did that required so much attention?"

He walked over to me and took the wine glass that I barely touched. He took the glasses to his dresser and pulled something out of his drawer. "Mostly drugs and weapons."

He said it like he wasn't out here committing crimes.

"So, you were a drug lord?"

"No. I left that to my uncle. But I'm sure you can figure some things out on your own."

I tried to think it over, but suddenly the room felt a bit wobbly. "W-what's happening?"

"I told you I have a past. One of the things I was particularly good at was getting information. You will tell me who you are and why you seem so familiar."

The fucking wine. I should have known better than to take a fucking sip. Damn. And all I wanted was some grade-A dick. "You f-fucking rat bastard."

I felt his hands on me. I tried to fight him off, but my body had a mind of its own. I wanted to fight. I really did. He's so fired, and I'm calling the police as soon as my fucking fingers start to work. My body starts to limp and all at once, darkness reaches up to grab me.

As I'm opening my eyes, all I see is pitch black. I try to move my arms and legs, but I can't. That's when my memory has me remembering where I am and who I'm with. The who's voice came up beside me.

"Hello Cosette," he greets.

"What the fuck is going on Angel?"

"Let's get this straight first and foremost. I need you to address me as Antonio. I love your little country/Floridian accent, but I need to hear my name on your lips."

"Fine, Antonio," she said through gritted teeth.

"What is the meaning of this? Am I fucking bound to a bed? Is this a fucking blindfold?"

"Yes, and yes. You didn't see me grab the blindfold out of my drawer? What a shame. I thought The Madame saw all."

"Don't mock me. Let me go."

His laugh makes my blood boil. Not like this. I don't like this. I start to breathe slowly, in through my nose and out through my mouth. Now was not the time to hyperventilate.

"Baby, you're not a hostage. Far from it. I am going to fuck you, but first I need some answers."

I couldn't even bring myself to laugh; I was so fucking scared. I will not be a victim. Fuck him! "I ain't telling you shit motherfucker!"

"Such a potty mouth for a sexy vixen like you. I'm finding I like this side of you. It makes my dick hard watching you struggle like this."

After what feels like a long time, my muscles become sore, and I stop struggling. "If I tell you what you want to know, will you release me?"

"I might release you from the bed, but you belong to me."

"I belong to no one you psycho."

"Oh baby, you do. And the sooner you get it through that thick skull of yours, the better."

"What?! What do you want to know?"

"Where do I know you from?"

"Nowhere. I've never met you before in my life. Next question."

“I love your name, Cosette. I found out when I went through your purse and saw your ID in your wallet.” Coming close to my ear, he whispered, “I even saw those boxes of Magnum condoms you brought with you. You naughty girl.”

Fuck! Why are my nipples hardening? Am I naked? “Why am I naked?” I knew I felt a draft.

“Because I like you that way! Anyways, my next question was, do you have a nickname? Cosette is rather long.”

“My close friends and family call me Cosi. Next question.”

“Aww, Cosi, you don’t think of me as a close friend?”

He’s a fucking lunatic. “Fuck no!”

“Yeah. Daddy sounds way better.”

I scoff. He’d better enjoy this shit while it lasts because he’s through. As soon as I made it out of this House of Horrors, I was going to the police. Not that they ever gave a damn about a black girl in distress. Ugh. I can’t have these dark thoughts right now.

“What other questions do you have for me?”

“Did you enjoy what we did previously and secretly hope that I would do it again and more?”

“Yes. Antoinette figured out what you and I had going on. So it wasn’t that much of a secret.”

“Antoinette is ‘Kitty’, correct?”

I just nod. “Now, can you remove the blindfold? You’re scaring me.”

“This was meant to gather answers that you would not have given me freely. And, yes, I will remove it in a moment. But first I want to have some fun.”

“I answered all your dumb ass questions, now let me go!” I roar.

He’s back on me in a flash. This time, I feel his body hovering over mine. His nose finds the sensitive part of my neck. I let out an involuntary moan. This is wrong. I should not be enjoying this. “Please stop. I don’t want this anymore.”

“Oh, but you do.” I feel his knee nudge my thighs open.

“Please stop.” I feel the tears coming. I can’t show this man how much this has my PTSD cutting up. Oh shit! I feel the tears coming down my face.

He must’ve seen my tears. “Shhh. Baby, I’m not going to hurt you. I don’t know what you’ve been through in your past, but I promise to bury every bad memory with new and better ones. You know deep down in that secretive heart of yours that I will never hurt you on purpose.”

“So you’ll hurt me anyway,” I say accusingly.

“Never on purpose. Please, my honor is hanging on by a very fine thread. I had to defend you at that club against that piece of shit Mouse. You have me on temporary work suspension, and now you’re naked before me.”

My breath hitches, but my tears miraculously slow down.

“You consume me, *Madame*. Every inch of that fucking club, I imagine what I want to do to you. What I want you to do to me.” I feel his hand around my throat. “I want to shove my dick down this pretty throat of yours.” I gasp. “Yeah, baby. The only air I want you to breathe is the one we share. And tonight, those tears will be for a very different reason.”

I want to clench my thighs shut, but his sweatpants are on, and his knee is rubbing against my clit. It's so subtle, but I feel my hips start to roll beneath him. Something is seriously fucked up with me. I feel my breath coming in shorter pants. "That's it, baby. Let my body give yours what it needs." Then he leans down in my ear again. "No other man will touch you, or you'll find pieces of his body mailed to you."

Fuck. Why is he so damn possessive? We haven't done anything that warrants this type of treatment. This isn't right.

But my body…wants him. Now!

"Antonio," I moan.

"Hmm?"

"Please fuck me. I can't take it anymore. Please."

That word seemed to be his undoing because my blindfold was removed instantly. Thank god the room was dimly lit. I saw my arms and legs shackled. The cuffs were leather and chained to his four-poster bed. He was between my thighs when he lifted one of my legs and started kissing my inner thigh. He kept kissing until he got to my toes.

I felt the wetness of his tongue first. Then his tongue swirled around my toes, making my back arch. His other big hand came to rest on the mound of my pussy. I was so lost in what his tongue was doing that I didn't feel his finger circling my clit until he pinched it between his index and middle fingers. His finger rolled over my clit, and I cried out. "Fuck baby. Your pussy is creaming already. We can't have that yummy go to waste." He pushed a finger inside my entrance and sucked on it. I couldn't take my eyes off him. I'm so turned on that my skin feels tight. I feel two fingers enter me again while he does the same thing to my other thigh and toes.

"Mmm. Have a taste, baby." I open my mouth automatically. I taste the tang and mild sweetness of my pussy. "I want more baby. Just

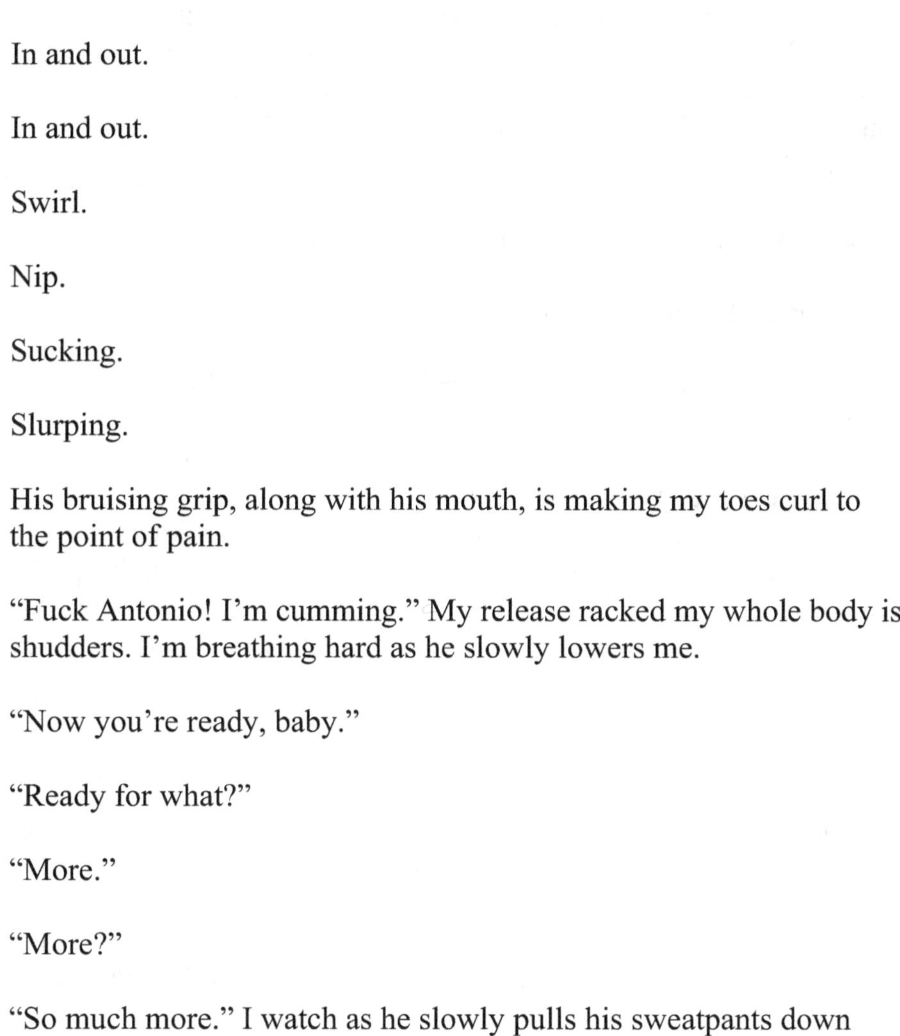

hold on and enjoy this." His eyes never leave mine. I watch him grip my hips and pull my pussy to him. His waiting tongue dives deep into my pussy. I cry out, not able to get a good grip on him because my wrists are still chained up, so I hold on to the chains instead. His mouth is relentless.

In and out.

In and out.

Swirl.

Nip.

Sucking.

Slurping.

His bruising grip, along with his mouth, is making my toes curl to the point of pain.

"Fuck Antonio! I'm cumming." My release racked my whole body is shudders. I'm breathing hard as he slowly lowers me.

"Now you're ready, baby."

"Ready for what?"

"More."

"More?"

"So much more." I watch as he slowly pulls his sweatpants down and removes his shirt. Watching his tattoos dance across his body in the dim light. I want to lick every inch of his him. His abs are flexing for me. Damn, this man is… Oh. My. Sweet baby Jesus.

The monster between his thighs is very intimidating. I've had so few lovers in the past. None of them looked like this. What if it doesn't fit? Fuck it! I'm going to take every inch. Discomfort be damned.

I'm watching him stroke it. I then see something shining in the light. "Yes baby. I have a few piercings down here. Do you like?"

I nod. My mouth is watering at the sight. It's so big. I wonder how much of it I can fit in my mouth. "Un-chain me. I won't run. I promise."

"Even if you did, you wouldn't make it far."

"Don't ruin this moment for us."

"There'll be more moments. I guarantee that," he said so confidently.

He unfastens the clasps on the cuffs. I crawl to the side of the bed he's on. I kiss him deeply. He doesn't disappoint. He kisses me back with all he desire he's feeling. I feel it down to my toes. He keeps pumping his dick while his other arm is wrapped around me. I push him back slightly so that I can stand up and lower myself to the floor on my knees.

He knows where this is going.

He tracks my every movement with his eyes. I see his jaw clenching, like he's restraining himself from touching me.

"Grab my hair." That was my only command before I started kissing his dick. The surprise that greeted my tongue was a full-on Prince Albert and Jacob's ladder. My tongue counted 8 piercings altogether. It was different. No man I had ever been with ever had something like this.

As I found my rhythm, I began sucking and stroking his dick.

It could've been my imagination, but it feels as if his dick grew in my mouth.

I get lost in the taste that is him. His hand grips my hair so tight it feels as if he's pulling my hair from the scalp. Somehow, it makes my nipples swell.

Fuck!

I want more of him. This isn't enough.

As if sensing my need, he pulls himself away from my mouth. "Get back on the bed. On your back."

I should be annoyed with the commands he's giving me. However, I do love a man who knows what he wants and goes for it.

I get on the bed and just let my legs spread open. He leans over me and kisses me deeply. He licks and sucks on my neck, then moves to my breasts. I'm so wet. "Antonio. I need you inside."

"Inside of what?"

"Please fuck my pussy, Antonio!" This man has me right where he wants me…And right where I want to be.

He positions his dick at my entrance and slowly pushes in.

Inch by delicious inch.

His piercings hitting every erogenous spot inside of me. "Mmm."

Once he's fully seated inside me, he pulls out a little, then slams inside me. "Fuck baby. *Sei tutta bagnata*."

Oh my. This is too much. He's so fucking deep. Fuck! "Antonio, deeper baby deeper."

“*Ti voglio tutta la notte. Mi fai impazzire.*”

I’m cumming all over his dick. The squelching sounds between us sound like beautiful music. This man is going to ruin my pussy for all other men.

All of a sudden, he pulls out and starts lapping at my pussy. Tears are starting to form in my eyes. I can’t take it. I’m too sensitive.

Everywhere.

I cum again. My juices all over his face. I see him wipe his face with his arm. He then grabs my legs and flips me over to my stomach. “Arch that back and put that juicy ass in the air.”

I do as I’m told. “Such a good girl for me. You’re taking my dick so good.” He enters me in one thrust. I cry out. “You. See. How. Good. You. Take. This. Dick. Mmm.”

I’m screaming into the bedsheets. He grips my hair. “Don’t you fucking dare hide your screams from me.”

He continues to pump relentlessly into my pussy. He’s pinching my nipples, and the tears are flowing freely now.

His release is so violent inside my pussy that it causes my whole body to shake as I cum for the final time before my body collapses.

We both just lay in the bed for a moment. His chest to my back. My thoughts are racing. I’ve never been fucked like that. How he turned my fear into desire. I don’t know what to think about that. What will this change at the club? Do I change the rules? I can’t be a hypocrite. I wonder what he’s thinking.

“I have to get going. I wasn’t planning on having a sleepover.”

He looks over at me. “You don’t need to leave. I have plenty of space.”

I laugh at that. “You can’t keep me in your sex dungeon.”

“Why? You have me working in yours?”

Oh, he has jokes. “I do, don’t I?”

“I was right. You’re such a smart ass.”

“Yeah. Well, so are you.”

He leans up on one elbow, peering down at me. “I want to see you more. And since I’m on this 5-day suspension, we could see each other without being discovered by the other staff at the club.”

I stay silent for a moment. What he’s suggesting makes sense. Oh. My. Goodness!!! “We didn’t use protection!”

“No, we didn’t. Are you not on birth control?”

“No, I’m not. I don’t sleep around.”

“I never said you did. But most women take that extra step.”

I’m so disappointed in myself. I can’t be so reckless. I don’t know if I can even have children after the trauma of my past. But I sure as hell don’t want any right now.

“Would you like me to go out and get a Plan B pill?”

“No. I’ll grab one on my way home.”

He sighs. “You’re so stubborn woman.”

“I am. So get used to it.”

“Does that mean that there will be more of me and you?”

I just smile at him as I get up from the bed to search for my clothing. I find my panties first. “You have to understand. That club is all I have. I have built something amazing for myself. And while this was great, I don’t see how we can continue this.” I gesture between us.

“It will continue. No other man will touch you ever again.”

I held his blue-eyed stare. There goes the serial killer look laced with,,,concern?

“You’re concerned about me?”

“You don’t get it Cosette.”

His using my actual name feels so…

Personal.

Intimate.

“You clearly think I was puffing out hot air. Every threat, every promise was a real thing.”

“Antonio, I don’t know why you’re being this intense for me. We don’t know each other well enough.”

“Does that mean that we can’t get closer?”

“I’ll be honest with you. I saw this going no further than a one-time fuck fest. Now I have to just roll with whatever comes.”

“I don’t want us to just roll with it. What if your life was in danger? Would you summon me then?”

"It's not that. And it's not because I don't like you or I'm not interested. It's just very complicated. You don't know what I've been through."

He starts sitting up in the bed, still gloriously naked. "Explain it to me then. I'm a simple man, but I can follow."

"I don't have to explain my emotional scars to anyone. Just know that my life was not always easy and that I have had to learn how to survive in this world as a woman, as a teenager."

My voice started to crack with emotion.

"There's nothing you can't tell me. I know we don't know each other as well as I would like, but I swear you can trust me."

I chuckle. "Says the man who drugged me to get answers from me."

"Would you have given them to me willingly?"

"No. I would have made you work for them. But now we'll never know. You seem to like taking things by force. And I don't particularly care for anyone who takes things by force. Mutual agreement and understanding are everything." Tears started to prick in my vision.

"Well, excuse the hell out of me for wanting you. I don't use a lot of words to express myself. Just actions. That's the only way I know how to operate."

"I thought you said you left that way of life. Looks like you're reverting."

"You don't get to judge me, Madame."

"You know, this was a mistake," I say as I look for my purse and keys. "Where did you put my shit?"

"So that's it? Are you going to run away? And here I thought you were so brave and fierce."

I walk up to him and slap that smirk off his face. I must've slapped him harder than I thought because a small drop of blood appeared on his lower lip.

He deserved it! Condescending motherfucker. "You don't get to talk to me that way."

"What? Can't handle the truth either? Oh, sweetheart. You're in for a rude awakening now that we're together."

"Have you lost your damn mind? We're not together. We never could be. For one, I'm your employer. And second, I could never be with an asshole who treats me like we're in the damn Stone Age."

He wipes at his lip and tastes his own blood. "My mother would have loved you," he says quietly.

"For the last time. Where is my shit?"

He points to a table situated in the corner of his bedroom. I grab my stuff and rush out the door. He doesn't follow me. Thank god.

I can't take this anymore. He's too much.

I can't have him trying to poke through my past to 'figure me out'. He's not the only man who has tried. However, he's the only one I've felt compelled to say more to.

I gotta get out of this house. After a minute, I located the front door and ran to my car. As soon as I was inside, I felt someone looking at me. When I look up, I see Antonio staring at me from what I think is his bedroom window. He doesn't look upset, just… lost.

I can’t worry about him right now. I have to get my head on straight. I can’t allow him to break down what I’ve worked so hard to build up.

My emotional wall.

My glorious emotional wall.

Impenetrable. Or so I thought.

I look at my phone and see 2 missed calls from Nette.

I call her back and she answers on the second ring.

“Bitch! I thought I was going to have to call the police and report you missing. Are you okay?”

After hearing her voice, I started crying. Hysterically. “Can I please come over? I need to vent.”

Chapter Ten

Antonio

I stare out of my bedroom window for a little longer. Even after I see her taillights disappear into the night. I shouldn't have let it go that far.

Not with her.

Not like that.

I go to sit at the edge of my bed, elbows resting on my knees, staring at the floor like it's going to give me answers.

It doesn't.

Nothing does. She did, though, just briefly. Only because I forced her hand.

I smiled when I found my hidden bottles of diazepam. I thought for sure she would have noticed me slip it into her wine. But my sleight-of-hand game hasn't changed. It's served me well in the past. Getting enemies to reveal things they wouldn't under normal circumstances. It was typically my last resort.

But the truth is—

I regret nothing. I don't regret touching her. Tasting her. She has the sweetest-tasting pussy I've ever licked. She felt so good. My dick definitely agreed after my almost violet release. I hope I didn't hurt her too much. I did get rough with her. I smile. Yeah, I regret not a damn thing.

Not for a second.

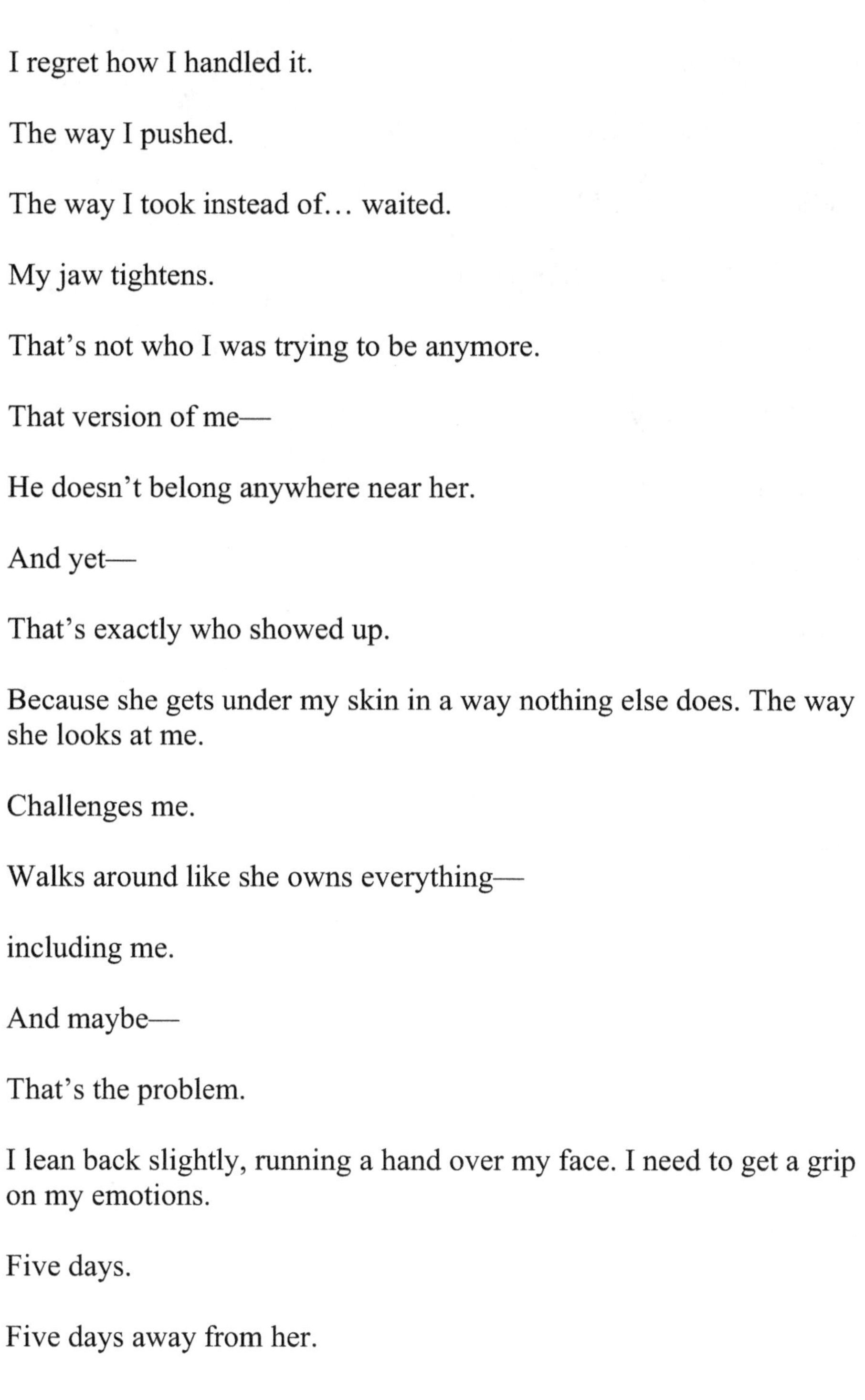

I regret how I handled it.

The way I pushed.

The way I took instead of… waited.

My jaw tightens.

That's not who I was trying to be anymore.

That version of me—

He doesn't belong anywhere near her.

And yet—

That's exactly who showed up.

Because she gets under my skin in a way nothing else does. The way she looks at me.

Challenges me.

Walks around like she owns everything—

including me.

And maybe—

That's the problem.

I lean back slightly, running a hand over my face. I need to get a grip on my emotions.

Five days.

Five days away from her.

From the club.

From everything I was starting to build.

Suspended. Because I lost control.

Because of Mouse. That piece of shit.

My expression hardens instantly at the thought of him.

That look in his eyes—Lust where it doesn't belong.

I've seen it before.

Men like him don't just *look.*

They take.

Or they try to.

And the way he stood in that hallway—

like he belonged near her—

like he had a right—

No.

My hands flex. My jaw clenches.

That won't happen again.

Not while I'm breathing. I'll skin him alive before the thought even crosses his brain.

My phone lights up on the nightstand.

I already know who it is.

I don’t need to look.

But I do anyway.

Unknown number.

Again.

I answer.

“What?”

A low chuckle slides through the line.

“You’ve always had such a temper.”

My body goes still.

“You’re calling too much,” I say flatly.

“You’re ignoring me,” he replies smoothly.

A pause.

“I don’t like being ignored.”

I lean back, eyes narrowing slightly.

“I told you. I’m out.”

“Are you?” he asks.

Too calm.

“I hear things.”

My grip tightens around the phone.

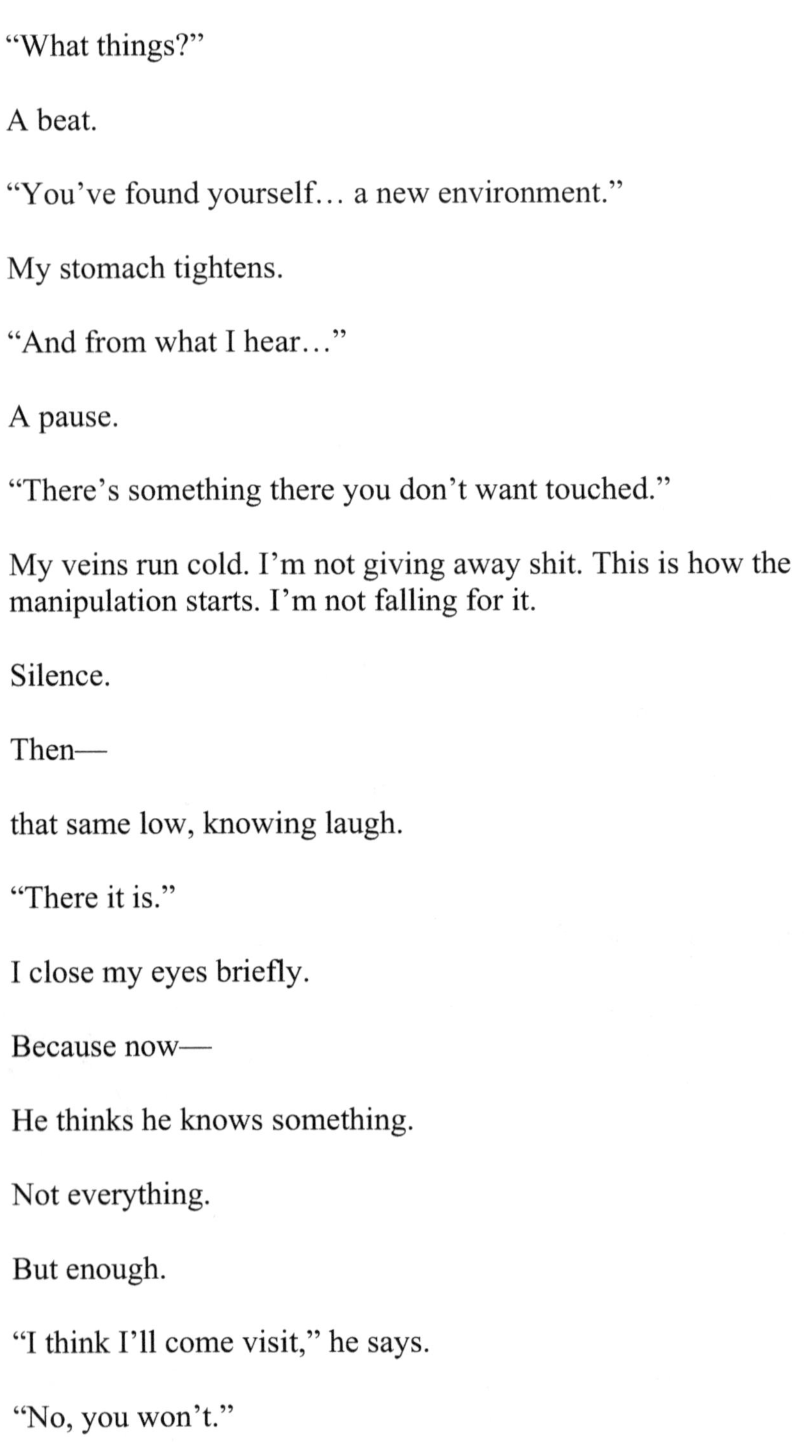

"What things?"

A beat.

"You've found yourself… a new environment."

My stomach tightens.

"And from what I hear…"

A pause.

"There's something there you don't want touched."

My veins run cold. I'm not giving away shit. This is how the manipulation starts. I'm not falling for it.

Silence.

Then—

that same low, knowing laugh.

"There it is."

I close my eyes briefly.

Because now—

He thinks he knows something.

Not everything.

But enough.

"I think I'll come visit," he says.

"No, you won't."

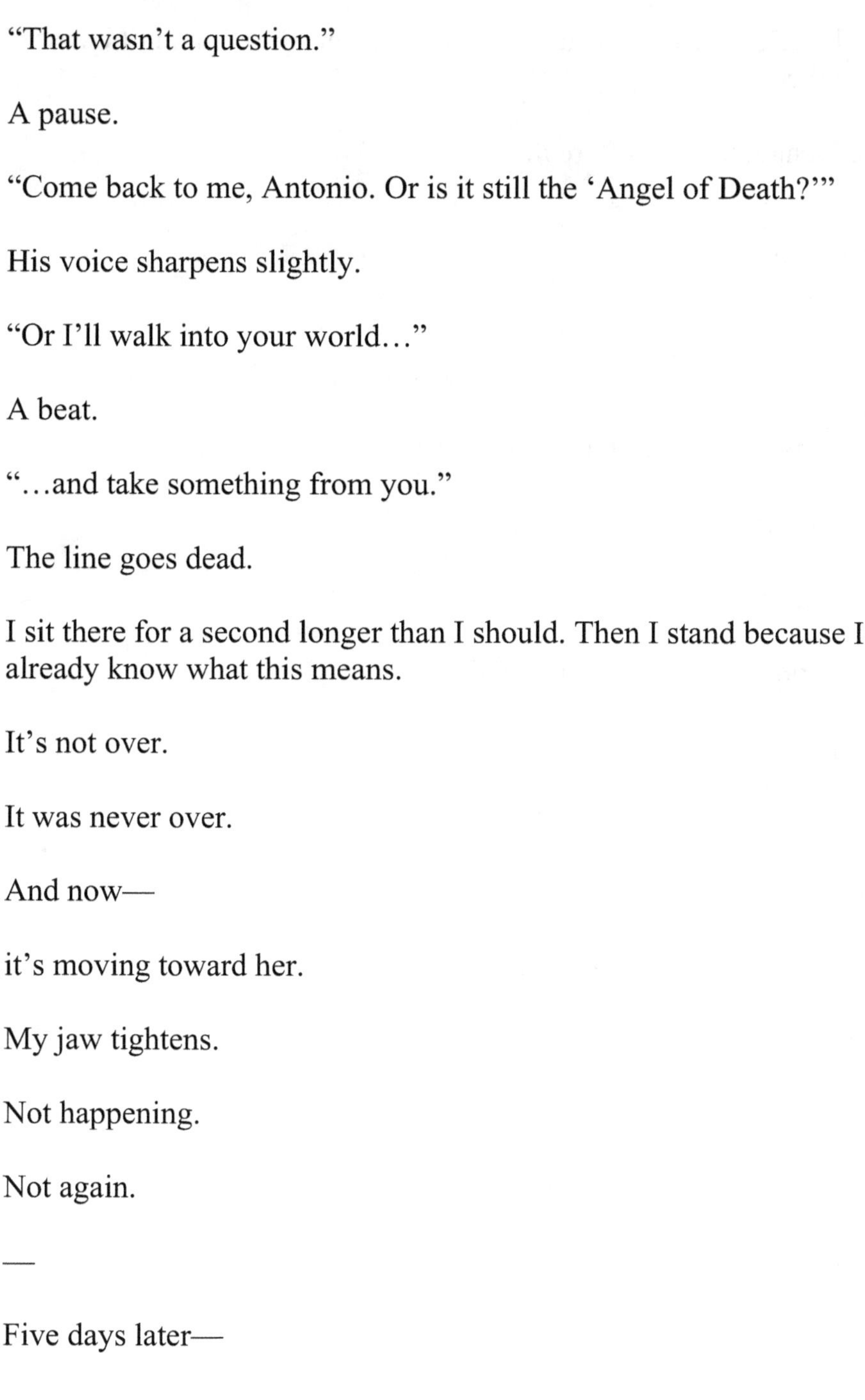

"That wasn't a question."

A pause.

"Come back to me, Antonio. Or is it still the 'Angel of Death?'"

His voice sharpens slightly.

"Or I'll walk into your world…"

A beat.

"…and take something from you."

The line goes dead.

I sit there for a second longer than I should. Then I stand because I already know what this means.

It's not over.

It was never over.

And now—

it's moving toward her.

My jaw tightens.

Not happening.

Not again.

—

Five days later—

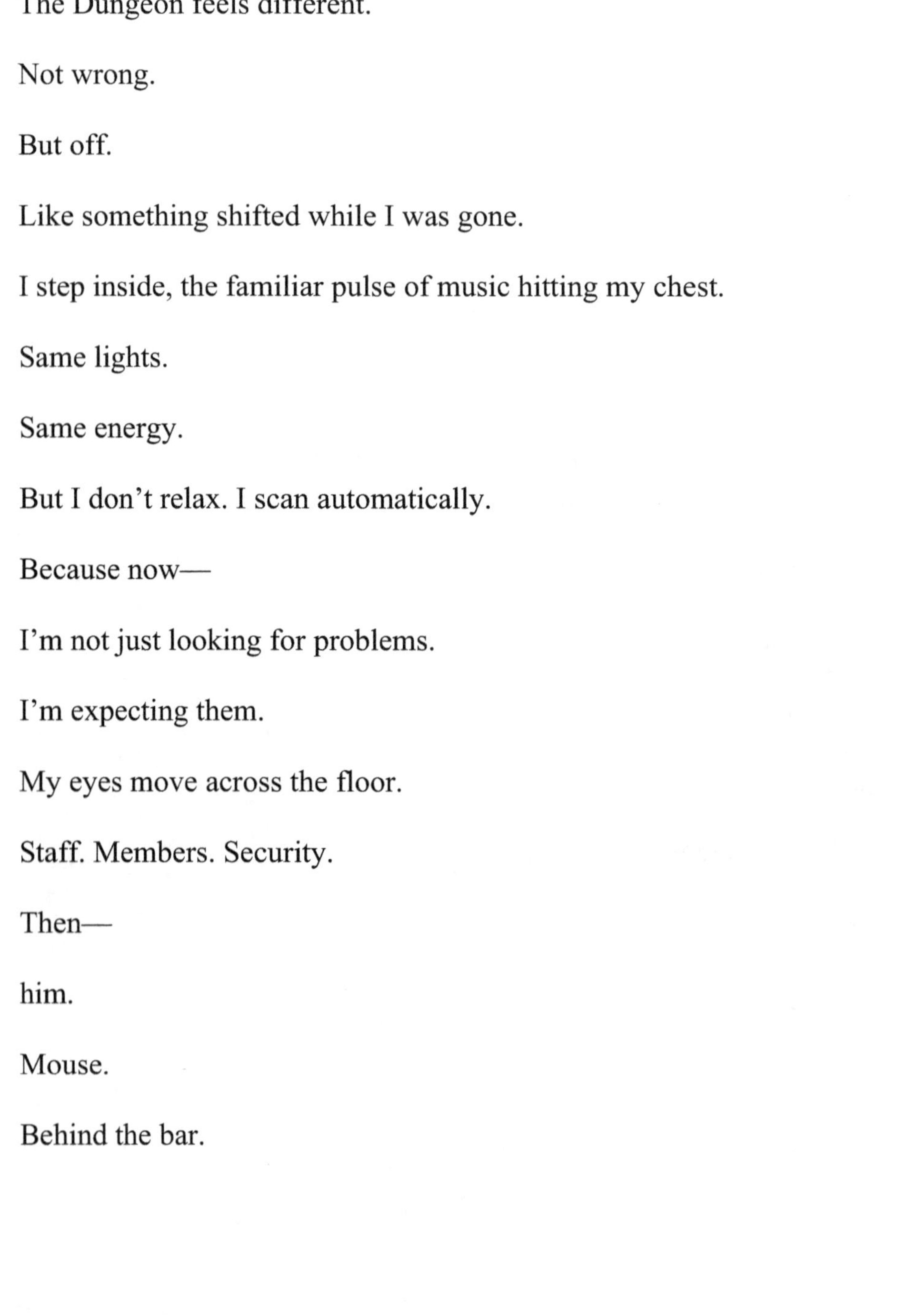

She hadn't called. We hadn't seen each other. But I couldn't blame her either.

The Dungeon feels different.

Not wrong.

But off.

Like something shifted while I was gone.

I step inside, the familiar pulse of music hitting my chest.

Same lights.

Same energy.

But I don't relax. I scan automatically.

Because now—

I'm not just looking for problems.

I'm expecting them.

My eyes move across the floor.

Staff. Members. Security.

Then—

him.

Mouse.

Behind the bar.

Like nothing happened. Stitches covering up my handiwork under his right eye.

Like he didn't get his ass handed to him.

That alone tells me everything I need to know.

He's not scared.

He should be.

But he's not.

Which means—

He thinks he has something.

Or someone.

Backing him.

My gaze hardens.

He doesn't notice me right away.

He's too busy watching.

Not the room.

She's up on the second level.

The Madame.

My jaw tightens.

There it is again. That look of obsession. I don't know why I didn't see it before.

That quiet—patient—creepy interest.

Snake. Just waiting patiently for his prey. He knows she's not interested, yet he still has that pitiful longing look on his face. Along with lust.

And now—

I'm sure of it.

He's not just a problem. Something feels very off.

Is he connected to something bigger?

Because men like him don't suddenly get bold for no reason.

They get bold—when they think they're protected.

My phone buzzes in my pocket.

A message.

Unknown number.

I don't need to open it.

I already know.

He's here.

Or close.

And suddenly—

everything lines up.

Mouse. Has to be.

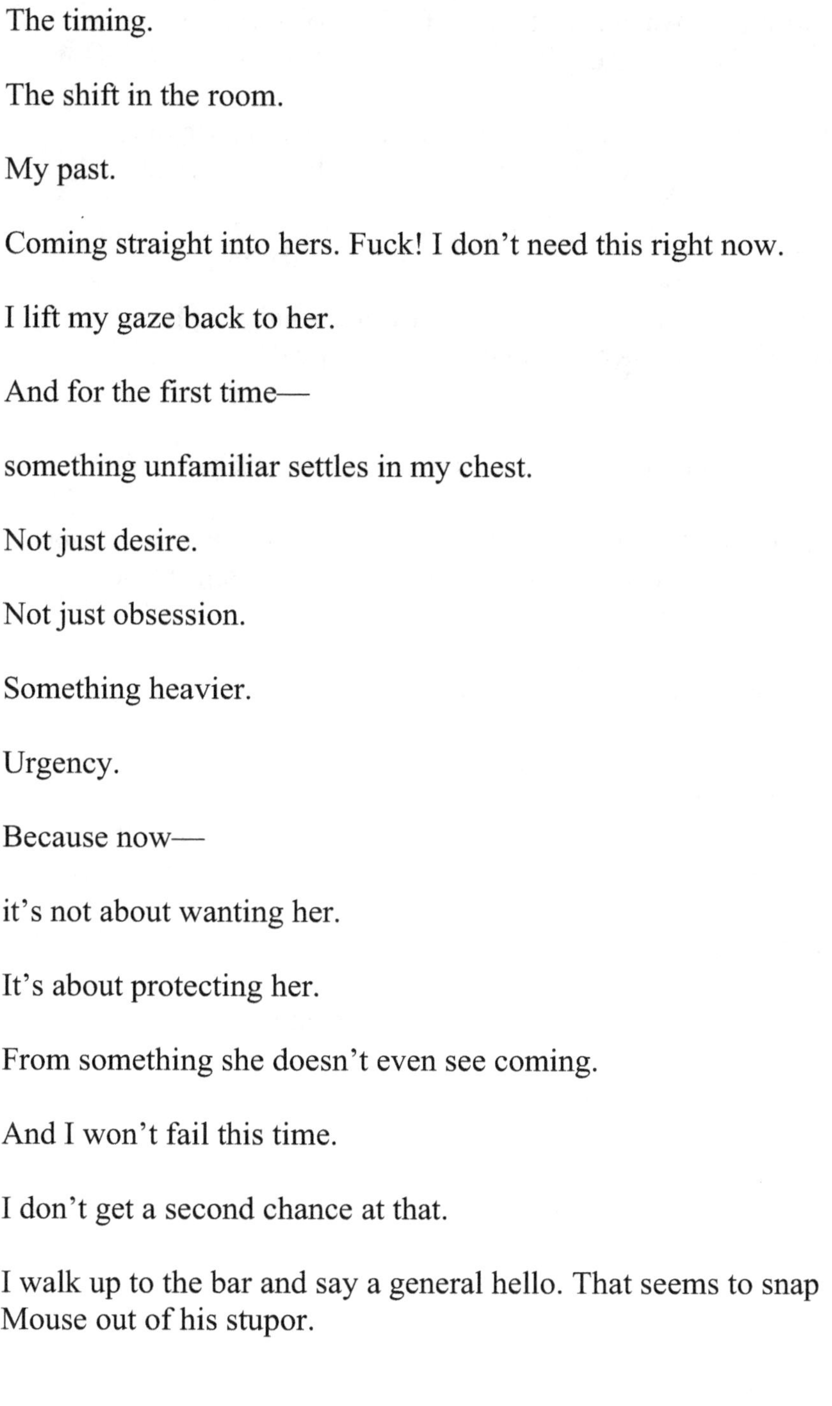

The timing.

The shift in the room.

My past.

Coming straight into hers. Fuck! I don't need this right now.

I lift my gaze back to her.

And for the first time—

something unfamiliar settles in my chest.

Not just desire.

Not just obsession.

Something heavier.

Urgency.

Because now—

it's not about wanting her.

It's about protecting her.

From something she doesn't even see coming.

And I won't fail this time.

I don't get a second chance at that.

I walk up to the bar and say a general hello. That seems to snap Mouse out of his stupor.

“Well, if it isn’t Angel. Back in the flesh. Thank you for the new scar. The ladies really dig it.”

My jaw clenches. “Yeah? I’m glad to be of service. Maybe now you’ll get your little dick wet by someone who really wants it.”

That seems to get a reaction out of him. So fucking predictable.

“Funny thing. Some of the guys and I were wondering if you were into men as well. Since you like looking at my dick, that just confirms it.”

I laugh. “Or it could mean I have an obsession with castration.”

His look darkens. “You touch me again, and you’ll have a lot more problems than you bargained for. Not to mention, you’ll lose your job.”

I shrug. His threats mean shit to me.

“The Madame isn’t a forgiving woman. Trust me. I know her better than you pretend to.”

“You almost sounded like a stalker. You know that’s a crime, right?”

“Not if it’s not proven in court.”

I turn and stare at him. “You really have a death wish.”

“No. But I will get what’s rightfully mine.”

I roll my eyes. Now he’s starting to bore me. “Well, when you actually know what that is, I’m sure there’ll be someone you can tell it to.”

“Like your uncle?”

My body stills.

I fucking knew it! In that moment, I knew I had to get to her before it was too late.

I storm off, leaving a very smiling Mouse behind.

Chapter Eleven

My Dearest Cosette,

Today is your 16th birthday. Your sweet 16. You've been gone for almost a year now, and it pains me to know that you are out there on your own. I refuse to believe you no longer walk this earth. When we are reunited, I will shower you with all the gifts you deserve. If your father were still alive, he would paint me as the worst mother, and you would be banned from my life. Being a single mother is no joke. Tough sacrifices get made. I have my regrets, things I can't take back even if I wanted to. You do mean the world to me, and I will spend the remainder of my life making things up to you. Until we meet again...

Love,

Mommy

Cosette

Antoinette has been a rock for me for the past week. My emotions were everywhere. Antonio really took me there. I had to gain my composure, or else I would have spilled my guts to him.

The dark parts of him that he keeps concealed, I'm too afraid to tap into that. I feel my trauma scars the more I'm around him. Both literally and figuratively. I know he saw the scars on my breasts and the scars on my back. The Boss did a number on me. But I can't let the years of therapy I've gone through to self-regulate my emotions set me back.

As for Antonio, I still want him. But I'm afraid to allow those parts of me to be revealed. And you can't be with someone if you can't be 100% honest with them.

For the past 10 years, this club has been my life. Through blood, sweat, and tears.

Antonio is twisted in his seductive methods. And maybe I'm twisted in some way, too. But, god, I've never been fucked so thoroughly in my life. I still feel the soreness between my thighs. And too, I love the thought that he came inside me. I know that's crazy, but it feels so warm and gooey inside my pussy.

Mmm. I need to stop. My nipples are getting hard, and I need to be Madame right now.

Something is off.

Not obvious. Not loud. But it's there—lingering beneath the music, beneath the laughter, beneath the carefully curated illusion I've spent years perfecting.

I feel it the moment I step onto the floor.

The Dungeon is running. Flowing. Everything looks exactly as it should. But it doesn't feel right.

My heels click against the polished floor as I move through the space, scanning everything like I always do. Nothing escapes me. Not for long. That's how I built this place—precision, awareness, control.

And right now, something is slipping.

My gaze lifts toward the bar and lands on Mouse.

He's working like nothing happened. Like he wasn't sent to the hospital. Like he didn't get himself suspended. Like he didn't cross a line he should've never even approached.

My expression doesn't change, but I slow slightly, watching him.

He moves differently tonight. Subtle—but I notice. Less chatter. Less ego. Too quiet. Too observant.

And he's not watching the customers.

He's watching me.

Our eyes meet for a moment. He doesn't look away immediately.

That alone is enough.

A flicker of something sharp moves through my chest. Not fear—I don't scare easily. But I don't ignore instincts either. And my instincts are telling me he's off.

I break eye contact first. Not because I have to, but because I choose to. He doesn't get that kind of access to me.

“Madame.”

I turn slightly at the voice behind me. Hazel looks more composed now, calmer than she was a week ago.

“You alright?” I ask.

She nods. “Yes, Madame. Just needed a moment.”

I study her for a second longer, making sure. This place doesn’t run if my people don’t feel safe.

“Good. Let me know if anything changes.”

“Umm, do you have time to chat on or around my break?”

“I should. Speak with Kitty to get yourself on my books so I don’t forget.”

She nods again and moves off.

I continue walking, but my attention keeps circling back to Mouse. Now that I’ve noticed it, I can’t unsee it.

He’s not working. Not really.

He’s positioning himself. Shifting angles. Placing himself where he can see more—where he can see me.

My jaw tightens. I’ve told this motherfucker on too many occasions that I’m not interested and that he needs to be professional at all times. Anyone with eyes can see that Antonio isn’t wrapped too tight mentally. And now it would seem, he’s a loose wire when it comes to me. Hulk watches me at all times as well. If Mouse were smart, he’d move the hell on.

This is not how my staff operates. That’s not how I trained them.

I change direction, heading toward the bar—but not directly. Never directly. I approach from the side, where he won't expect me.

When I step into his line of sight, he startles. Just slightly, but enough.

"Madame," he says quickly.

I rest my hand lightly against the bar, calm and composed.

"How's your face?" I ask.

His expression flickers. "I'm good. Just a scratch."

I nod slowly. "Lucky."

Silence stretches between us. He shifts, uncomfortable now.

Good.

"You seem distracted," I say.

"Just focused, Madame."

Liar.

"On what?"

He doesn't hesitate this time. "You."

There it is.

No filter. No hesitation. Just something ugly and unwelcome.

My expression doesn't change, but something inside me sharpens.

"You're here to work," I say evenly.

"I am."

He doesn't believe that. Neither do I.

"Then do that," I reply. "And stay out of places you don't belong."

His jaw tightens, but he nods. "Yes, Madame."

I hold his gaze for one more second, letting the weight of my words settle, then I turn and walk away.

But I can still feel it.

That look.

Like something crawling along my back.

Like something or someone is watching.

Waiting.

My steps don't falter, but inside, something is already moving.

Because this is how it starts—small, subtle, something out of place… until everything breaks.

"Cosette."

I stop.

I don't turn right away. I know that voice. I know what it does to me—even now.

I inhale slowly, then turn.

Antonio stands a few feet away, closer than he should be.

His presence hits me instantly. Heavy. Different. Not just desire anymore—something else. Something more urgent.

His eyes lock onto mine, and I see it.

Concern.

Real concern.

“You shouldn’t be out here alone,” he says.

“I’m not alone,” I reply, gesturing slightly around us. “My entire staff is here.”

“That’s not what I mean.”

His voice drops, and the air between us shifts again.

“What do you mean?”

He steps closer. Too close. But I don’t move.

“There’s something wrong,” he says.

“I’m aware.”

His jaw tightens. “You don’t understand.”

“Then explain it.”

He hesitates.

That tells me everything.

“You’re keeping something from me,” I say.

His eyes flick briefly toward the bar—toward Mouse—then back to me.

Now I know.

It's not just me feeling it.

It's him too.

"What is it?" I press.

"Danger," he says quietly.

The word lands heavily between us.

"You're going to need to be more specific."

But even as I say it, I feel it again—that shift in the room. Like something tightening around us.

Antonio steps closer, his voice low enough that only I can hear.

"My past is here," he says. "And I think it already found you."

Everything inside me goes still.

This isn't instinct anymore.

This is confirmation.

My gaze slowly lifts back to the bar.

Back to Mouse.

And this time, when our eyes meet, I don't look away.

Because now I'm not just observing.

I'm preparing.

And whatever this is—whatever's coming—it just made a mistake.

It stepped into my world.

And I don’t lose control of what’s mine.

Chapter Twelve

Antonio

His eyes will be the first to go. After warning Cosette, we devise a plan to make sure she has security clocking her every move. She agreed to fire Mouse. The atmosphere felt too off to allow him to continue working here. He was now a threat, not only to The Dungeon but also to those in it.

His look has become very noticeably different. More hungry, more hostile.

I notice it before I even realize I've stopped moving. I can't make another scene here. But I need to get him under control before he does something else he'll truly regret. Once he's fired, I'll make some calls to have him handled properly.

Mouse stands behind the bar like he belongs there, like nothing happened, like he didn't just threaten my uncle on me.

He's surer of himself.

It's in his posture. In the way he leans just slightly forward when she walks past. In the way his eyes follow her—not respectfully, not professionally—but with something else.

Something possessive. Something ugly. Lusting after her.

My jaw tightens. That shit will never happen.

He doesn't notice me approaching at first.

That's his second mistake. He's truly a dead man.

I step closer, slow, deliberate. Not enough to draw attention, but enough to step into his space.

Close enough that he feels it.

His head turns slightly.

And then his eyes land on me.

There's no fear there.

Not anymore.

Just a smirk.

"Look who's back," he says under his breath.

I don't respond right away. I just look at him. Let the silence stretch long enough to make him uncomfortable.

It doesn't work. Cocky little bitch.

He holds my gaze like he's been waiting for this.

That alone tells me everything.

"Your eyes are doing that disrespectful thing again," I say finally.

His lips twitch. "And your point?"

A beat passes.

"You're still standing," he adds. "I'm impressed. I thought you were handled. Your uncle did say you were a tough one. Maybe he's biding his time when it comes to you."

I lean slightly against the bar, casual on the outside, anything but on the inside.

"You got something to say," I tell him, "You should say it carefully."

His smirk widens.

"Oh, I plan to."

He pauses.

"I saw you," he says quietly.

My expression doesn't change.

"You see a lot of things," I reply.

"Yeah," he says. "But that day… that was interesting. Hearing her moan for another man."

He leans in slightly, lowering his voice.

"Didn't think The Madame had such low standards."

My hand tightens slightly against the bar.

"You talk about her again," I say, my voice low and steady, "you won't live long enough to see the next day."

He chuckles.

Soft.

Disrespectful.

"Touchy," he says. "You must really like her."

I don't answer that.

I don't need to.

He already knows.

That's why he's doing this. Baiting me.

"Careful," he adds, eyes flicking briefly toward the second level where she stands. "Men have gotten hurt over less."

My head tilts slightly.

"And you think you're not one of them?"

He shrugs.

"I think I'm the one who sees what's really going on."

A pause.

Then—

"I think your uncle would be really interested in that."

Everything in me goes still.

Not visibly.

Never visibly.

But inside—

"How do you know anything about my uncle?" I ask.

His smile doesn't fade.

"That's the thing about you," he says. "You think you're the only one with connections."

A beat.

"You're not as off the grid as you think. I've looked into you."

There it is.

Confirmation.

My suspicion hardens into certainty.

He's not just a snake.

He's someone's snake.

And I already know whose.

"You've been asking about me," I say.

He shrugs again.

"Maybe I've been listening. You're a low-life criminal born with a silver spoon in your mouth. Heard your dad was shit on the job too, and that your uncle has thought of you as a liability ever since. Can't say I disagree with him."

My hand moves before I decide to.

Fast.

Gripping his neck and slamming him back against the wall behind the bar.

The impact is loud enough to turn a few heads.

Not enough to stop me.

"Who have you been talking to?" I ask, my voice low and lethal.

His breath stutters slightly from the hit—but he's still smiling.

Still.

Smiling.

"You don't scare me Ang…," he says.

That's his last mistake.

My fist connects with his jaw before he finishes the sentence.

Hard.

His head snaps to the side, blood already starting to form at the corner of his mouth.

The room shifts.

People are watching now.

I don't care.

He swings back.

Sloppy.

Desperate.

I dodge it easily and hit him again.

And again.

Each hit cleaner than the last.

Each one fueled by something deeper than anger.

By the image of him watching her.

By the sound of his voice, saying my uncle's name.

By the fact that he thought he could stand here—

Talk about her—talk about my father.

like he had any place in her world.

“You don’t say his name,” I growl.

Another punch.

“You don’t look at her.”

Another.

“You don’t breathe in her direction.”

He collapses, but I don’t let him fall.

I pull him back up.

Because I’m not done.

Not even close.

“Angel.”

The voice cuts through the noise.

Hulk.

I barely register it.

A hand grabs my shoulder.

That’s all it takes.

Instinct takes over.

I turn—fast—grabbing the arm without thinking, twisting it hard in the opposite direction.

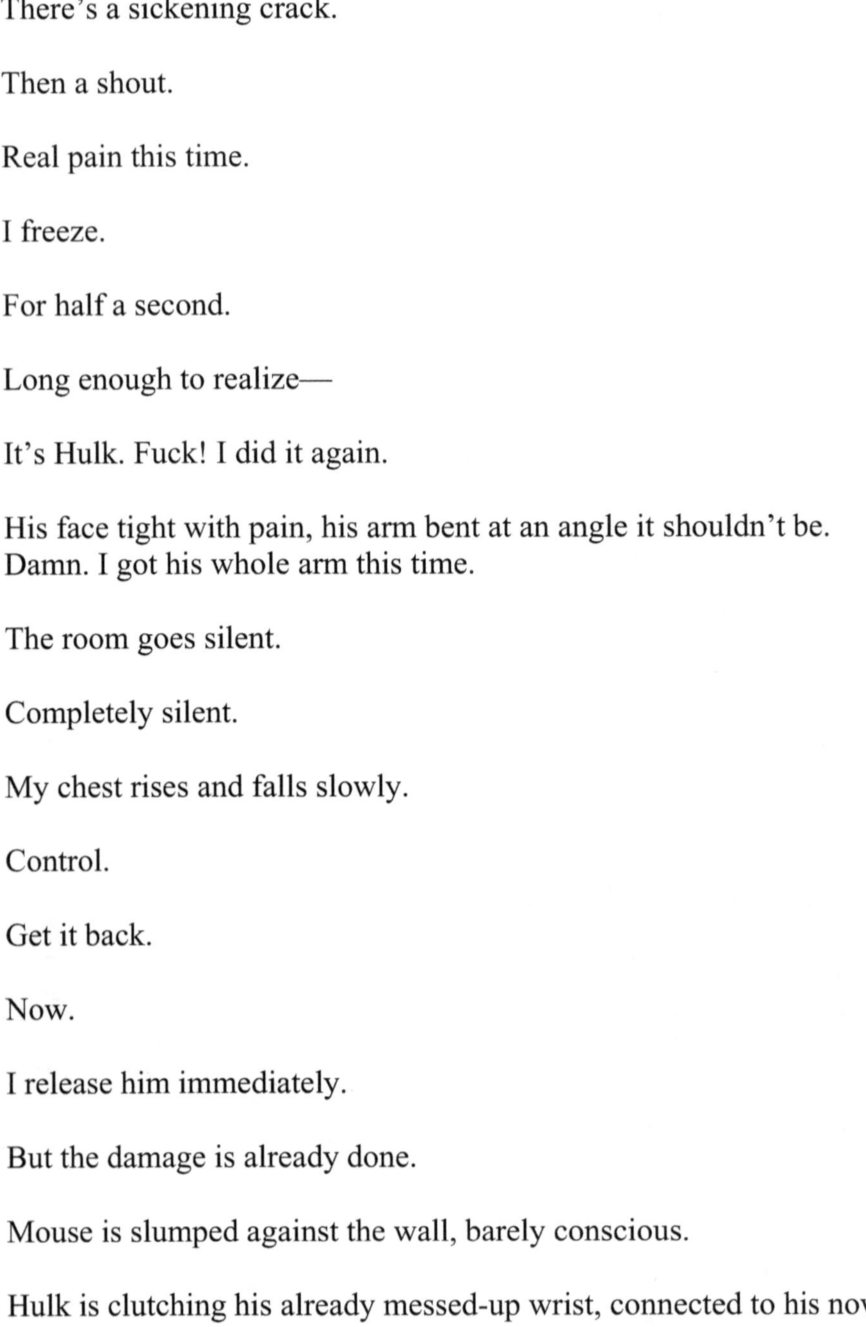

There's a sickening crack.

Then a shout.

Real pain this time.

I freeze.

For half a second.

Long enough to realize—

It's Hulk. Fuck! I did it again.

His face tight with pain, his arm bent at an angle it shouldn't be. Damn. I got his whole arm this time.

The room goes silent.

Completely silent.

My chest rises and falls slowly.

Control.

Get it back.

Now.

I release him immediately.

But the damage is already done.

Mouse is slumped against the wall, barely conscious.

Hulk is clutching his already messed-up wrist, connected to his now dislocated arm.

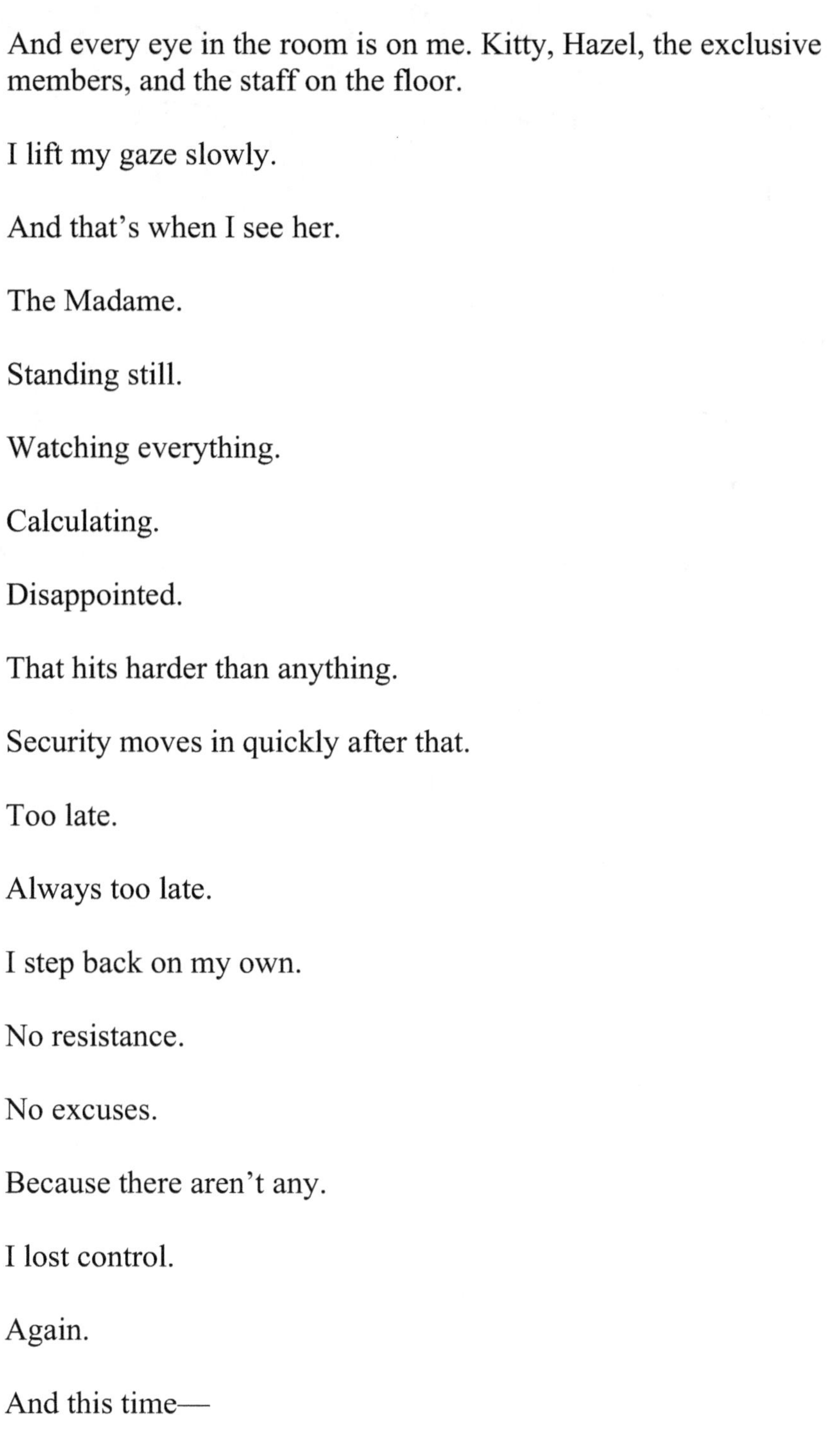

And every eye in the room is on me. Kitty, Hazel, the exclusive members, and the staff on the floor.

I lift my gaze slowly.

And that’s when I see her.

The Madame.

Standing still.

Watching everything.

Calculating.

Disappointed.

That hits harder than anything.

Security moves in quickly after that.

Too late.

Always too late.

I step back on my own.

No resistance.

No excuses.

Because there aren’t any.

I lost control.

Again.

And this time—

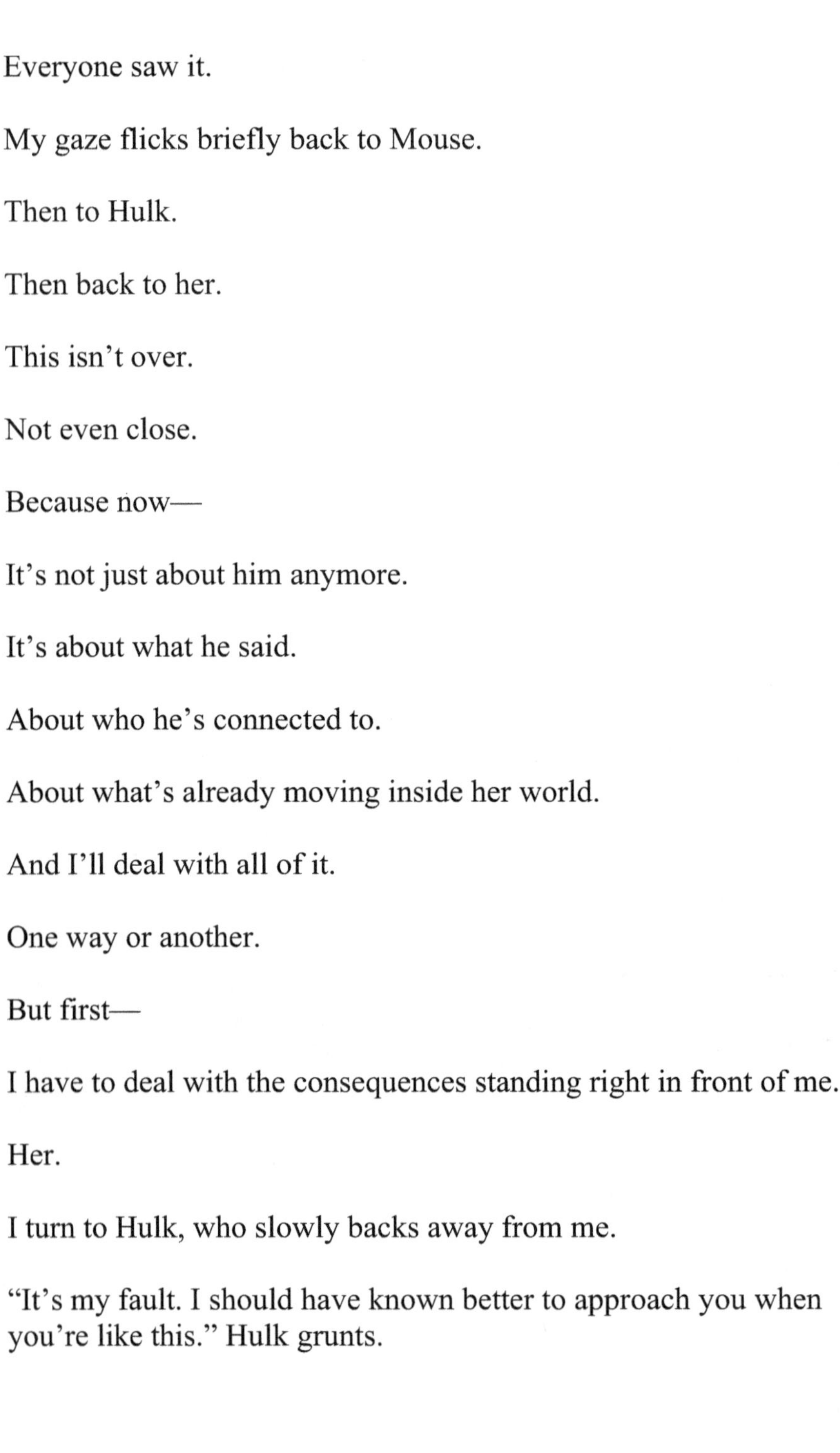

Everyone saw it.

My gaze flicks briefly back to Mouse.

Then to Hulk.

Then back to her.

This isn't over.

Not even close.

Because now—

It's not just about him anymore.

It's about what he said.

About who he's connected to.

About what's already moving inside her world.

And I'll deal with all of it.

One way or another.

But first—

I have to deal with the consequences standing right in front of me.

Her.

I turn to Hulk, who slowly backs away from me.

"It's my fault. I should have known better to approach you when you're like this." Hulk grunts.

I shake my head. “Old battle habits. My bad, Hulk. I’ll get everything back in order. If Madame doesn’t fire me.”

Hulk, clearly in pain, just nods and walks off. I should’ve at least grabbed him some ice. I feel terrible. But why the fuck would you grab someone who’s clearly pissed off?

“Angel. Mouse. My office now!” Her voice is booming now. Fuck! She’s pissed.

Chapter Thirteen

Cosette

I don't speak until the door closes.

Silence fills my office, heavy and deliberate.

I let it sit.

Let it stretch.

Let it remind both of them exactly where they are.

My space.

My rules.

My authority.

Mouse stands to the left, trying to look composed despite the swelling and bleeding in his face. It took 2 security guards to drag him in. Antonio stands across from him, still, unreadable, dangerous. Knuckles bruised and covered in Mouse's blood.

Neither of them speaks.

Good.

"Do either of you want to explain what just happened out there?" I ask calmly.

Mouse answers immediately.

"He attacked me," he says, quick and rehearsed. "Unprovoked."

I don't react.

I turn my head slightly.

"Angel?"

"I handled a problem," he says.

Of course he did.

My gaze shifts back to Mouse.

"Unprovoked?" I repeat.

"Yes, Madame. I was doing my job."

The lie sits in the room like smoke.

Thick.

Obvious.

And insulting.

I exhale slowly, stepping around my desk.

"You're not very good at lying," I say.

His expression flickers.

Just slightly.

But I see it.

"I don't know what you mean," he replies.

"Then let me make it very clear."

I turn toward the door.

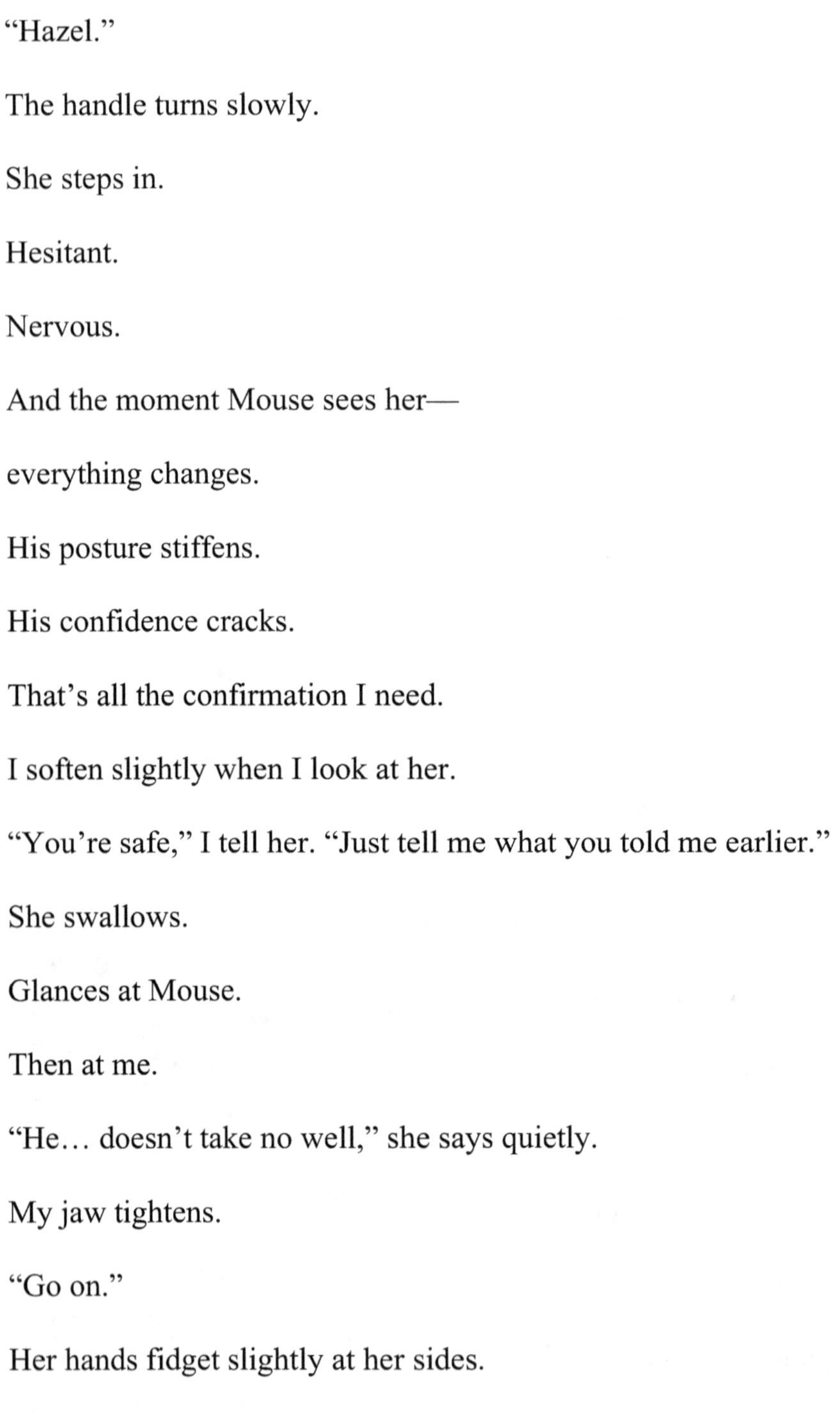

"Hazel."

The handle turns slowly.

She steps in.

Hesitant.

Nervous.

And the moment Mouse sees her—

everything changes.

His posture stiffens.

His confidence cracks.

That's all the confirmation I need.

I soften slightly when I look at her.

"You're safe," I tell her. "Just tell me what you told me earlier."

She swallows.

Glances at Mouse.

Then at me.

"He… doesn't take no well," she says quietly.

My jaw tightens.

"Go on."

Her hands fidget slightly at her sides.

"I turned him down a few weeks ago," she continues. "After my shift. He followed me to the back hallway. Said I thought I was better than him."

My stomach turns.

But I keep my face neutral.

Steady.

"He grabbed me," she adds, voice shaking now. "Not hard enough to leave marks… but enough. And he told me if I didn't fuck him, I wouldn't last long here."

Silence.

Heavy.

I don't look at Mouse yet.

Because I don't need to.

I already know what I'm going to see.

I nod once.

"You can go," I tell her gently.

She leaves quickly.

The door closes again.

And now—

there's no hiding.

I turn slowly.

"Do you want to try that again?" I ask.

Mouse exhales through his swollen lips.

Shifts his weight.

"She's a fucking liar," he says. "Women like her do that."

That's all it takes.

"You're done," I say.

Flat.

Final.

His head snaps up.

"What?"

"You're fired."

The words land like a gunshot.

"You can't fire me over some bullshit like that," he snaps. "There's no proof."

He takes a deep breath. "Madame, I've been a loyal employee for 3 years. You'd fire me over that bitch?"

I step closer.

Calm.

Unbothered.

"I don't need proof," I say. "I need judgment. And mine is better than yours."

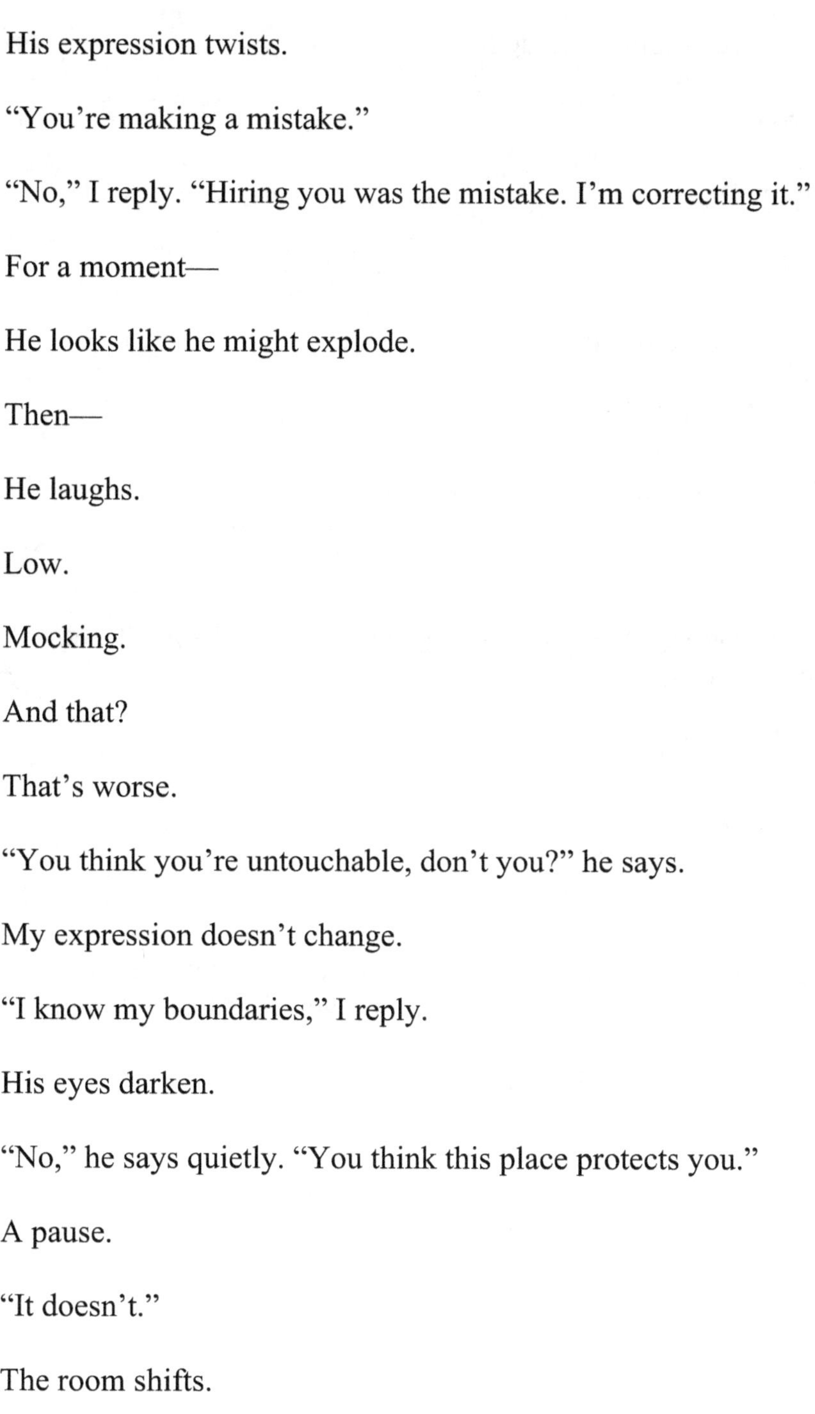

His expression twists.

"You're making a mistake."

"No," I reply. "Hiring you was the mistake. I'm correcting it."

For a moment—

He looks like he might explode.

Then—

He laughs.

Low.

Mocking.

And that?

That's worse.

"You think you're untouchable, don't you?" he says.

My expression doesn't change.

"I know my boundaries," I reply.

His eyes darken.

"No," he says quietly. "You think this place protects you."

A pause.

"It doesn't."

The room shifts.

Antonio moves slightly beside me.

Not in front.

Not over me.

Beside.

Exactly where I need him.

"You don't get to threaten me in my office," I say.

Mouse steps forward.

Just enough.

"You rejected me," he says, voice tightening. "Like I wasn't even worth considering."

"You weren't," I say.

His jaw tightens.

"You think you're better than me, bitch?"

"I know I am. And watch your fucking mouth when you're speaking to me. Or your job won't be the only thing you'll be losing tonight."

That lands exactly how I want it to.

His composure cracks completely.

"I'll make you regret this decision," he says. "You and your little slave."

Antonio steps forward now.

Fully.

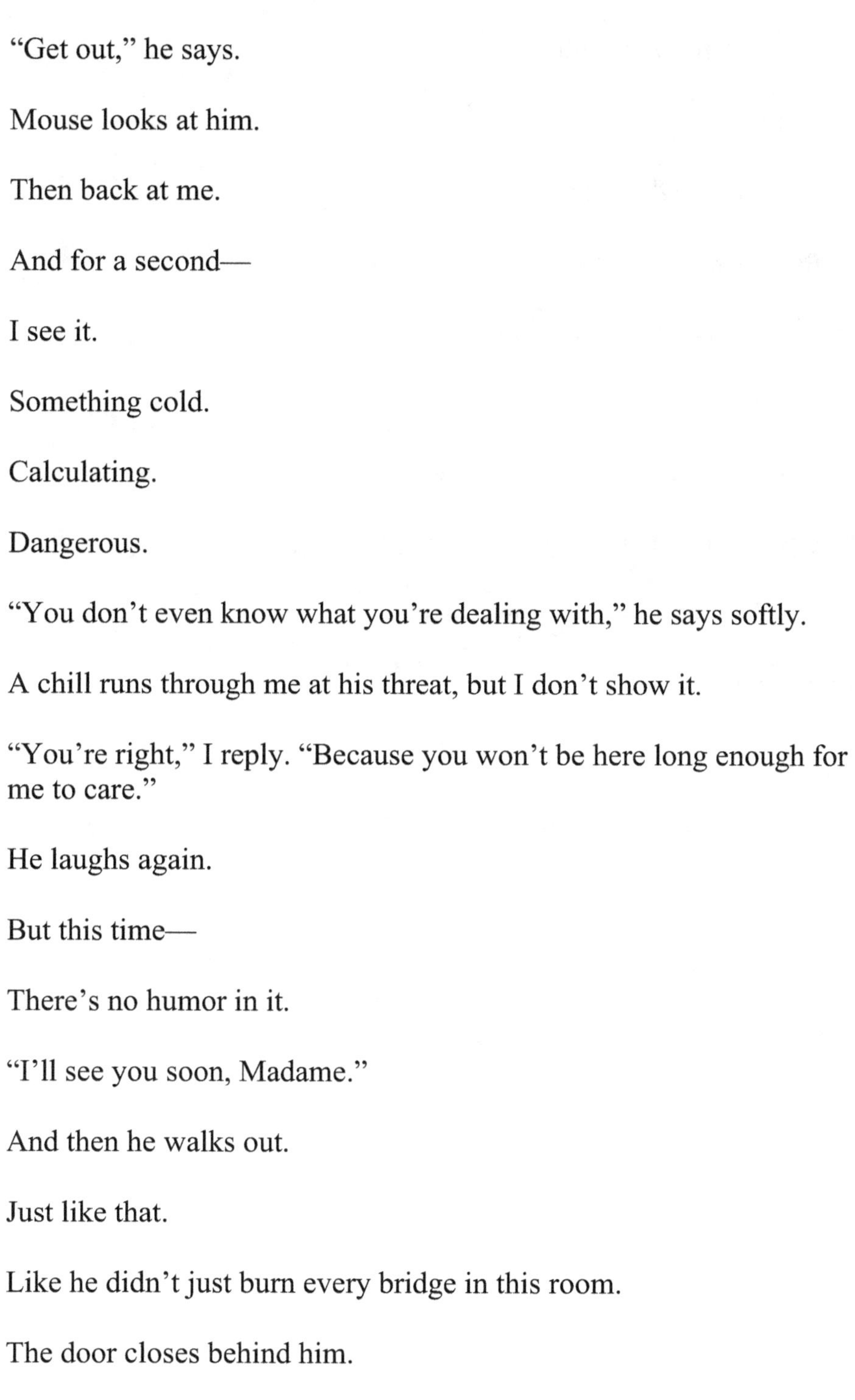

"Get out," he says.

Mouse looks at him.

Then back at me.

And for a second—

I see it.

Something cold.

Calculating.

Dangerous.

"You don't even know what you're dealing with," he says softly.

A chill runs through me at his threat, but I don't show it.

"You're right," I reply. "Because you won't be here long enough for me to care."

He laughs again.

But this time—

There's no humor in it.

"I'll see you soon, Madame."

And then he walks out.

Just like that.

Like he didn't just burn every bridge in this room.

The door closes behind him.

And the silence that follows—

feels different.

I don't move right away.

Neither does Antonio.

"Lock the back corridors down," I say.

My voice is steady.

Even if my instincts are screaming.

"No one is alone in this building tonight."

"Yes, Madame," he says immediately.

I turn to him slowly.

Really look at him.

"You were right," I admit.

A beat.

"He's a problem."

Antonio's expression doesn't change.

"I know."

Silence settles between us.

Then—

"I need someone I can trust," I say.

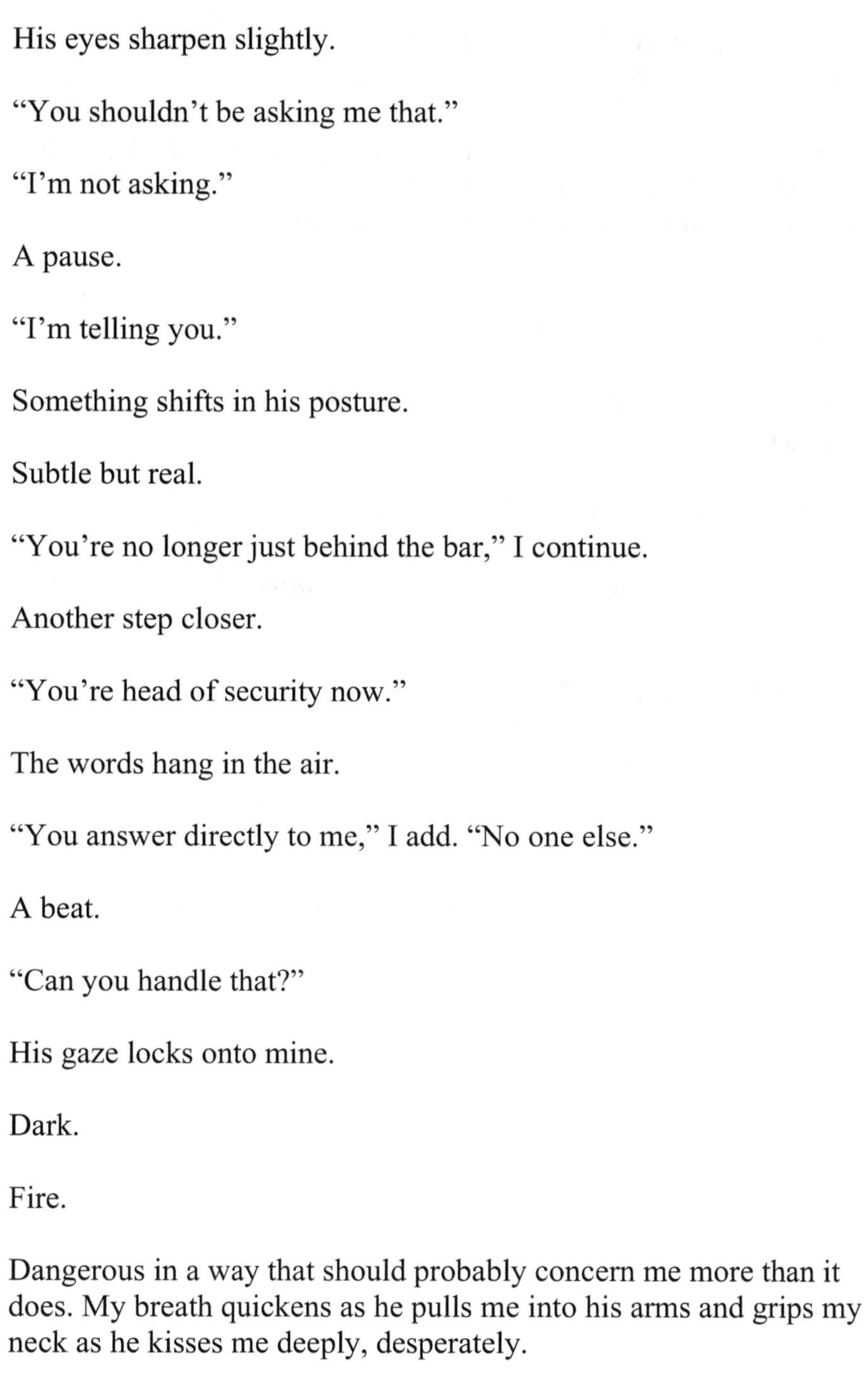

His eyes sharpen slightly.

"You shouldn't be asking me that."

"I'm not asking."

A pause.

"I'm telling you."

Something shifts in his posture.

Subtle but real.

"You're no longer just behind the bar," I continue.

Another step closer.

"You're head of security now."

The words hang in the air.

"You answer directly to me," I add. "No one else."

A beat.

"Can you handle that?"

His gaze locks onto mine.

Dark.

Fire.

Dangerous in a way that should probably concern me more than it does. My breath quickens as he pulls me into his arms and grips my neck as he kisses me deeply, desperately.

I kiss him right back. It was like he knew I needed his touch, his kisses. "Mmm," I moan.

I hear the zipper on his pants, but it didn't register until I felt him lift my dress. He lifted me up as I wrapped my legs around his waist. His dick pushed inside me in one delicious thrust.

Holding him tight, I kiss him with all the need and passion in my being. God, this man sets my body on fire.

His pumps come hard and fast. He bites and sucks, and kisses my lips and my neck.

"Yes, baby. Grip my dick with that pussy."

My release is near. I hear his pants getting shorter and shorter. He's close too.

"Cum with me, Antonio."

Our release racked both of our bodies. I feel his seed releasing into my hungry pussy. I just cling to him for a moment longer before he sets me on my feet.

Once he catches his breath, he holds my face in both hands and says, "Yes. It would be my honor to protect you. You didn't even need to ask."

"Music to my ears." I smile, looking into his beautiful eyes.

"You're mine, Cosette."

"I know."

No hesitation.

Of course not.

He nods once.

“Good.”

Because something just changed tonight.

Not just in this room.

Not just with Mouse.

But in the entire structure of what I’ve built.

And for the first time in a long time—

I’m not just managing a business.

I’m preparing for danger I can’t fully see or understand.

And this time—

I won’t be caught off guard. I’ll be ready for whatever with Antonio next to me.

Chapter Fourteen

Antonio

I don't celebrate wins. Not real ones, and definitely not the kind that come with consequences.

Head of security.

The title sits in my mind. Not because I don't understand it, but because I understand it too well. Access. Authority. Proximity. To her.

That's what she gave me—whether she realizes it or not.

I'm still trying to process my feelings for her. We have only had interactions at the club and at my house. I want to know more about her. But with this new threat hanging over us, it feels like it'll be impossible. At least for now.

I never felt I needed a significant other in my life. But damn, this woman consumes me. I have to come back to these thoughts and feelings at another time. I need to prioritize. Deal with my uncle first, then have a nice chat with my feisty chocolate goddess.

I step outside The Dungeon, the cool night air hitting my skin as the door closes behind me. The noise from inside dulls instantly, replaced by something quieter.

This is where I think best. Outside. Away from distractions. Away from her.

Because when I'm near her, I don't think clearly.

And right now, I need clarity.

Mouse is gone. Fired. But that doesn't make him irrelevant. It makes him more dangerous. Men like him don't walk away clean. They don't accept rejection. They don't forget humiliation.

They retaliate.

The way he looked at her before he left—that wasn't over. That was a promise.

My jaw tightens.

I reach into my pocket and pull out my phone. I need to reach out to some contacts for extra backup. Not sure if they'll take my call. I'm leaving the business without any explanation to anyone. There's already a message waiting. Unknown number.

Of course.

I open it.

`You're making this harder than it needs to be.`

I don't respond.

Another message comes through almost immediately.

`You always were stubborn.`

I exhale slowly through my nose.

I feel my phone vibrate. Unknown number. Again? What the hell!

I answer on the first ring.

"Antonio."

That voice—calm, controlled, like none of this means anything.

“You’re getting bold,” I say.

A soft chuckle follows. “No, I’m getting impatient.”

I lean against the wall, eyes scanning the alley out of habit.

“You sent him,” I say.

A pause. Then, “I don’t know what you’re talking about.”

Lie.

“You’re sloppy. He mentioned you.”

Silence stretches, then— “Ah. So, you’ve met my pet Mouse.”

My grip tightens around the phone.

“You don’t get to send people into my space.”

“Your space?” he repeats, amusement laced in his tone. “You’re living in a fantasy, Antonio. You don’t own anything.”

“I own my decisions.”

“And one of those decisions was walking away from me.”

There it is. The truth underneath everything.

“This is your way back,” he continues. “You come back to the family. You take your place.”

“No.”

Immediate. Firm. Final.

A pause. Then his tone shifts, just slightly.

"You always were emotional."

"This isn't emotional. This is done."

Another pause, longer this time.

"Then I suppose I'll have to motivate you."

My body stills.

"You stay away from her."

"You're very attached to this woman."

I don't answer. I don't need to.

"I wonder if she knows who she's dealing with," he adds.

My voice drops. "You don't go near her."

"Or what?" he asks softly. "You'll kill me?"

We both know the answer to that.

"Yes."

No hesitation. No emotion. Just truth.

Another pause. Then, "That's my boy."

The line goes dead.

I lower the phone slowly. My pulse is steady. Too steady.

Because now this isn't a possibility anymore.

This is happening.

He's moving.

I take my phone and dial an old contact of mine who owes me a favor for saving his life back in the day.

"Gordo."

"Tony. Is it really you?"

"Yeah. Listen, I know you haven't spoken to me in a while…"

"Listen, you know I don't give a fuck about time. The Angel of Death took out more bodies than necessary to secure my business. Because of you, my famililia and I can eat. Whatcha' need?"

I breathe a sigh of relief. "I need some additional security to be provided to my girl and me. Her place of business and both of our homes. I know it's a big job, but I need someone I can trust with this. My uncle is up to something, and I need to prepare for whatever's coming."

"I can supply about 50 men. All loyal to me and not that sick fuck Eugenio. I can't confirm anything, though. I'm wrapping up a job now."

"That'll work. I'll call you in a few hours with more details. Thanks Gordo."

"My pleasure."

Mouse was just the beginning.

I push off the wall and head back inside.

The moment I step through the doors, everything sharpens again—the lights, the music, the movement.

But now I'm not seeing it as a bartender.

I'm seeing it as security.

My eyes scan every entry point, every blind spot, every corridor. A guard repositioned. A hallway checked. A door secured.

No one questions it. They feel the energy shift too.

Places like this don't break all at once. They crack slowly, quietly, until something forces them open.

And I can feel it coming.

Close.

Very close.

My gaze drifts to the upper level.

She's there, watching like she always does.

She meets my eyes briefly.

And this time, there's no flirtation.

No tension.

Just understanding.

She knows something is wrong.

She just doesn't know how wrong yet.

My attention shifts back to the floor, but I don't relax. Not even for a second.

Because now this isn't about desire.

This isn't about tension.

This is about survival.

And if anything comes for her—

anything—

I won't hesitate.

I'll burn every fucking thing down to stop it.

Even if it means becoming the man I tried to leave behind.

Chapter Fifteen

Cosette

The Dungeon has never felt like this before.

Not unsafe. Not chaotic. Just… different.

Like every corner is being watched twice.

I stand on the upper level, hands resting lightly against the railing as I scan the floor below. Everything is running smoothly. Music, movement, laughter—it's all exactly how it should be.

But beneath it, there's tension.

And I don't miss tension.

Security has doubled. Not obviously. Not in a way that would alarm my members. But I see it. The repositioning. The rotation patterns. The way certain doors are now monitored instead of being casually checked.

Antonio.

My eyes find him almost immediately.

He's not behind the bar anymore. He's moving. Constantly. Observing. Adjusting. Watching.

Not just like a man doing a job.

Like a man preparing for something.

And that alone is enough to make me start asking questions.

I turn and head toward my office. I don't rush. I never rush. But my mind is already moving ahead of me.

Because something isn't adding up.

The house. The money. The way he fights. The way he moves like he's been trained—not taught.

And now? The way he's securing my entire establishment like it's under threat… without telling me exactly what that threat is.

That, I don't like.

I close my office door behind me and walk straight to my desk, pulling open the drawer where I keep employee files.

His file is still there.

Right where I left it.

Antonio. Angel.

Even the name situation is a problem.

I flip through the paperwork slowly, scanning for something I might've missed the first time.

Address.

My eyes land on it again.

That same restricted community.

I sit back in my chair, staring at it.

That neighborhood isn't just expensive. It's exclusive. Members live there. People with real money. Old money. Protected money.

And he just… lives there?

No.

That doesn't happen by accident.

My fingers tap lightly against the desk.

"You're hiding something," I murmur.

A soft knock pulls me out of my thoughts.

"Come in."

Antoinette steps inside, closing the door behind her. One look at my face and she sighs.

"Oh, this is about him," she says.

I don't deny it.

"He's changing things," I say.

"Security," she replies, leaning against the door. "I noticed."

"More than that. He's anticipating something."

"And you don't like not knowing what."

"No."

I don't operate in the dark. Not anymore.

"Then ask him," she says.

I let out a small laugh. "You think he's just going to tell me?"

She shrugs. “You’d be surprised what men will say when they’re obsessed.”

I roll my eyes. “He’s not obsessed.”

She just looks at me.

I exhale. “Okay… he’s intense as hell.”

“That’s one word for it.”

A quiet pause settles between us.

Then she says it.

“He scares you. He’s basically claimed you.”

My head lifts instantly. “No.”

Too fast.

“Cosette.”

I lean back slightly, forcing calm into my voice. “He doesn’t scare me. He just… doesn’t feel predictable.”

“And you like control.”

“I require control. But when we’re together, I find myself wanting to give him all the control.”

She grins. “I know.”

Silence.

Then I say it.

“I’m going to look into him.”

She straightens slightly. "How deep?"

"As deep as I need to."

Because something is off. And I don't ignore that feeling.

Not anymore.

"Just be careful," she says. "Men like him usually come with history."

"I figured that much out already."

She smiles faintly. "Keep me posted."

"I always do."

She leaves, and I'm alone again.

I look back down at his file.

Then at my phone.

I don't hesitate.

I dial.

He answers on the second ring.

"Madame."

His voice does something to me. Annoying. Unwanted. Real.

"Where are you?" I ask.

"At the club."

"I know that. Where in the club?"

A pause. "Why?"

I lean back slightly in my chair. "Because I want to see you."

Silence.

Then, "I'll be there in a minute."

The line goes dead.

Of course it does.

I set the phone down slowly.

Because this conversation?

It's long overdue.

A knock comes again.

"Come in."

The door opens.

And there he is.

He steps inside like he belongs here.

Like this space is his, too.

I don't speak right away.

I just look at him.

Really look at him.

Because now I'm not just seeing the man I'm attracted to.

I'm seeing the man I don't understand.

And that makes him dangerous.

"You wanted to see me," he says after a while.

I nod slightly.

"I did."

A pause.

Then I lean forward slightly, eyes locked on his.

"What exactly is going on, Antonio?"

He doesn't answer right away.

Of course he doesn't.

His gaze studies me, like he's deciding how much to say… or how much to hide.

"That depends," he finally says.

"On what?" I ask.

"On how much you're ready to hear."

My jaw tightens slightly.

"Try me."

A beat passes between us.

Then—

"You're not safe," he says.

I don’t flinch.

“I’ve built this place to be one of the safest environments in this city,” I reply.

“That was before,” he says.

Before.

The word lands harder than it should.

“Before what?” I ask.

His eyes hold mine.

“Before I got here.”

Silence stretches between us.

“You think you’re the problem?” I ask.

“I think I brought one with me.”

Something cold settles in my chest.

“What kind of problem?” I ask.

The corner of his jaw tightens.

“The kind that doesn’t knock before it enters,” he says. “The kind that doesn’t respect boundaries.”

My mind immediately flashes to Mouse.

To his eyes.

To his words.

To the way he said, *you'll regret this.*

"Is this about him?" I ask.

Antonio's gaze sharpens.

"It's about more than him."

That's not reassuring.

"Then stop speaking in riddles and tell me what I'm dealing with."

A pause.

Then—

"My past," he says.

The room feels smaller.

"Be specific."

His expression darkens slightly.

"You don't want that."

"You don't get to decide what I want," I say.

His eyes flicker.

There it is again—that tension between us.

"You gave me a position," he says. "Let me do my job."

"I don't give blind trust," I reply. "I make informed decisions."

Another pause.

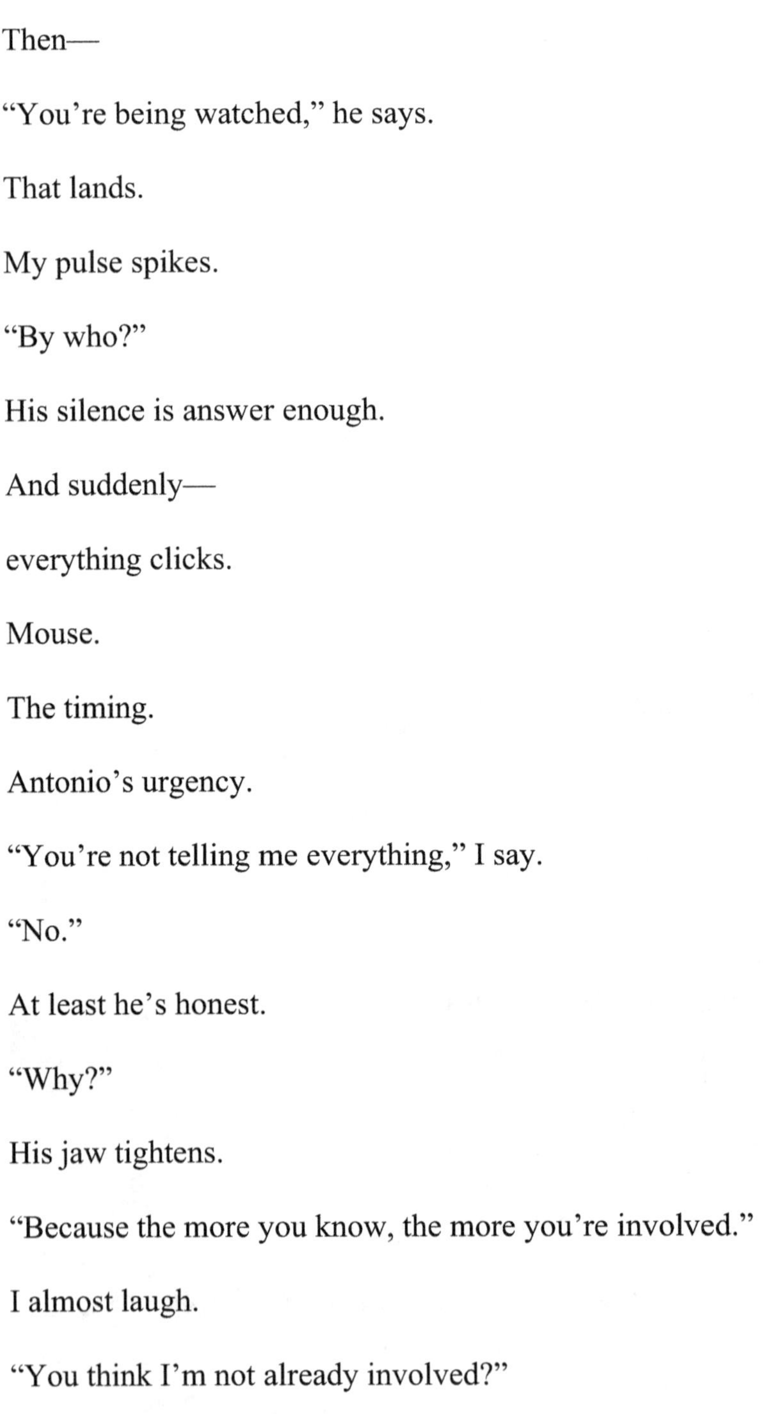

Then—

"You're being watched," he says.

That lands.

My pulse spikes.

"By who?"

His silence is answer enough.

And suddenly—

everything clicks.

Mouse.

The timing.

Antonio's urgency.

"You're not telling me everything," I say.

"No."

At least he's honest.

"Why?"

His jaw tightens.

"Because the more you know, the more you're involved."

I almost laugh.

"You think I'm not already involved?"

A beat.

"You are," he admits. "But there are levels to this."

"And you're deciding which level I get access to?"

"I'm trying to keep you alive."

The words hang between us.

I lean back slowly in my chair.

Studying him.

Reassessing everything.

"You don't get to make decisions for me," I say quietly.

"I know."

"But you will anyway."

A pause.

"Yes."

At least he doesn't lie.

I exhale slowly.

Because this?

This is bigger than I thought.

And I don't like being blindsided.

Not ever.

"Then we're going to do this differently," I say.

His brow lifts slightly.

"How?"

"You stop deciding what I can handle," I reply. "And you start telling me the truth."

Silence.

Then—

"I'll tell you enough," he says.

Not good enough.

But it's something.

"For now," I say.

Because this conversation isn't over.

Not even close.

And whatever he brought into my world—

I'm going to uncover it.

One way or another.

Chapter Sixteen

Antonio

Cosette doesn't like not knowing. I know this.

I saw it in her eyes the moment she asked me what was going on.

Pressure.

She feels it now.

Good.

That means she'll be more careful.

It also means I'm running out of time.

I step out of her office and don't look back. Not because I don't want to—but because if I do, I might say too much. Or worse, not enough.

Neither helps her.

Neither keeps her safe.

I move through the club with purpose, scanning as I go. Every entrance. Every exit. Every blind spot. My men aren't here yet, but I've already started shifting things into place.

Temporary fixes.

They won't hold.

Not against what's coming.

I step outside again, pulling my phone from my pocket before the door even closes behind me.

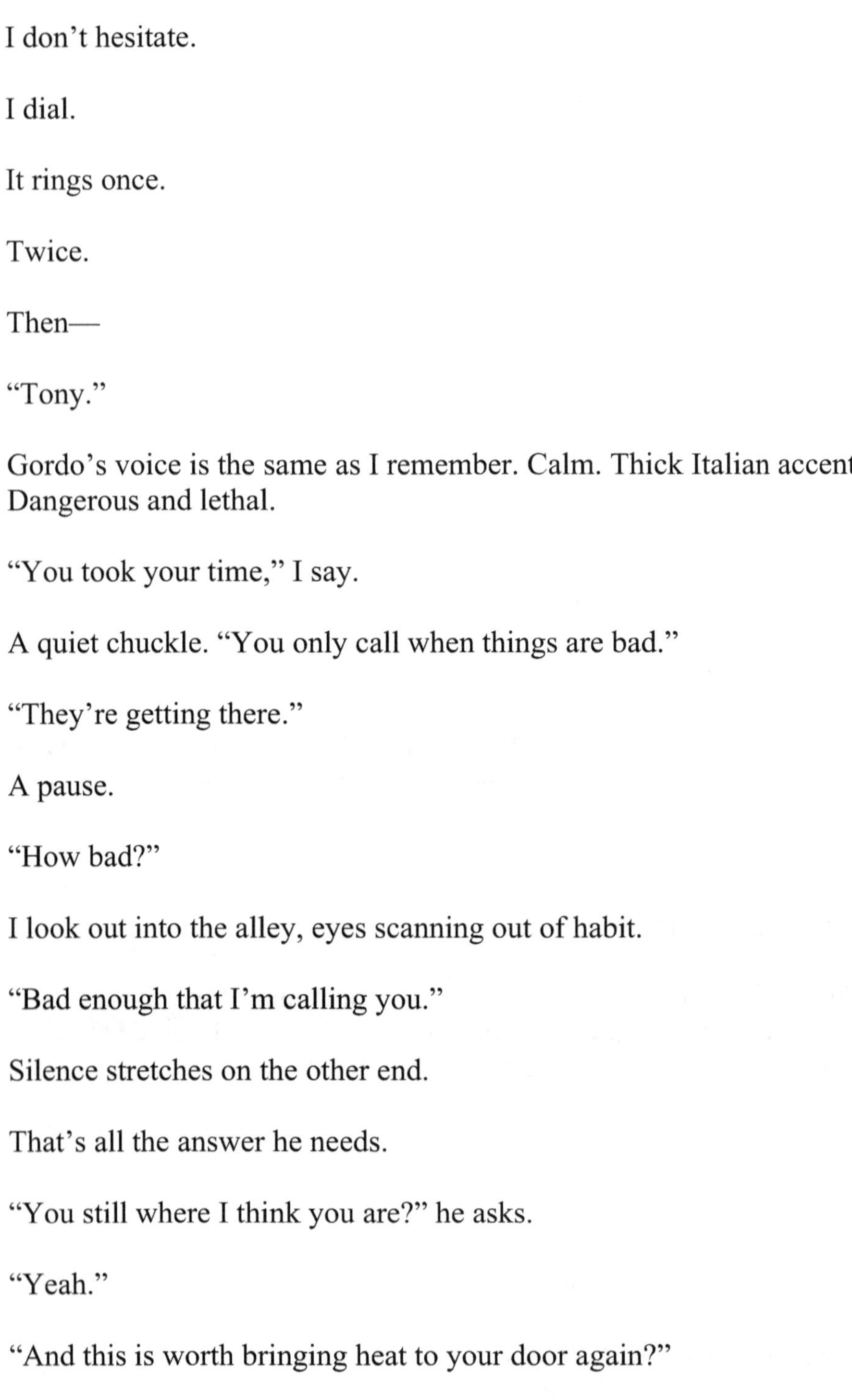

I don’t hesitate.

I dial.

It rings once.

Twice.

Then—

“Tony.”

Gordo’s voice is the same as I remember. Calm. Thick Italian accent. Dangerous and lethal.

“You took your time,” I say.

A quiet chuckle. “You only call when things are bad.”

“They’re getting there.”

A pause.

“How bad?”

I look out into the alley, eyes scanning out of habit.

“Bad enough that I’m calling you.”

Silence stretches on the other end.

That’s all the answer he needs.

“You still where I think you are?” he asks.

“Yeah.”

“And this is worth bringing heat to your door again?”

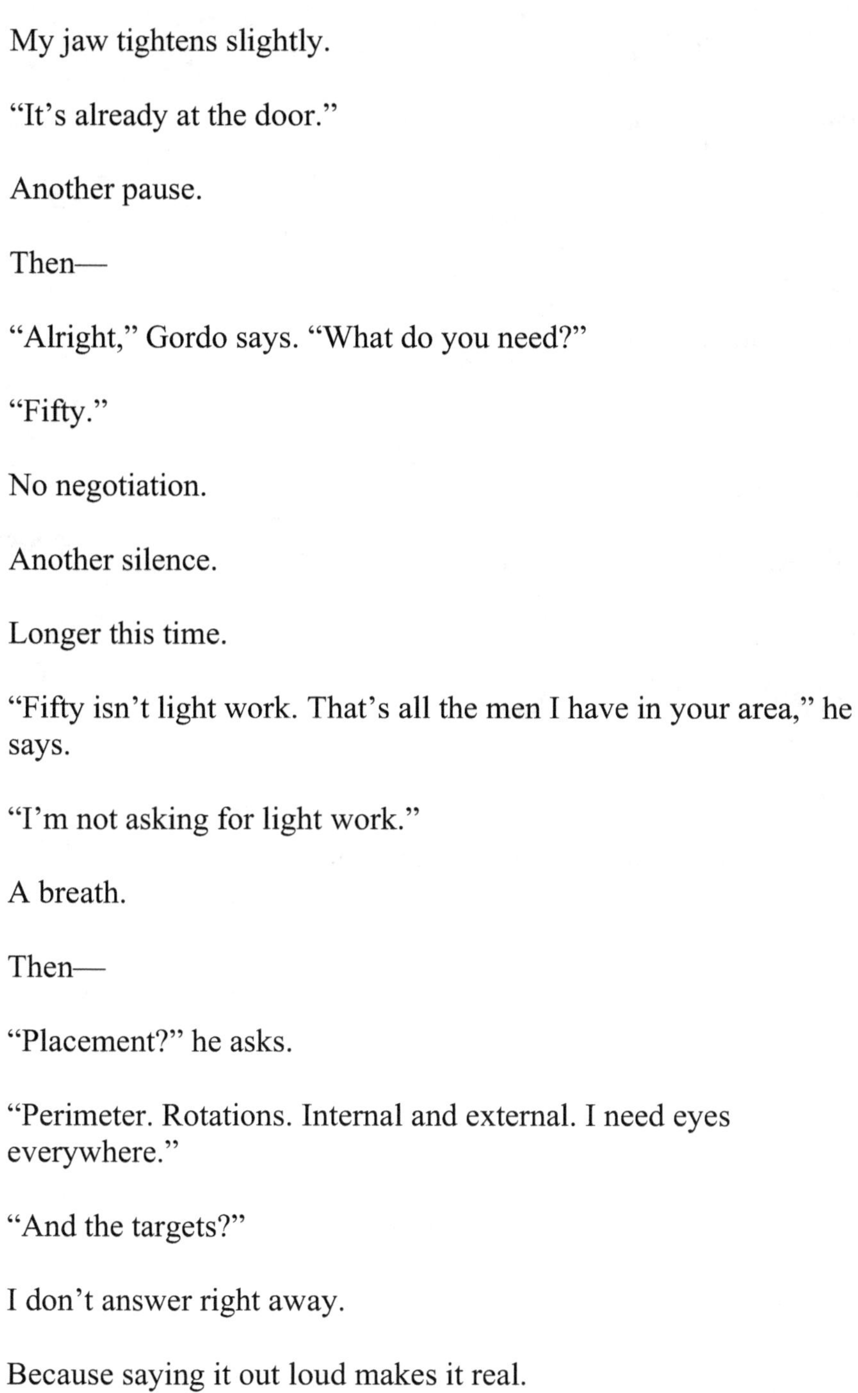

My jaw tightens slightly.

"It's already at the door."

Another pause.

Then—

"Alright," Gordo says. "What do you need?"

"Fifty."

No negotiation.

Another silence.

Longer this time.

"Fifty isn't light work. That's all the men I have in your area," he says.

"I'm not asking for light work."

A breath.

Then—

"Placement?" he asks.

"Perimeter. Rotations. Internal and external. I need eyes everywhere."

"And the targets?"

I don't answer right away.

Because saying it out loud makes it real.

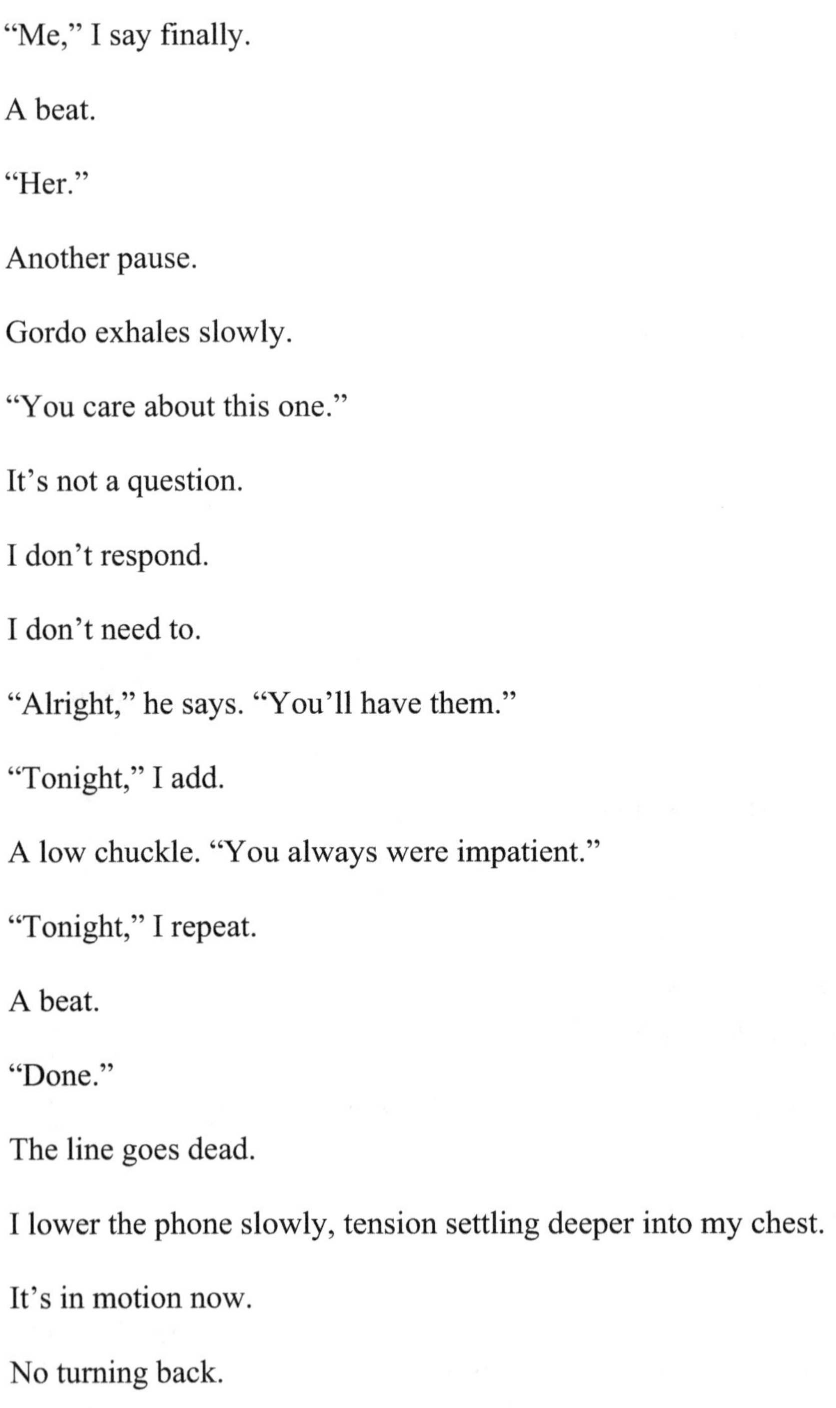

"Me," I say finally.

A beat.

"Her."

Another pause.

Gordo exhales slowly.

"You care about this one."

It's not a question.

I don't respond.

I don't need to.

"Alright," he says. "You'll have them."

"Tonight," I add.

A low chuckle. "You always were impatient."

"Tonight," I repeat.

A beat.

"Done."

The line goes dead.

I lower the phone slowly, tension settling deeper into my chest.

It's in motion now.

No turning back.

I head back inside, my mind already running through logistics. Entry points. Shift changes. Blind zones that need to disappear. The club is only one part of this.

The bigger problem?

Her. She means more to me than I thought.

I pull up her address from memory.

I shouldn't have it.

But I do.

Because I planned for this before she even knew she needed protection.

Her house isn't exposed.

But it's not secured as it should be either.

That changes tonight.

My phone buzzes again.

A message from Gordo.

`Two teams en route. More within the hour.`

Good.

Fast.

Efficient.

Exactly why I called him.

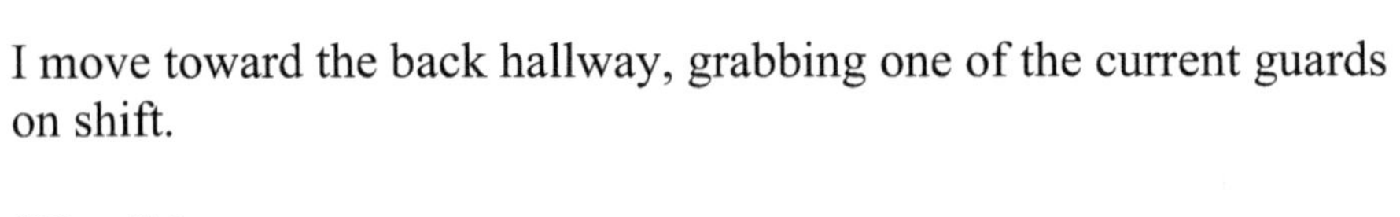

I move toward the back hallway, grabbing one of the current guards on shift.

"You," I say.

He straightens immediately. "Yes—"

"Front and back doors stay covered at all times. No gaps. No rotations without clearance from me."

He nods quickly.

"Anyone unfamiliar?"

"They don't get in."

"Yes."

"And no one leaves alone. Especially the Madame. Remember, eyes on her at all times," I add.

His expression tightens slightly.

"Yes, sir."

I step back out onto the main floor and pause, letting my eyes adjust to the lighting again.

Then I see her.

Cosette.

Still upstairs.

Still watching.

She hasn't moved much.

That means she's thinking.

That means she's already putting pieces together.

Good.

But not fast enough.

Not for what's coming.

My phone buzzes again.

Another message.

`External coverage in position.`

That was fast.

I glance toward the entrance subtly.

Nothing looks different.

That's exactly how it should be.

Invisible.

Effective.

Lethal if necessary. I know Gordo's men come equipped with all the heat we'll need.

I shift my attention back to the room.

Everything is still running.

Still functioning.

Still unaware.

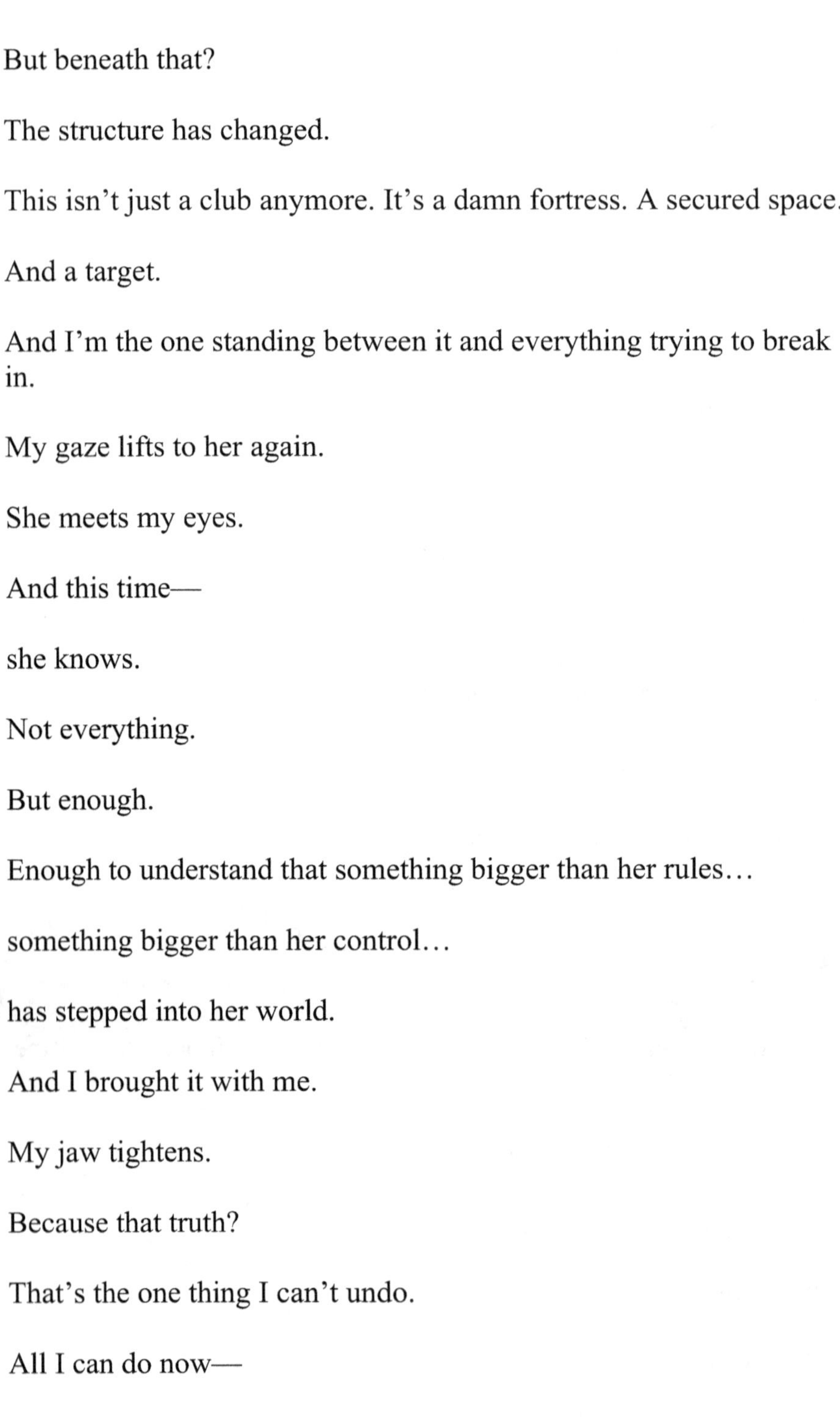

But beneath that?

The structure has changed.

This isn't just a club anymore. It's a damn fortress. A secured space.

And a target.

And I'm the one standing between it and everything trying to break in.

My gaze lifts to her again.

She meets my eyes.

And this time—

she knows.

Not everything.

But enough.

Enough to understand that something bigger than her rules…

something bigger than her control…

has stepped into her world.

And I brought it with me.

My jaw tightens.

Because that truth?

That's the one thing I can't undo.

All I can do now—

is make sure it doesn't destroy her.

Or anything she built.

Because if it does—

I won't just lose her.

I'll lose the only thing that's made me want to be better than what I was.

And that?

That's not an option.

Chapter Seventeen

Dear Cosette,

What have you done? Now The Boss wants me. Did you repay your debt to our family? Did you fight him? I don't even know if I'll ever see you again now. I just needed you to hold on a little longer. He would have released you to me eventually. No, I don't know what you've been through. You've been away from me for two years now. Surely, that's enough time to repay our debts. I'm so afraid of what you've done that he now wants me to come to him. And if I refuse, he'll most likely have someone hunt me down. Please don't be the reason our family is forever fucked. We can't afford to piss The Boss off. I hope I get to give you all these letters. Sorry if I'm coming off like a bitch. This man has controlled our family for so long. I hear approaching cars outside our home. Hopefully, this won't be my last letter.

Mommy

Cosette

Things have definitely changed. And I hate it.

It's right there.

In front of me.

Walking my floor.

I stand on the upper level again, but this time I'm not observing for pleasure or routine. I'm counting.

Faces.

Movements.

Positions.

And there are at least ten men in this room I've never seen before.

That's ten too many.

They're not members.

They're not staff.

And they're definitely not random.

They move differently.

Too coordinated.

Too aware.

Too controlled.

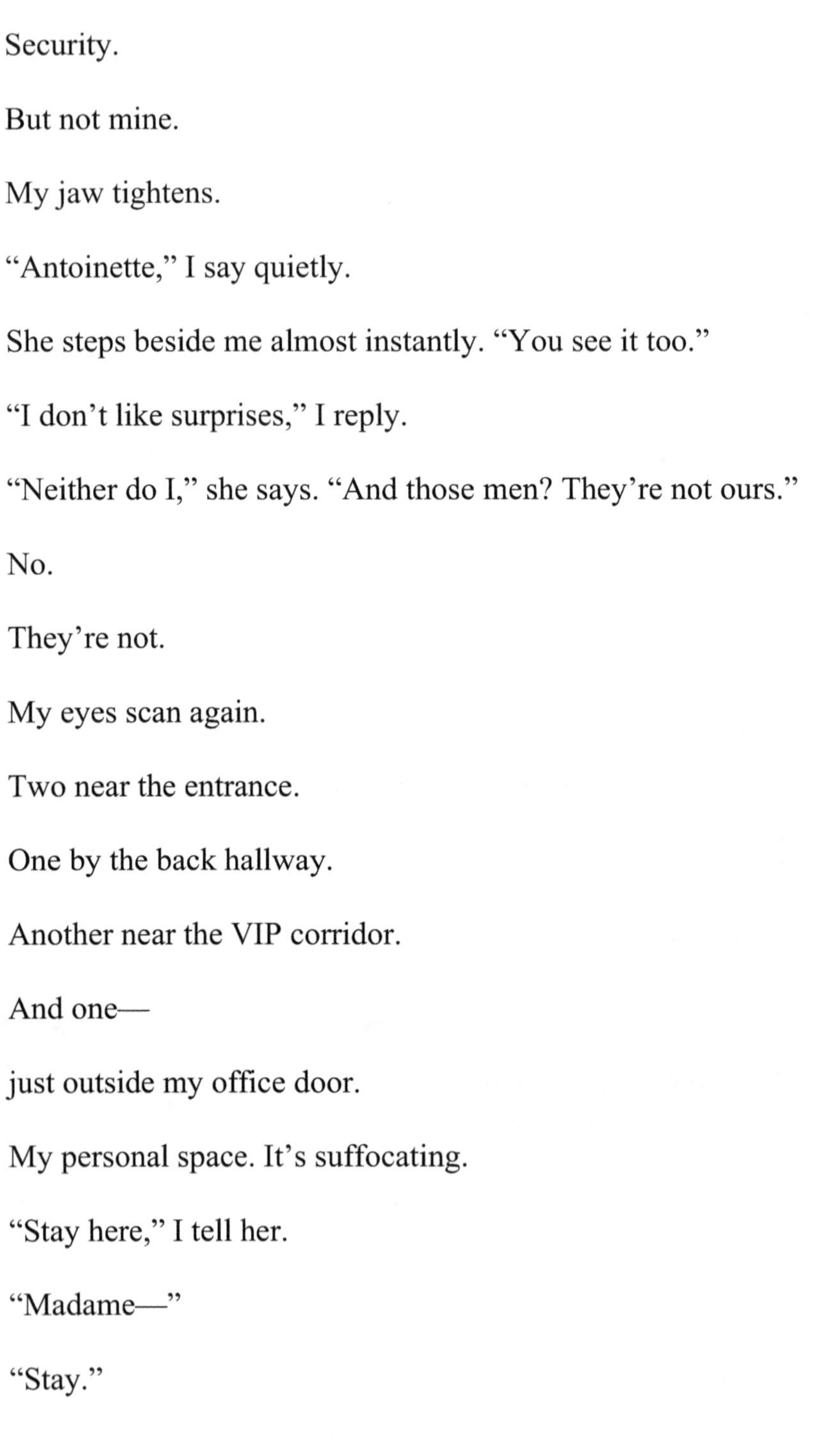

Security.

But not mine.

My jaw tightens.

"Antoinette," I say quietly.

She steps beside me almost instantly. "You see it too."

"I don't like surprises," I reply.

"Neither do I," she says. "And those men? They're not ours."

No.

They're not.

My eyes scan again.

Two near the entrance.

One by the back hallway.

Another near the VIP corridor.

And one—

just outside my office door.

My personal space. It's suffocating.

"Stay here," I tell her.

"Madame—"

"Stay."

My tone leaves no room for argument.

She exhales but nods.

I turn and head downstairs.

I don't rush or show urgency.

Because panic is contagious.

If this is a threat, I need to know how deep it goes.

If this is protection…

I already know who gave the order.

Antonio.

I find him near the back corridor, speaking quietly to one of the unfamiliar men. The man nods once and moves off without question.

That alone tells me everything.

He's in charge.

Of them.

Of this.

Of something he didn't ask me about.

I step into his line of sight.

He notices me immediately.

Of course he does.

His body shifts slightly.

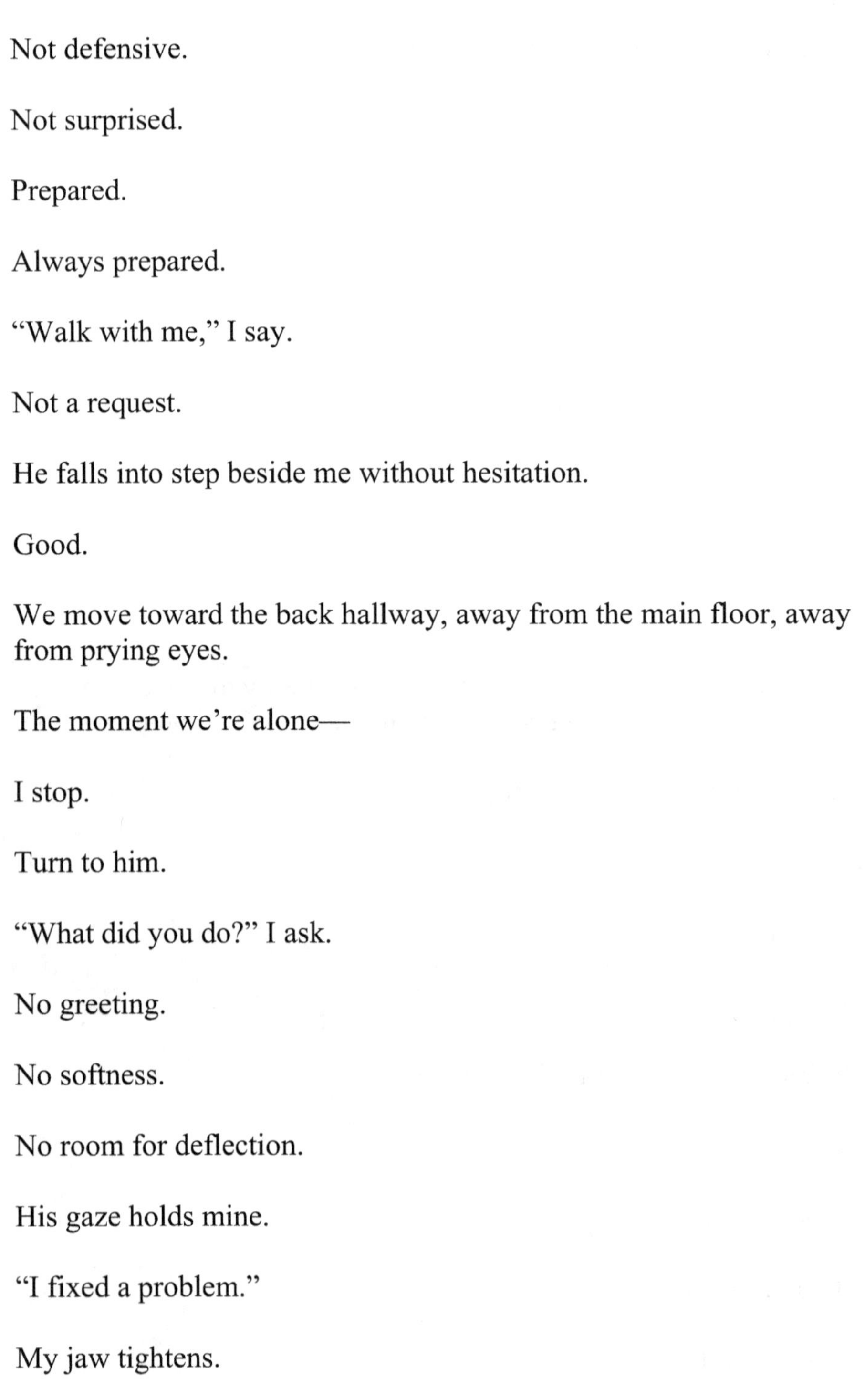

Not defensive.

Not surprised.

Prepared.

Always prepared.

“Walk with me,” I say.

Not a request.

He falls into step beside me without hesitation.

Good.

We move toward the back hallway, away from the main floor, away from prying eyes.

The moment we’re alone—

I stop.

Turn to him.

“What did you do?” I ask.

No greeting.

No softness.

No room for deflection.

His gaze holds mine.

“I fixed a problem.”

My jaw tightens.

"You don't fix things in my club without telling me," I say.

"You wanted protection," he replies.

"I wanted information," I correct. "Not an army."

A pause.

Then—

"They're not here for the club," he says.

"Then who are they here for?" I ask.

He doesn't answer right away.

And that?

That's answer enough.

"For me?" I press.

A beat.

Then—

"Yes."

Silence stretches between us.

"You brought fifty men into my world," I say slowly, "without my permission."

"They're not inside your world," he says. "They're around it."

"That's not fucking better."

"It's necessary."

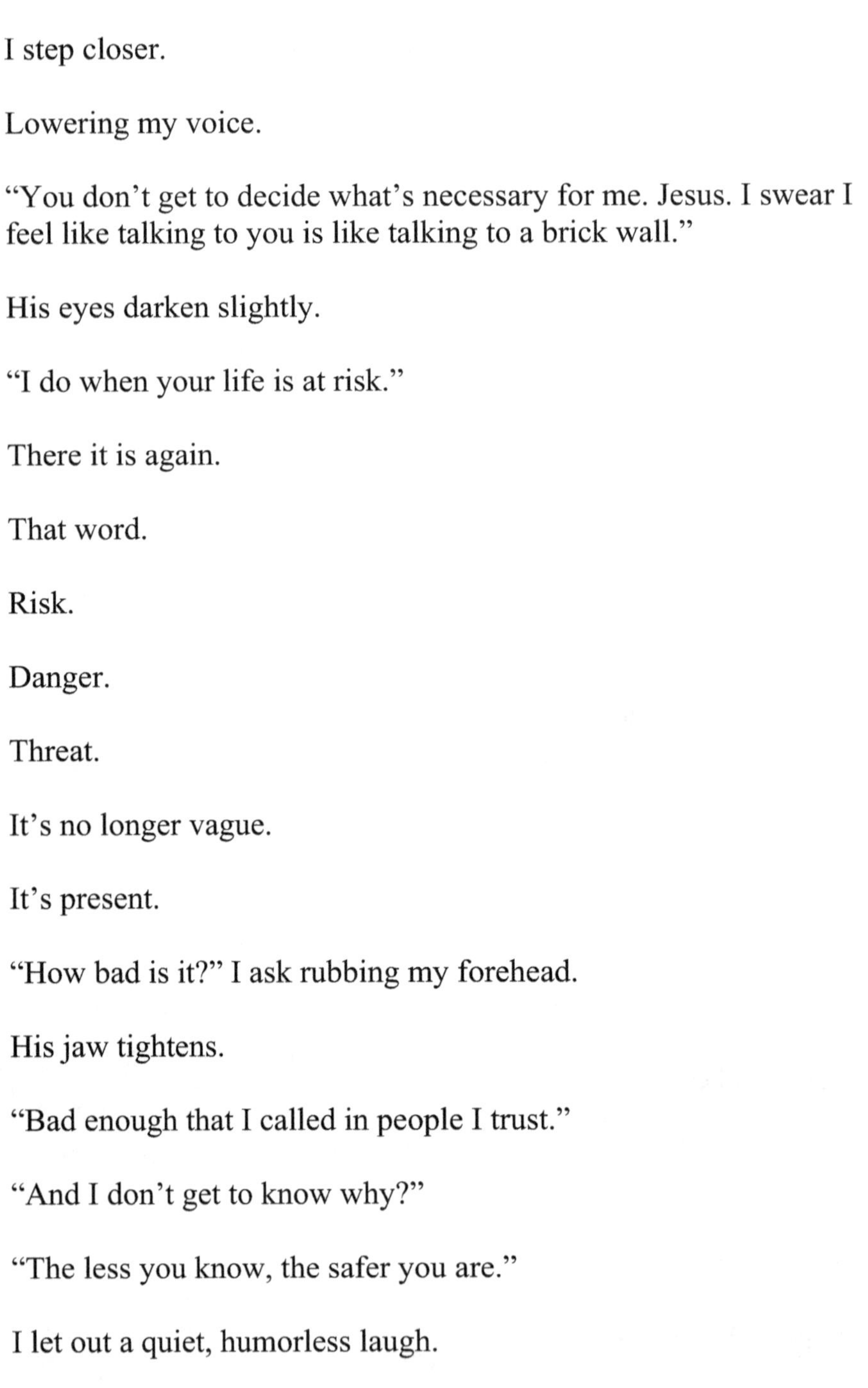

I step closer.

Lowering my voice.

"You don't get to decide what's necessary for me. Jesus. I swear I feel like talking to you is like talking to a brick wall."

His eyes darken slightly.

"I do when your life is at risk."

There it is again.

That word.

Risk.

Danger.

Threat.

It's no longer vague.

It's present.

"How bad is it?" I ask rubbing my forehead.

His jaw tightens.

"Bad enough that I called in people I trust."

"And I don't get to know why?"

"The less you know, the safer you are."

I let out a quiet, humorless laugh.

"That's not how this works."

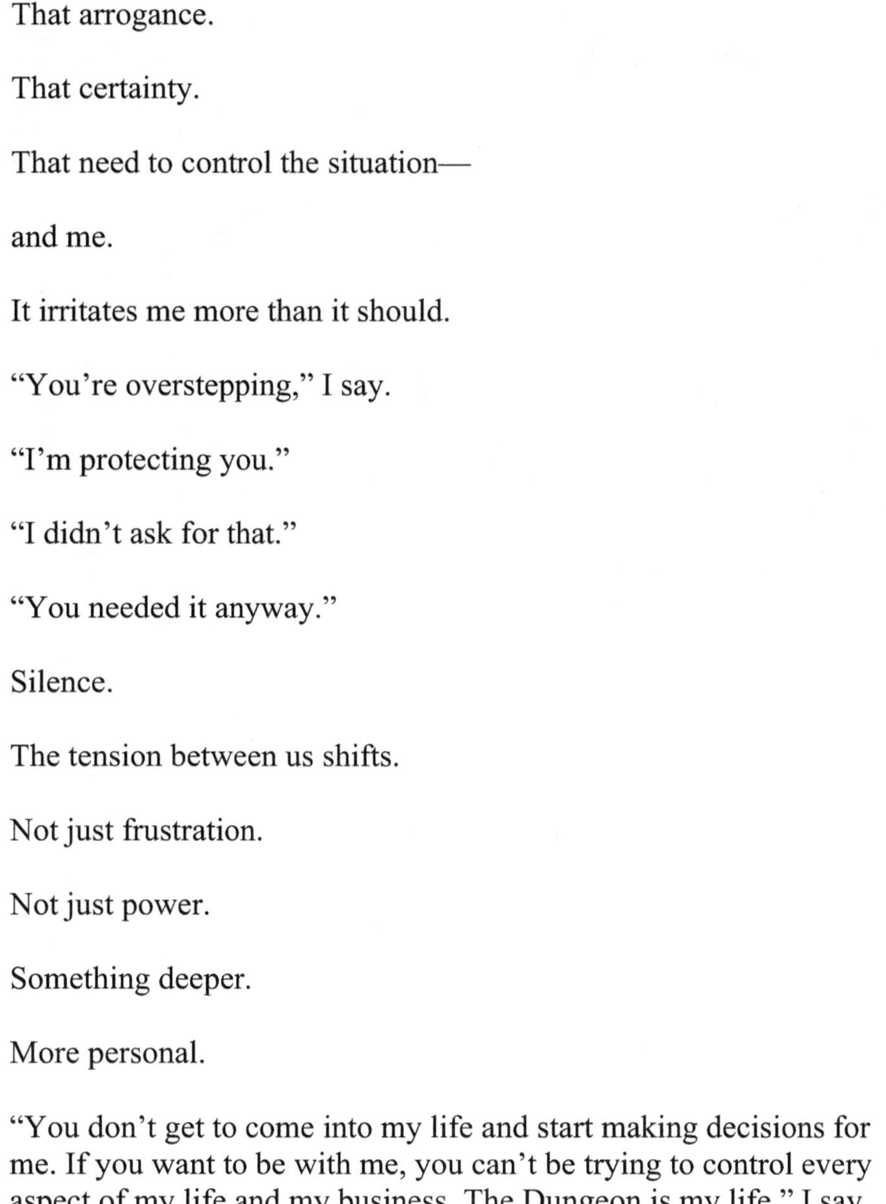

"It is now."

That arrogance.

That certainty.

That need to control the situation—

and me.

It irritates me more than it should.

"You're overstepping," I say.

"I'm protecting you."

"I didn't ask for that."

"You needed it anyway."

Silence.

The tension between us shifts.

Not just frustration.

Not just power.

Something deeper.

More personal.

"You don't get to come into my life and start making decisions for me. If you want to be with me, you can't be trying to control every aspect of my life and my business. The Dungeon is my life," I say quietly.

"I'm not making them for you," he replies. "I'm making them for what's coming."

My chest tightens slightly.

"Then tell me what's coming."

A pause.

Then—

"My past," he says.

Again.

Always vague.

Always just out of reach.

I study him.

Really study him.

The way he holds himself.

The way he speaks.

The way he moves like a man who's lived in something darker than he lets on.

"You're not just some bartender," I say.

His expression doesn't change.

"No."

"I figured that much out," I reply. "People don't live in gated communities like that off tips."

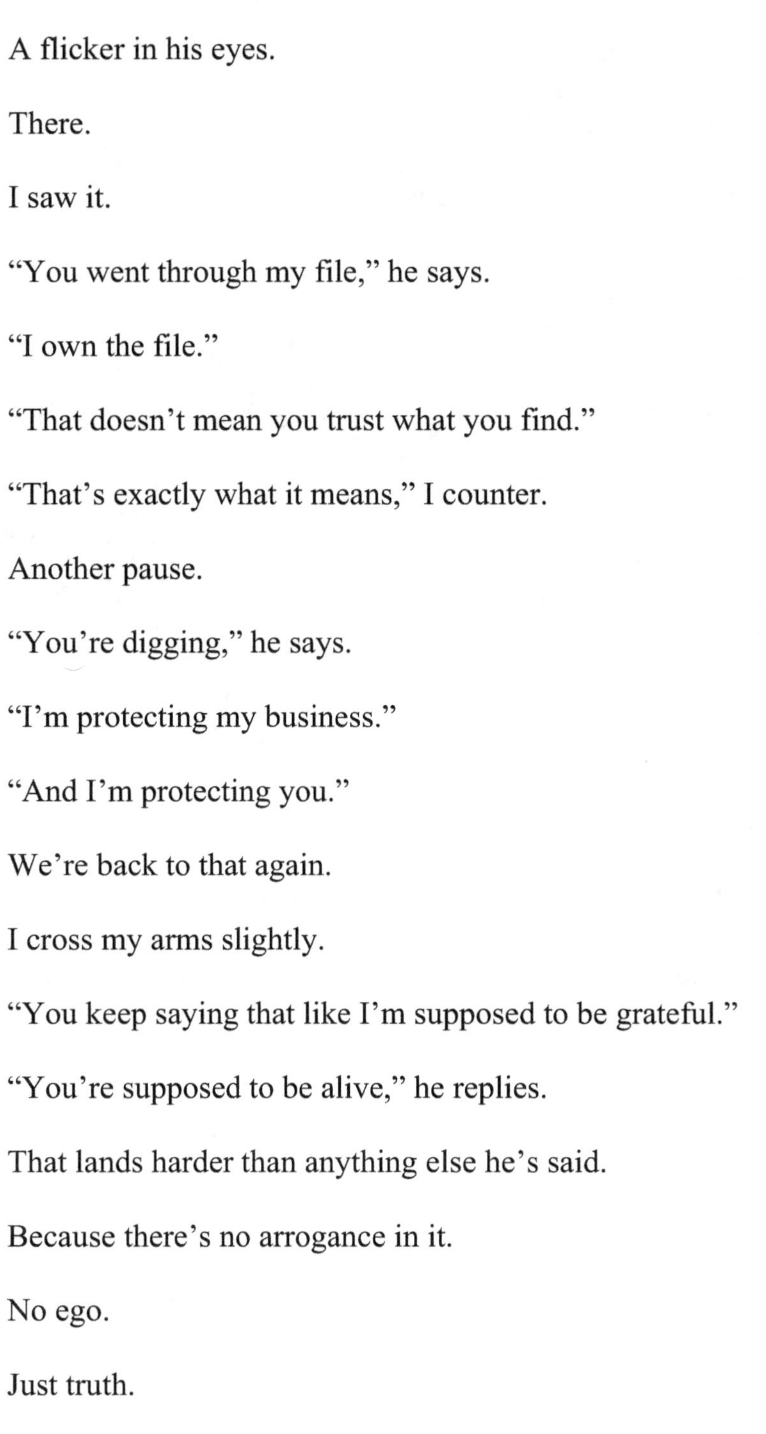

A flicker in his eyes.

There.

I saw it.

“You went through my file,” he says.

“I own the file.”

“That doesn’t mean you trust what you find.”

“That’s exactly what it means,” I counter.

Another pause.

“You’re digging,” he says.

“I’m protecting my business.”

“And I’m protecting you.”

We’re back to that again.

I cross my arms slightly.

“You keep saying that like I’m supposed to be grateful.”

“You’re supposed to be alive,” he replies.

That lands harder than anything else he’s said.

Because there’s no arrogance in it.

No ego.

Just truth.

And that?

That's what unsettles me.

"Who are you, Antonio?" I ask quietly.

A long pause.

Then—

"Someone who walked away from something he shouldn't have," he says.

"That's not an answer."

"It's the only one you're getting right now."

Frustration builds in my chest.

Because I hate being in the dark.

I hate not knowing.

And I especially hate feeling like I'm being managed.

"You don't get to control this situation. My own mother didn't even give a damn about my protection like this," I say without thinking.

"No," he agrees. "But I can control how it ends."

I take a deep breath.

"And what do you mean your mother didn't give a damn about you."

Shit! I can't tell him about my past now. This isn't the place or the time. And my stomach still knots up at the thought of my horrible past.

"That's not important."

"The hell it isn't. You talk about my secrets and wanting to know things. Let's clear the air now. Once and for all."

My eyes narrow slightly, just catching what he said before.

"And how does it end?"

His gaze locks onto mine.

"With you safe."

The way he says it—

like it's the only outcome he'll accept—

does something to me.

Something I don't like.

Something I don't fully understand.

I exhale slowly.

"This isn't over," he says.

"I know."

"I will find out what you're not telling me."

"I expect you to try."

That almost sounds like a challenge.

I step back slightly.

Creating space.

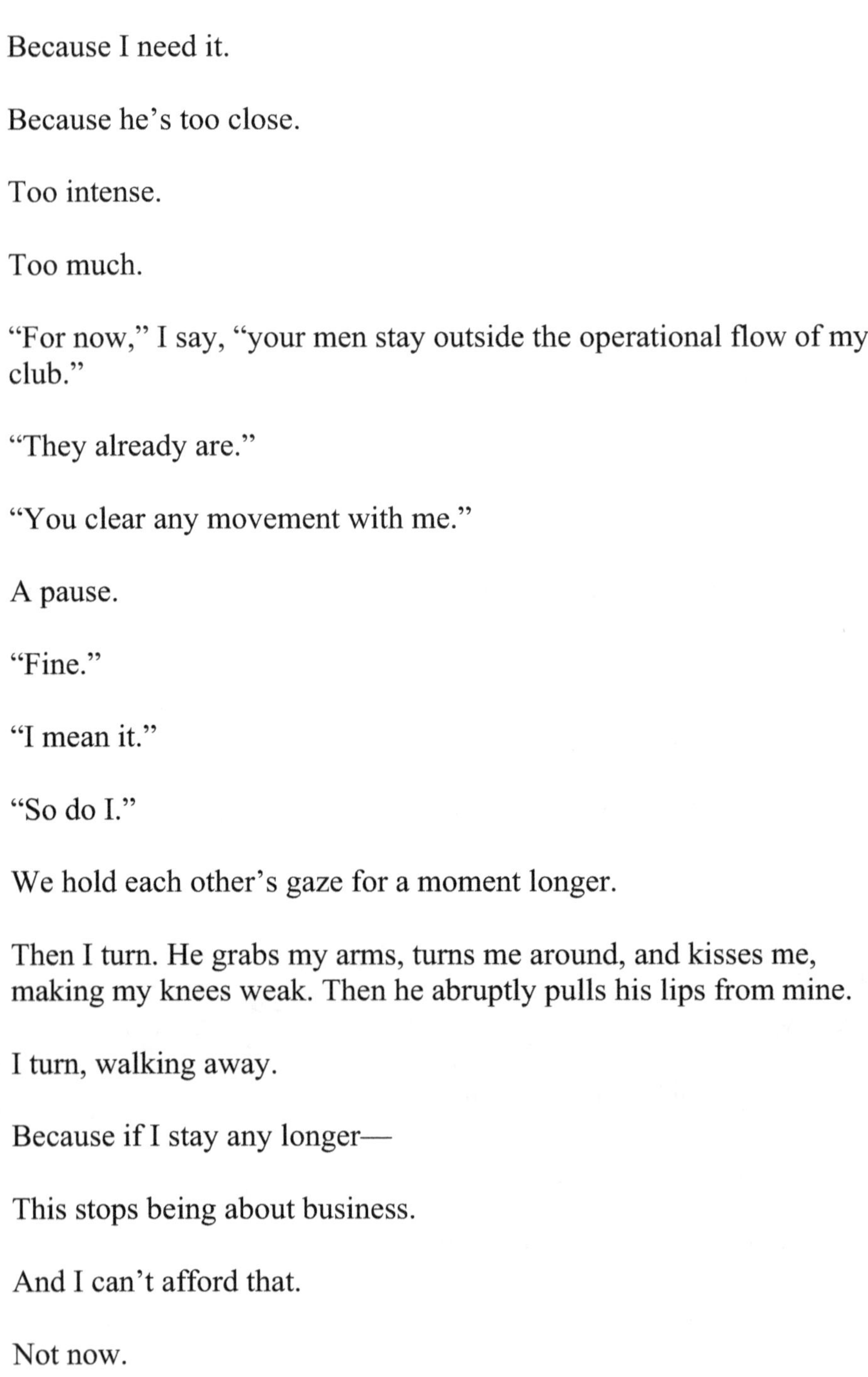

Because I need it.

Because he's too close.

Too intense.

Too much.

"For now," I say, "your men stay outside the operational flow of my club."

"They already are."

"You clear any movement with me."

A pause.

"Fine."

"I mean it."

"So do I."

We hold each other's gaze for a moment longer.

Then I turn. He grabs my arms, turns me around, and kisses me, making my knees weak. Then he abruptly pulls his lips from mine.

I turn, walking away.

Because if I stay any longer—

This stops being about business.

And I can't afford that.

Not now.

Not with everything shifting around me.

Not with danger creeping closer.

But as I move back toward the main floor—

I can feel it.

Not just the tension in the air.

Not just the presence of unfamiliar men.

But him.

Behind me.

Watching.

Protecting.

Changing everything.

And whether I like it or not—

My world just got a lot bigger.

And a lot more dangerous.

I think back to the letters that I found in my family home. When I escaped, that was the first place I went to. It took me 5 hours and a boat ride to get back home. My mother was nowhere to be found. It looked like the house had been abandoned. There was still rotting food in the sink. While I was going through her belongings, I found a stack of letters addressed to me. It explained my mother's betrayal. She sold me to The Boss to satisfy some fucking debt that my father owed to him at the time of his death.

My own mother pimped me out to the most ruthless child trafficker in all of Florida and put me in a horrible position to get raped repeatedly by multiple men. Their pet. Their plaything. And the sickest part of it all, I didn't hate it all. My innocence was permanently gone, but some men were more gentle than others. I learned what my body enjoys during sex and what it hates.

Does that mean I have a sick way of looking at intimacy and sex? Yes. But I learned to live through it. I survived. Got my GED, went to college, and got a Master's in Business Management. I kept my head down until I could build my business from the ground up. A woman of color doing big business with the men of this world.

This is the world that I created, and I will not see it brought down. Antonio owes me answers. If he doesn't give them to me soon, I'll have to cut ties.

Maybe that's what he secretly desires.

Antoinette approaches me. "Hey, are you okay?"

"No. I didn't get the answers that I needed."

"So what's the play?"

"Continue digging. I have a feeling I'm close to the truth."

Nette nodded once.

Together, we walked back to the upper level to continue surveillance over my newly arrived security detail.

Chapter Eighteen

Antonio

She's already digging.

I can see it in the way she looks at me now.

That's dangerous.

Not because she's wrong for wanting to know more—but because she's getting closer to something that doesn't stay buried once it's uncovered.

And I don't have time to ease her into it.

I step away from the main floor, moving into the back corridor where the noise dulls just enough for me to think. One of Gordo's men stands near the exit, posture relaxed but eyes sharp.

Good.

They're already settling in.

Efficient.

Disciplined.

Exactly what I needed.

"Perimeter's clean," he says as I pass.

"For now," I reply.

He nods once. No questions.

That's the difference between men like this and everyone else.

They don't need explanations.

They trust the situation is already worse than it looks.

My phone buzzes.

Gordo.

I answer immediately.

"Talk."

"You've got movement," he says.

My body stills slightly.

"Where?"

"Not on your club," he replies. "On her."

My grip tightens around the phone.

"Explain."

"Vehicle's been circling her residence for the last hour. Same car. Same route. Not random."

My jaw tightens.

"What kind of vehicle?"

"Black sedan. Tinted. Clean. Too clean."

Professional.

Not sloppy.

Not impulsive.

Targeted.

“Anyone get a look at the driver?”

“Not yet,” Gordo says. “But they’re patient.”

That’s worse.

“Keep eyes on it,” I say. “No engagement yet.”

“You want us to pull him?”

“Not until I know who he belongs to.”

A pause.

“You thinking it’s him?”

Eugenio.

“Yeah,” I say.

Another pause.

Then—

“You brought this to her,” Gordo says.

Not accusing.

Just stating facts.

“I know.”

Silence stretches between us for a second.

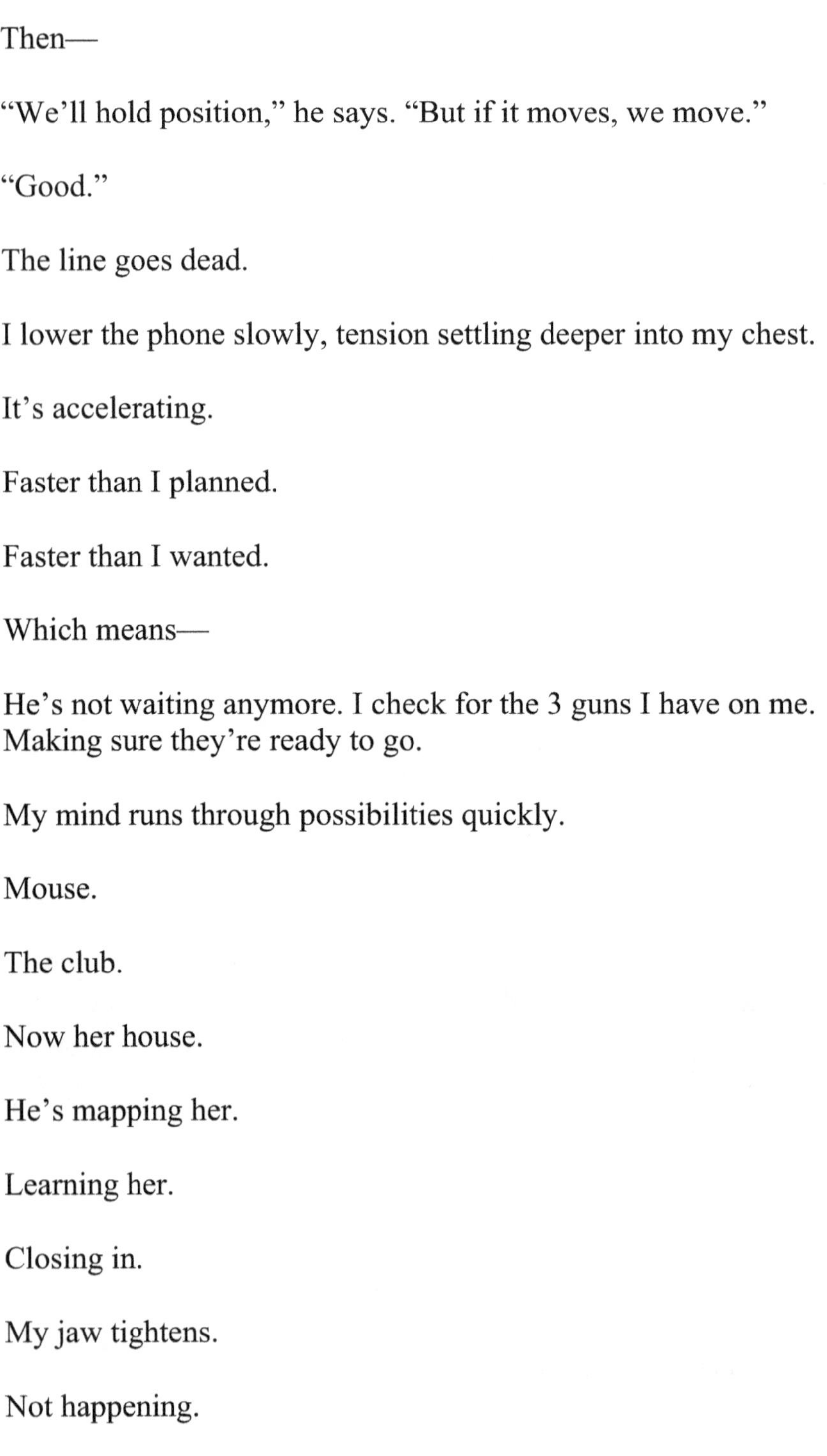

Then—

"We'll hold position," he says. "But if it moves, we move."

"Good."

The line goes dead.

I lower the phone slowly, tension settling deeper into my chest.

It's accelerating.

Faster than I planned.

Faster than I wanted.

Which means—

He's not waiting anymore. I check for the 3 guns I have on me. Making sure they're ready to go.

My mind runs through possibilities quickly.

Mouse.

The club.

Now her house.

He's mapping her.

Learning her.

Closing in.

My jaw tightens.

Not happening.

I turn and head back toward the main floor, but I don't go to her.

Not yet.

Because if I walk up to her right now and tell her someone is watching her house—

She's not going to panic.

She's going to act.

And acting without knowing the full scope?

That's how people get hurt. Not thinking gets people killed. I'll be damned if I allow that to happen.

Instead, I shift direction.

I need more information.

And there's only one person who might have it.

I step outside again, dialing before the door even closes behind me.

It rings once.

Then—

"Thought you'd call back," Gordo answers.

"I need everything you've got on that car," I say.

"Already running it."

"Faster."

A quiet chuckle. "You're not the only one who knows how to move."

I pace slightly, scanning the street.

"This isn't random," I say. "He's escalating."

"Yeah," Gordo replies. "And you know what that means."

I do.

It means the next move won't be subtle.

It won't be observation.

It'll be action.

"Double the coverage on her house," I say. "No gaps."

"Already done."

"Inside?"

A pause.

"Not yet."

I exhale slowly.

"That changes tonight."

"You sure?" Gordo asks. "That's a line you don't uncross."

I know.

Putting men inside her space—

That's not just protection.

That's invasion.

But so is what's coming.

"She doesn't know yet," I say.

"She's going to notice."

"She already is."

A pause.

Then—

"You're in deep," Gordo says.

I don't respond.

Because that's not the problem.

The problem is—

I don't care.

"Send two inside," I say. "Quiet. Invisible. I don't want her feeling like she's being watched."

"She is being watched."

"Not by us," I reply.

Silence.

Then—

"Alright," Gordo says. "I'll handle it."

Another long silence. "Is she worth it?"

Not hesitating, "Abso-fucking-lutely."

The line cuts.

I lower the phone again, running a hand over my jaw.

This is moving too fast.

Too close.

And now—

it's not just about me anymore.

It's about her safety.

Her life.

Her world.

Everything she built.

I step back inside and immediately find her again.

Upper level.

Same spot.

Always watching.

Observing. Thinking. Calculating. Adapting.

She's already alert.

And that?

That's one of the reasons she's still alive.

My eyes lock onto hers for a brief second.

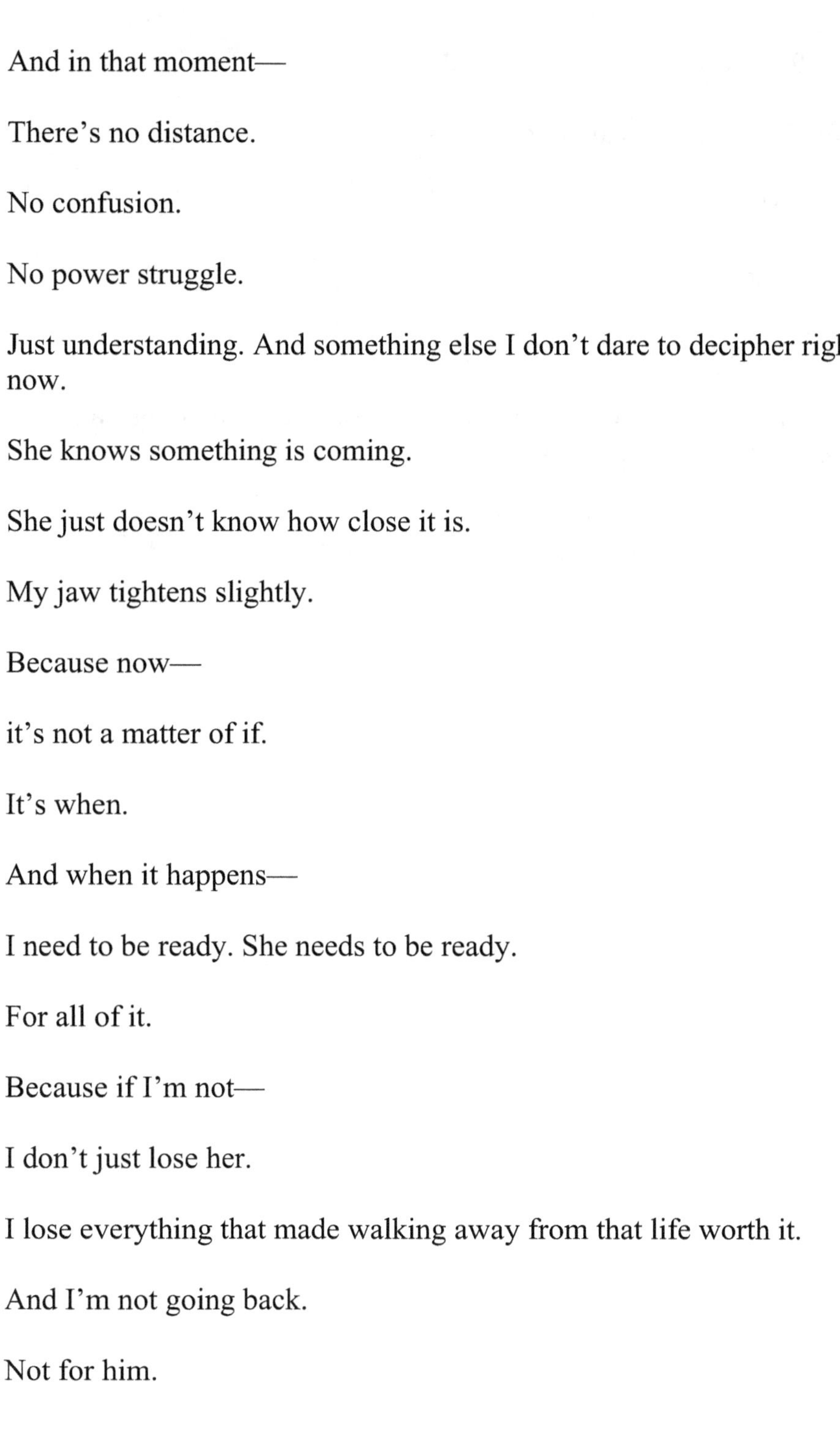

And in that moment—

There's no distance.

No confusion.

No power struggle.

Just understanding. And something else I don't dare to decipher right now.

She knows something is coming.

She just doesn't know how close it is.

My jaw tightens slightly.

Because now—

it's not a matter of if.

It's when.

And when it happens—

I need to be ready. She needs to be ready.

For all of it.

Because if I'm not—

I don't just lose her.

I lose everything that made walking away from that life worth it.

And I'm not going back.

Not for him.

Not for anyone.

But if he thinks he can touch her—

take her—

break her—

He's going to learn the hard way—

I'm still very capable of becoming exactly who I used to be. Who I need to be to the woman who's grown to mean so much to me.

Chapter Nineteen

Cosette

"What would you like to do about the entertainment lineup?"

"Let's rotate them and make sure they have enough time on the individual stages."

Once Antoinette and I finish up with business, she follows me to my office for a quick status update on Antonio.

"I couldn't find anything. Whoever he is or was, it's been covered up pretty well."

"Isn't that what someone who was involved in some deep shit would do? Bury any information on themselves?" she asks.

"Yes. But for now, let's just worry about this imminent threat Antonio has been speaking of."

"You still don't know?"

I shake my head.

"That's fucked up. It's your damn club. Your damn safety. I'd be lying if I said I wasn't scared."

I take her hands in mine. "I am too, but I have to show a brave face."

She squeezes my hand in response. "I know he cares a lot about you, but he needs to get this shit under control. The whole staff feels the tension. Like they know something is on the horizon too."

"Yeah. It'll all work out. I promise."

I hug her tightly.

"Well then, Madame, can I get you anything before you call it a night?"

"Nah. I'm okay. Just call me if anything pops off."

She hugs me once more, and I grab my belongings to head to my car.

Walking to the back hallway near the exit. I look for security to escort me to my car. Antonio said I needed someone with me at all times. I see one of the 'other security guys' and ask him to escort me.

"Sorry, Madame. I'm not allowed to leave this post without someone to take my place. If you wait a moment, I can escort you."

I exhale. "No. I'll look for someone else."

I huff and walk away. After what felt like forever, I went in search of Antonio. Surely he'd be able to walk me to my car. I go down another empty hallway, near the back alleyway. He usually goes out this way to talk on the phone or get some quiet time.

I knew something was coming as soon as I stepped into the hallway.

I felt it.

In the walls. In the air. In the way everything shifted just slightly out of place.

But I didn't expect it to happen like this.

One second, I'm leaving The Dungeon, Antoinette's voice still echoing behind me, talking to some of the staff, reminding me to call her when I get home.

The next—

Everything goes dark.

A hand clamps over my mouth.

Another around my waist.

I fight.

Instinct.

Immediate.

Violent.

But whoever has me—

They're prepared.

Too prepared.

Something sharp presses into my neck.

A sting.

Then—

nothing.

—

When I wake up, I don't move.

I've learned that the hard way.

Breathing slow.

Controlled.

Measured.

My eyes stay closed as I listen first.

Always listen first.

Silence.

Too quiet.

Then—

footsteps.

Slow.

Unhurried.

Familiar.

My stomach turns before my eyes even open.

Because I know that sound.

I remember it. Those god-forsaken Italian leather shoes.

Even after all these years.

I open my eyes.

And my world shatters.

Eugenio Palomari, The Boss, stands across the room, watching me like he never lost me.

Like I was always his.

Time doesn't move.

My body goes numb.

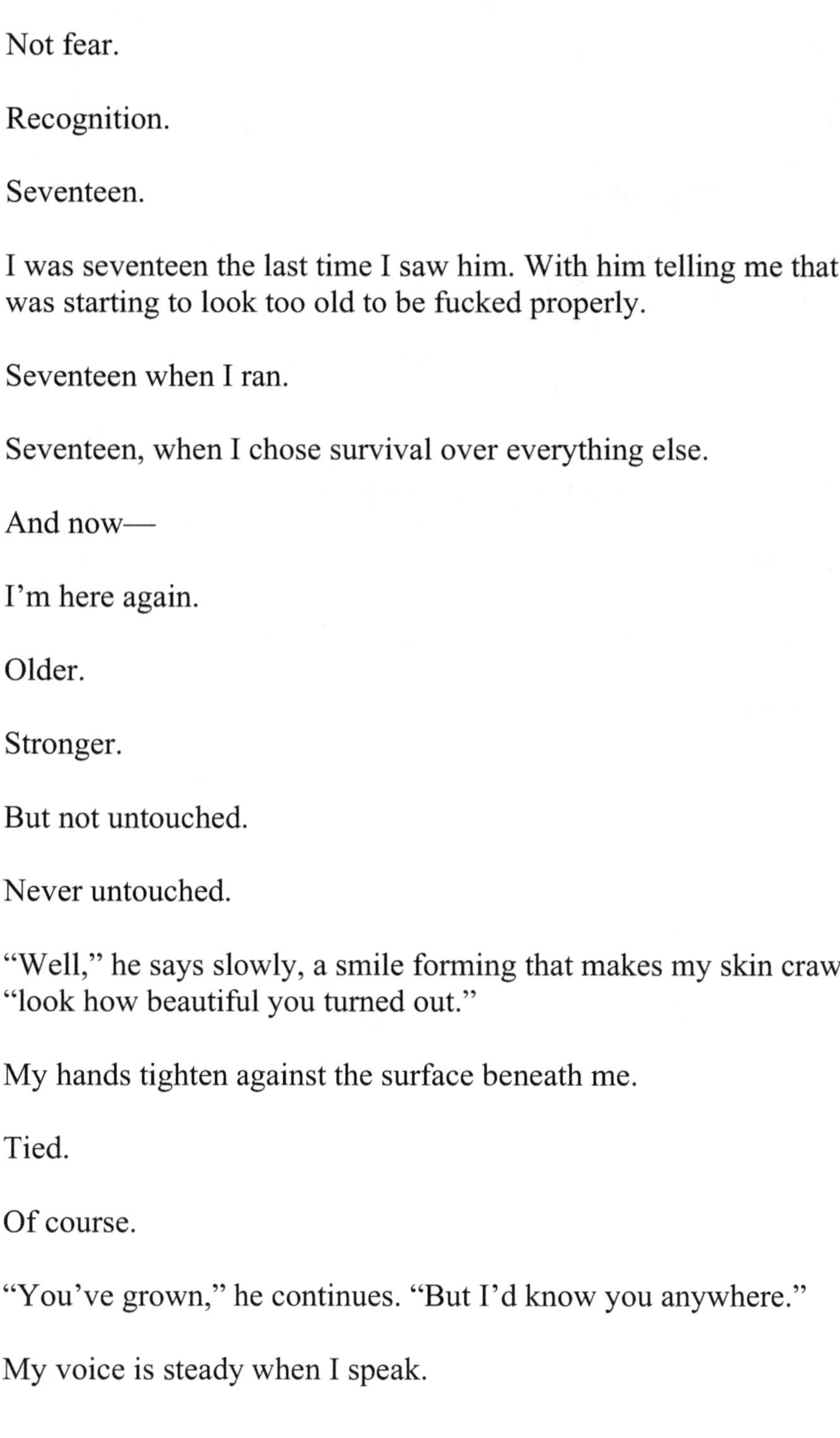

Not fear.

Recognition.

Seventeen.

I was seventeen the last time I saw him. With him telling me that I was starting to look too old to be fucked properly.

Seventeen when I ran.

Seventeen, when I chose survival over everything else.

And now—

I'm here again.

Older.

Stronger.

But not untouched.

Never untouched.

"Well," he says slowly, a smile forming that makes my skin crawl, "look how beautiful you turned out."

My hands tighten against the surface beneath me.

Tied.

Of course.

"You've grown," he continues. "But I'd know you anywhere."

My voice is steady when I speak.

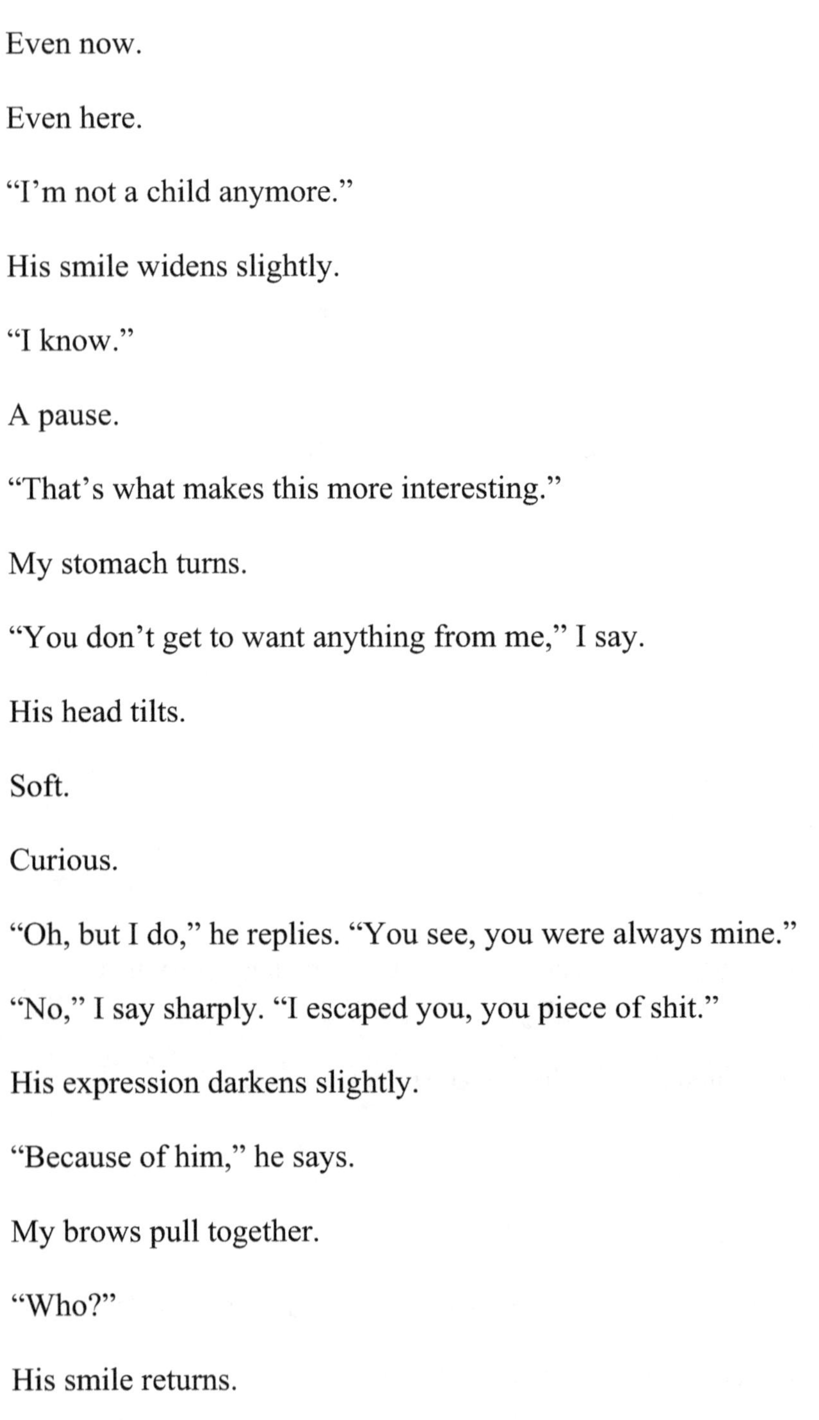

Even now.

Even here.

"I'm not a child anymore."

His smile widens slightly.

"I know."

A pause.

"That's what makes this more interesting."

My stomach turns.

"You don't get to want anything from me," I say.

His head tilts.

Soft.

Curious.

"Oh, but I do," he replies. "You see, you were always mine."

"No," I say sharply. "I escaped you, you piece of shit."

His expression darkens slightly.

"Because of him," he says.

My brows pull together.

"Who?"

His smile returns.

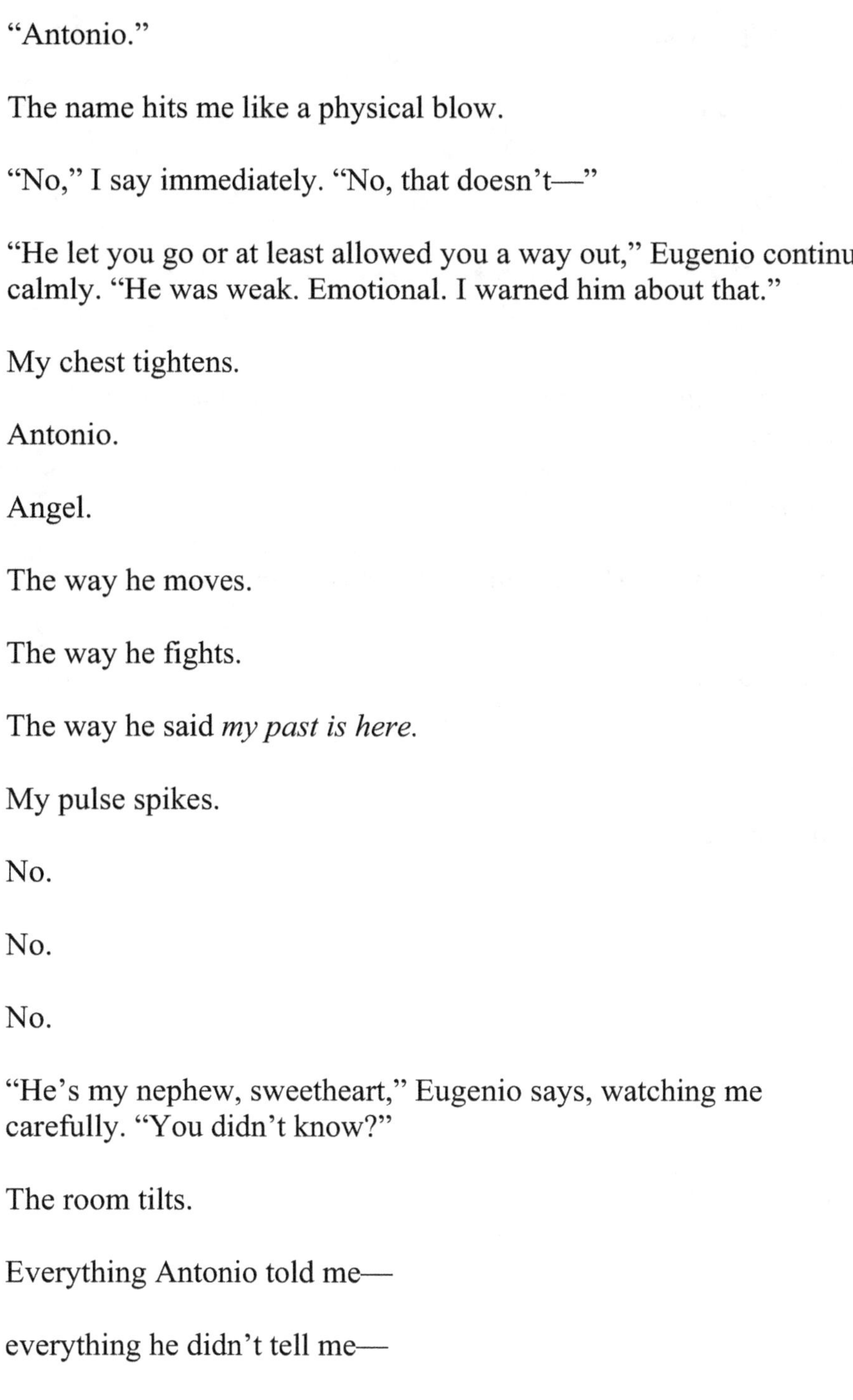

"Antonio."

The name hits me like a physical blow.

"No," I say immediately. "No, that doesn't—"

"He let you go or at least allowed you a way out," Eugenio continues calmly. "He was weak. Emotional. I warned him about that."

My chest tightens.

Antonio.

Angel.

The way he moves.

The way he fights.

The way he said *my past is here.*

My pulse spikes.

No.

No.

No.

"He's my nephew, sweetheart," Eugenio says, watching me carefully. "You didn't know?"

The room tilts.

Everything Antonio told me—

everything he didn't tell me—

slams into place all at once.

The protection.

The control.

The secrecy.

The lies.

“You brought him into your world,” Eugenio continues. “That was… unexpected.”

My throat tightens.

“He was supposed to be watching,” he adds. “Not… getting attached.”

My stomach drops.

Watching.

Not protecting.

Watching.

A setup.

A game.

And I fell for it all.

My chest tightens painfully.

“You’re a liar,” I say, but it sounds weaker than I want it to.

Eugenio chuckles.

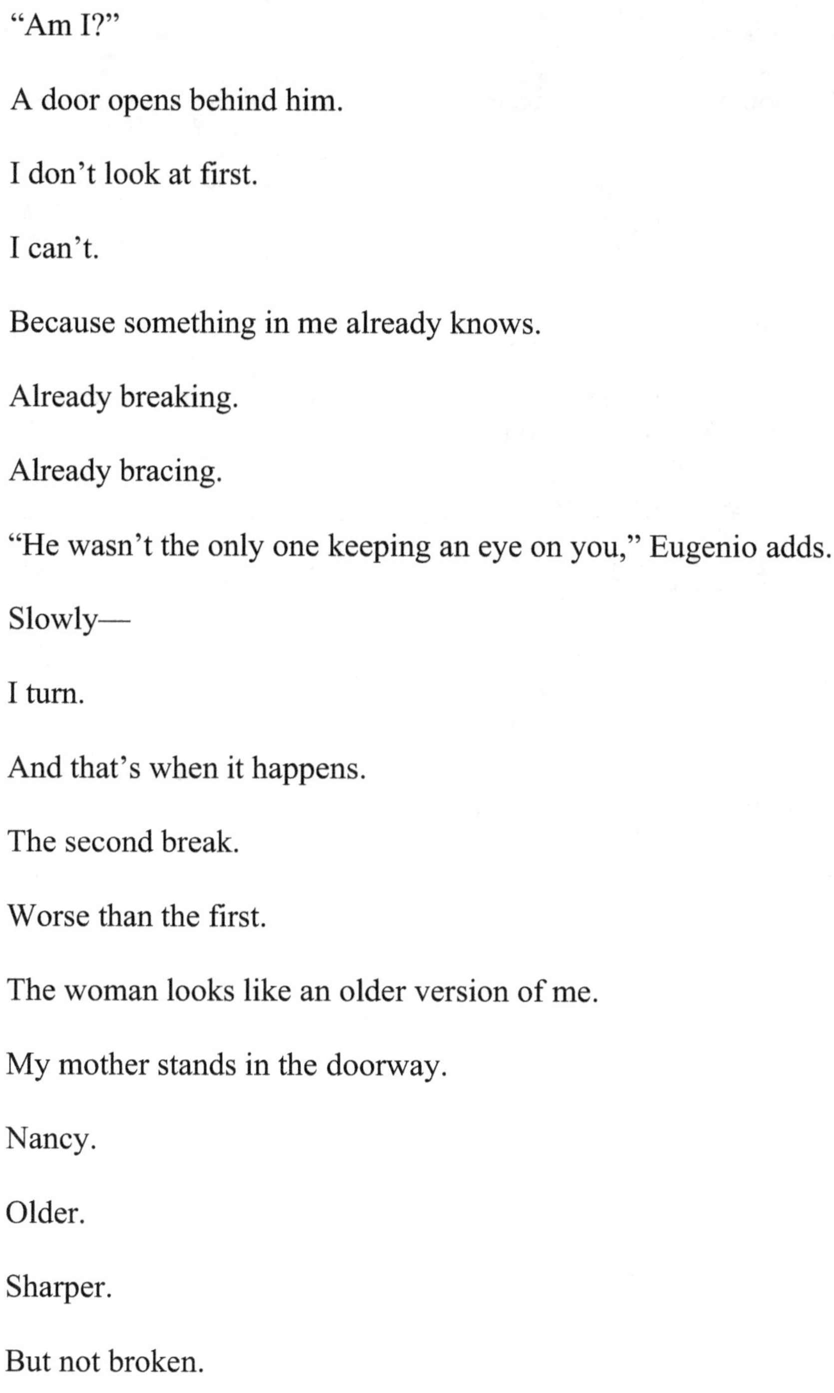

"Am I?"

A door opens behind him.

I don't look at first.

I can't.

Because something in me already knows.

Already breaking.

Already bracing.

"He wasn't the only one keeping an eye on you," Eugenio adds.

Slowly—

I turn.

And that's when it happens.

The second break.

Worse than the first.

The woman looks like an older version of me.

My mother stands in the doorway.

Nancy.

Older.

Sharper.

But not broken.

Not grieving.

Not the woman I had convinced myself she was all these years.

No.

This bitch—

is something else entirely.

"Well," she says, looking me up and down with something that almost resembles disappointment, "there you are."

My breath leaves my body.

"You…" I whisper.

All those letters.

Every single one.

The apologies.

The explanations.

The excuses.

I had no choice.

I did what I had to do.

I love you.

My chest tightens.

"You wrote to me," I say.

Her expression doesn't soften.

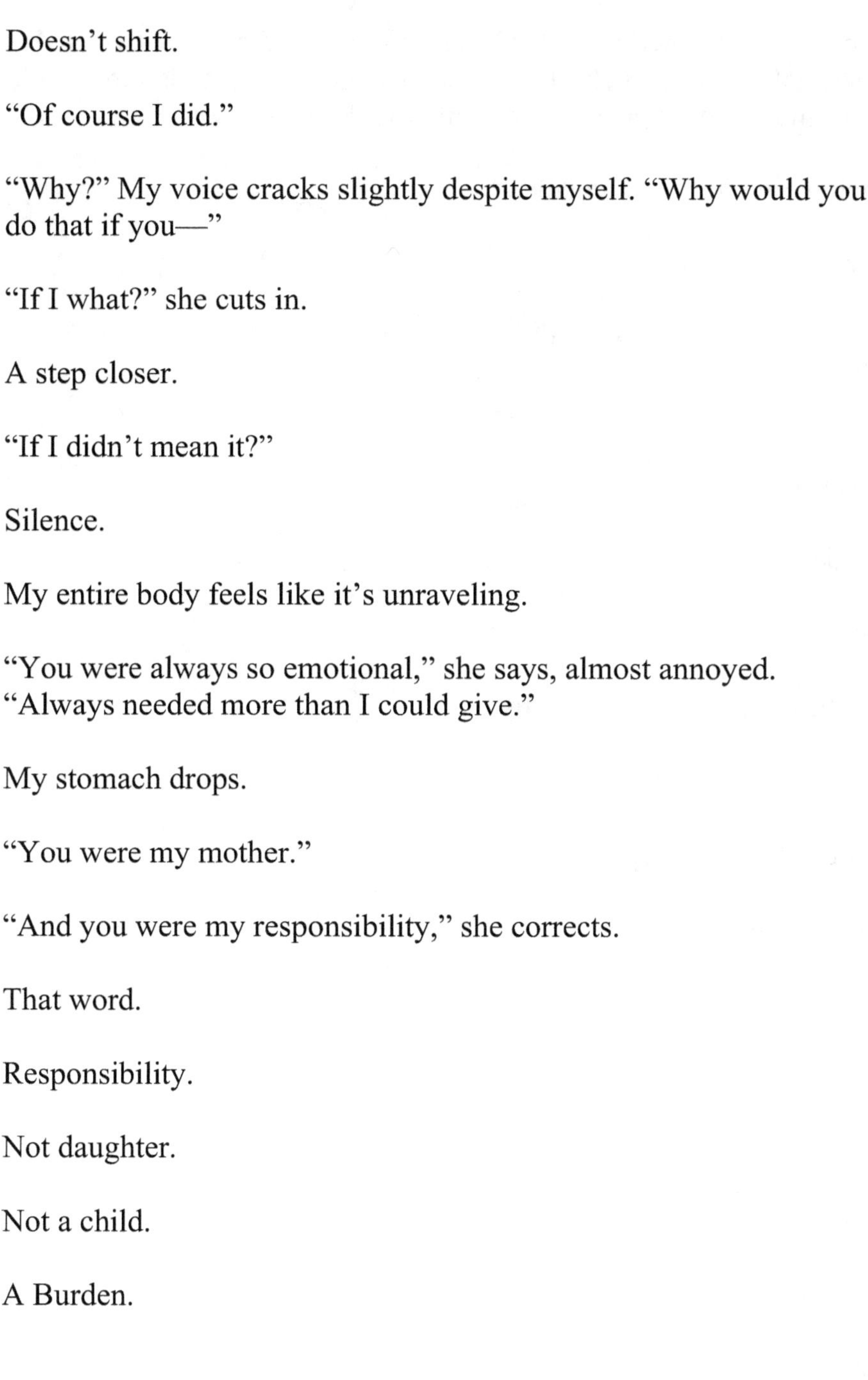

Doesn’t shift.

“Of course I did.”

“Why?” My voice cracks slightly despite myself. “Why would you do that if you—”

“If I what?” she cuts in.

A step closer.

“If I didn’t mean it?”

Silence.

My entire body feels like it’s unraveling.

“You were always so emotional,” she says, almost annoyed. “Always needed more than I could give.”

My stomach drops.

“You were my mother.”

“And you were my responsibility,” she corrects.

That word.

Responsibility.

Not daughter.

Not a child.

A Burden.

"You think I wanted that life?" she continues. "You think I wanted to struggle? To be stuck? To deal with a child I didn't plan for, while everything else fell apart? Your father fucked me over."

Each word lands like a blade.

"You sold me," I say.

Flat.

Empty.

Because now—

I understand.

All of it.

Her lips press together slightly.

"I made a decision."

"You sold me," I repeat.

"Don't simplify it," she snaps. "You were a liability."

There it is.

The truth.

Raw.

Ugly.

Unfiltered.

"You ruined my life," she adds.

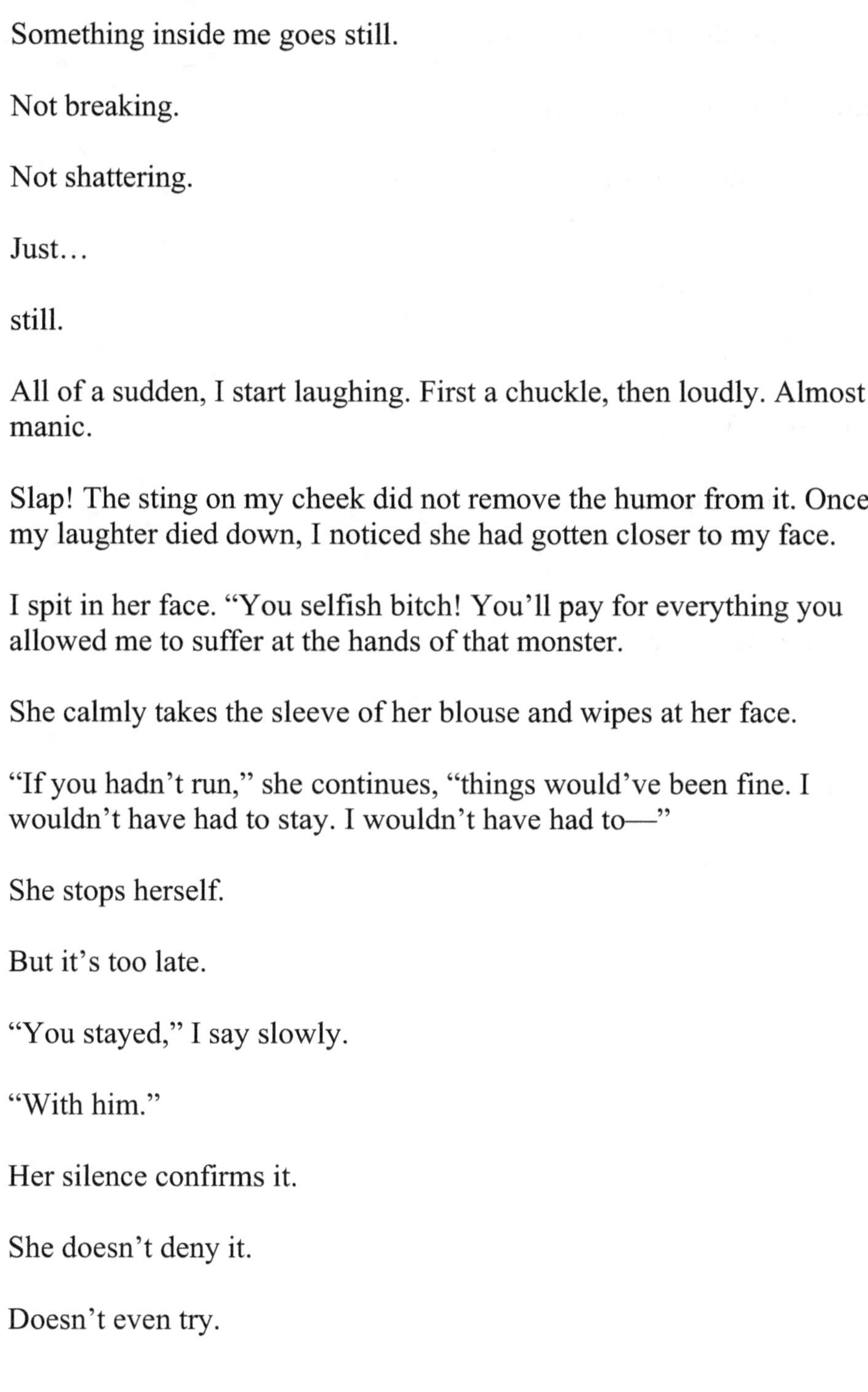

Something inside me goes still.

Not breaking.

Not shattering.

Just…

still.

All of a sudden, I start laughing. First a chuckle, then loudly. Almost manic.

Slap! The sting on my cheek did not remove the humor from it. Once my laughter died down, I noticed she had gotten closer to my face.

I spit in her face. “You selfish bitch! You’ll pay for everything you allowed me to suffer at the hands of that monster.

She calmly takes the sleeve of her blouse and wipes at her face.

“If you hadn’t run,” she continues, “things would’ve been fine. I wouldn’t have had to stay. I wouldn’t have had to—”

She stops herself.

But it’s too late.

“You stayed,” I say slowly.

“With him.”

Her silence confirms it.

She doesn’t deny it.

Doesn’t even try.

"You're with him," I say again.

Eugenio smiles behind her.

"She adjusted. But I must say, your pussy was a lot sweeter than your mother's," he says.

My stomach turns.

This isn't grief.

This isn't survival.

This is a choice.

"You never loved me," I say.

It's not a question.

It's a realization.

Final.

Her expression hardens.

"No," she says simply.

And that—

That's what does it.

Not the kidnapping.

Not Eugenio.

Not even Antonio.

The truth.

The final piece.

The confirmation that every part of my past was exactly what I feared it was.

A lie.

My eyes close briefly.

Just for a second.

And when they open again—

I'm not the same person who woke up tied to this chair.

Something colder settles in.

Something clearer.

"You should've stayed gone," Eugenio says.

I look at him.

Really look at him.

At the man who thought he broke me.

At the man who thinks he owns me.

At the man who doesn't realize—

I'm not that girl anymore.

"You should've killed me when you had the chance, bastard," I reply calmly.

His smile fades slightly.

Good.

Because now—

This isn't about survival anymore.

This is about something else entirely.

And if Antonio really did bring me into this—

If he really was watching me—

If this was all some twisted plan—

Then he didn't just betray me.

He handed me back to the worst part of my life.

And for that?

There will be consequences.

For all of them.

"Now that the surprises are out of the way, let discuss some things. I only wanted my nephew to come back and work for me. You were an added bonus. Nancy, please leave the room."

My mother turns from me and leaves. Not even giving me a sideways glance.

"I would say it was nice seeing you again, Cosette, but I'd be lying." Her mother closes the door as she leaves.

"Well, that was uncalled for," Eugenio states, taking off his suit jacket. "She's just a little sour because I prefer a younger body to hers. Her body does it for me sometimes, but I need someone young and vibrant."

The bile that rises in my throat is almost thick enough to make me gag.

"What do you want with me?"

"Well, of course, I'm going to torture you until my nephew tries to make his grand entrance. But before I do that, I'm going to fuck you."

The look on my face lacks the surprise or panic he was expecting. "Oh. Got a little brave, did you?"

"No. I deal with dumb ass motherfuckers daily. You're nothing special."

His face darkened. "Watch your tone with me. As you probably recall, I don't take kindly to disrespect."

He walks over to me. The numbness I feel barely registers his presence. "I escaped before. I can and will escape again."

"Not before I kill you. I have no problem fucking a corpse."

He then pulls out a gun and points it at my head. I don't flinch. I've wished for death many times. This moment is no different. At least if he fucks my dead body, I'll feel nothing still.

"Do what you feel you need to do."

"You don't get to make the orders. Here, I'm The Boss. Everyone here does what I tell them to do."

I just sit there. I just want this nightmare to be over.

"Oh, and by the way, I have a present for you. Come in," he shouts at the door. And in walks the fucking snake Mouse.

"Madame. You look amazing per usual.

Looking at the damage Antonio caused makes me smile... "And you look like Antonio didn't beat your ass well enough."

His smile fades as he takes in my words. He looks ready to hit me, until Eugenio stops him. "Relax Mouse. She's just baiting you. If you're going to have a crack at one of the kids we have lined up for auction, you need to brace yourself for the insults. Never tolerate disrespect, but you have to keep a cool head."

Mouse doesn't stop staring at me. He just nods. "You're going to learn your place Madame."

"You no longer work for her. Her title isn't needed anymore. Address as Cosette."

I seethe. Mouse smiles widely.

Turning to Eugenio, he says, "May I have at her boss before you take your turn?"

"No. Her body was first claimed by me. I doubt my nephew's dick kept her stretched out. I can remember a time in the past when she bled each time I took her. Her ass, especially. We'll see if she can bleed again."

With a dark smile, Eugenio starts unfastening his pants.

I dare him to stick his dick anywhere near my teeth.

As if knowing my thoughts, he starts rubbing at his shriveled old dick. After what felt like forever, I noticed that he had trouble getting it up. I start laughing hysterically.

"What's wrong, champ? Unable to get an erection? Aww. Am I not to your liking anymore?"

Slap! Slap! He hit me hard. “You’ll shut up, you bitch. Mouse, strip her naked, keep her bound, and start fucking her. Maybe the sight of you two will excite me.”

Mouse gives a sinister smile, “With pleasure, boss.”

I close my eyes for a moment, visualizing Antonio’s big ass dick, thrusting inside of me, making me scream his name.

“Oh. You’re smiling. That means you’re ready for us.”

“No, it just means the two of you couldn’t please me, even if you both were fucking me at the same time. Antonio had no issues in that area ever. I’d fuck him on command if he asked. I belong to him and always will.”

That seemed to get their attention because both of them were fuming. “Not so fun when the rabbit got the gun, is it?”

Mouse comes up to me. I struggle against the rope that has my hands bound behind me. Mouse grabs my hair and yanks it back. He tries to kiss me. I bite his lip as hard as I can.

“Ahh Fuck! You bitch!” A piece of the skin from his lip was hanging off.

“Looks like you need a band-aid.”

The sarcastic barb lands where I need it to.

Just then, he throws me onto the floor and pulls my pants down. He gets his dick ready to penetrate me. In one thrust, he’s inside. The pain that seared my insides made my eyes water. But I refuse to give Mouse one hint of emotion.

He keeps going. Gripping my face and holding it at an odd angle so that he could see my face without me having access to bite anything.

I just lay there and wait for him to finish. This isn't anything new. It's just been so long since I was treated this way.

Mouse barely lasts five minutes. When he grunted his finish, I started laughing uncontrollably. "What was that? Was that the ecstasy you promised me?"

That earned me a punch to the face. That brought stars to my vision and made my ears ring. I hear Eugenio in the back yelling, "Enough!"

Mouse pulls up his pants and walks out the door. Eugenio is still standing there trying to get his dick hard.

I laugh through my blood-stained teeth. "You're wasting your time, boss. Just kill me. I will never desire you or fulfill your disgusting fantasies. Just let me go."

Giving up on giving himself an erection, he tucks his limp dick back in his pants and squats down to where I am. He looks me over. "You grew into a very beautiful woman, but I'd rather have someone younger. Yeah, that's it. Maybe someone 12 or 10. What do you think, Cosette? Do you think that would help?"

My body goes so still, I don't know if I'm still breathing.

Taking my silence as acceptance, "Let me go pick one."

"NO!"

He's already out the door.

I won't survive this.

Where is Antonio? I'm mad at him but I don't think this is completely his fault.

Once this is over, he has to answer all my questions. That's if this doesn't end in me being in a body bag.

Not realizing that some time had passed, I heard the door open. When I open my eyes, I see Eugenio walking in with a crying little boy, looking no older than 7.

Fuck! Fuck! Fuck!

"Shh, it's okay, little one. This lady is going to watch as I make you scream my name."

I start gagging on the bile in my throat.

Antonio, please get here, I silently pray.

Chapter Twenty

Antonio

Something's wrong.

Antoinette is rushing towards me with a concerned look on her face.

"What is it?"

"She never called me when she got home. That's not like her."

And I know.

I always know.

I nod at Antoinette and let her know all will be well. But the storm brewing inside of me is not.

I'm already moving when my phone rings.

"Talk," I snap.

"It's her."

Gordo.

My chest tightens instantly.

"What about her?"

A pause. Too long.

"She never made it home."

Everything inside me goes still.

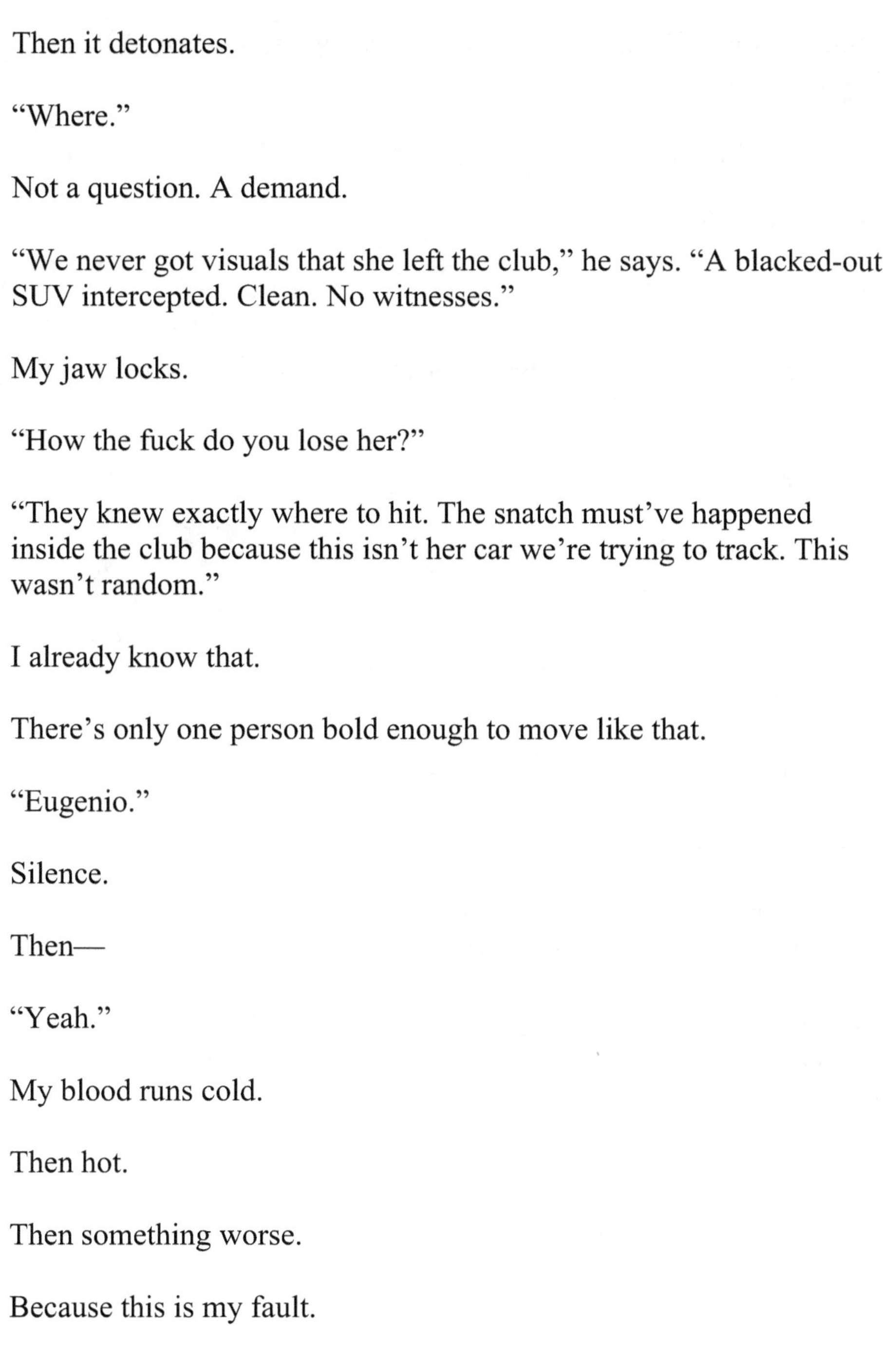

Then it detonates.

“Where.”

Not a question. A demand.

“We never got visuals that she left the club,” he says. “A blacked-out SUV intercepted. Clean. No witnesses.”

My jaw locks.

“How the fuck do you lose her?”

“They knew exactly where to hit. The snatch must’ve happened inside the club because this isn’t her car we’re trying to track. This wasn’t random.”

I already know that.

There’s only one person bold enough to move like that.

“Eugenio.”

Silence.

Then—

“Yeah.”

My blood runs cold.

Then hot.

Then something worse.

Because this is my fault.

I brought this to her. I let him get close enough to see her, to track her, to take her.

“Location,” I say.

“We’re working it.”

“Faster.”

“We’ve got a lead—warehouse district. Old property tied to one of his shell companies.”

That’s enough.

“I’m on my way.”

“Antonio—”

I hang up.

I don’t need a warning. I don’t need a plan.

I need her back.

Now. That fucking warehouse is a bad omen. My uncle has done some horrendous shit in that warehouse. What will he do to Cosette?

The drive is reckless. Red lights blur past. Speed limits mean nothing. My grip tightens on the wheel as one thought loops over and over in my mind—her, alone, with him.

I know what he is.

I know what he’s capable of.

And if he even—

No.

I shut that down.

Because if I let that thought take over, I won't make it there.

And I need to make it there.

The warehouse sits exactly where Gordo said it would—dark, quiet, isolated. Perfect for someone who doesn't want to be found.

Too bad for him, old habits die hard. He's a creature of habit that I've spent years studying.

When I step out of the car, Gordo's men are already positioned.

"Inside," one of them says.

"How many?"

"Unknown."

Doesn't matter.

"Where is she?"

"Second floor."

I don't hesitate. I place my silencer on the gun in my hand.

The door splinters under my kick, the sound echoing through the building.

Good.

Let him hear me.

With my Glock raised, the first man positioned just inside the door drops immediately. The second doesn't even get his weapon up before I break his arm. I move through them fast, efficient, brutal.

This isn't a fight.

It's a message.

I take the stairs two at a time, adrenaline burning through me. I hear voices before I see anything.

His.

And hers.

My chest tightens.

Alive.

That's all that matters.

I kick the door open.

Everything stops.

She's there.

Tied, but on her side. Her pants down by her thighs, exposing her bare ass and pussy.

"Mine," I growl.

Alive.

My eyes lock onto hers—and something in my chest cracks.

Because she's not looking at me like I saved her.

She's looking at me like I betrayed her.

"What—"

Then I see him.

Eugenio.

Standing behind her like a dark cloud. He's dragging a little boy. Looks no more than 7. The boy is completely naked. His face is tear-streaked, and blood is running down his legs along with what looks like urine.

That sick fuck! I don't know what this man has done to Cosette, but to also harm this child… I want to vomit.

Something inside me snaps.

"Still emotional," he says calmly.

I don't respond.

I move.

Fast.

He reaches for a weapon, but I'm already on him. My fist connects with his jaw, sending him back. I don't stop. Each hit lands harder than the last, fueled by years of restraint—and the one mistake he just made.

Touching that child. For all the children he's harmed.

Taking her.

"You don't touch her," I growl, slamming him into the wall. "You don't look at her."

He laughs, blood spilling from his mouth.

"You sound just like me."

That's when I notice the blade too late. I feel a sharp pain in my abdomen and a twist. White-hot pain burns through me.

My uncle pushes me off of him.

"You should've rejoined me as I said. You decided this fate for yourself."

I stagger a bit until I refocus and reach for my gun. But my movements are sloppy. The first gunshot hit my arm. The second, my leg.

I hear Cosette scream out my name. I see the little boy crying and huddled up in the corner of the room. Faint gunshots ring out in the distance. No one has come to see where the gunshots are coming from on the inside. Gordo must be handling things outside.

"Now, before I officially end your life, you'll witness me fucking this little vixen of a woman, whom you helped to escape from me years ago. Thank you, by the way."

The look of recognition, then shock, then horror plays across my face. Memories flood back from that night. I told her to use her brain and leave as soon as her legs could carry her. I told her to follow the lights outside and that they would guide her to the road. That frightened young girl. Nipple clamps marring her skin. The scars on her body when we fucked the first time. Everything hitting me all at once. My Cosette.

"And when I'm done with her, I'll of course kill her too. No sense in leaving loose ends, right Angel? We don't do that in this family. Then I'll let you watch as I fuck my little boy toy here. No one will hear anyone's screams. And I don't give a fuck how many men you brought with you."

I wheeze, “You’re a dead man.”

I hear him begin to laugh. “How poetic. We all have to go at some point. I’m just ending your life sooner.

With all my remaining strength, I grab him by the throat and slam him down hard. He struggles, shock written on his face. I squeeze his throat until his face starts changing colors.

Good.

I slam his head into the concrete floor, hearing a loud crack. He lies there unmoving, but it’s not enough. I stick both of my thumbs into his eyes, forcefully removing them.

“You should’ve stayed away.”

It’s done.

Over.

Final.

Permanent.

Silence fills the room.

I turn back to her.

Cosette.

“You’re okay,” I say.

But she doesn’t respond.

She just stares at me.

Cold.

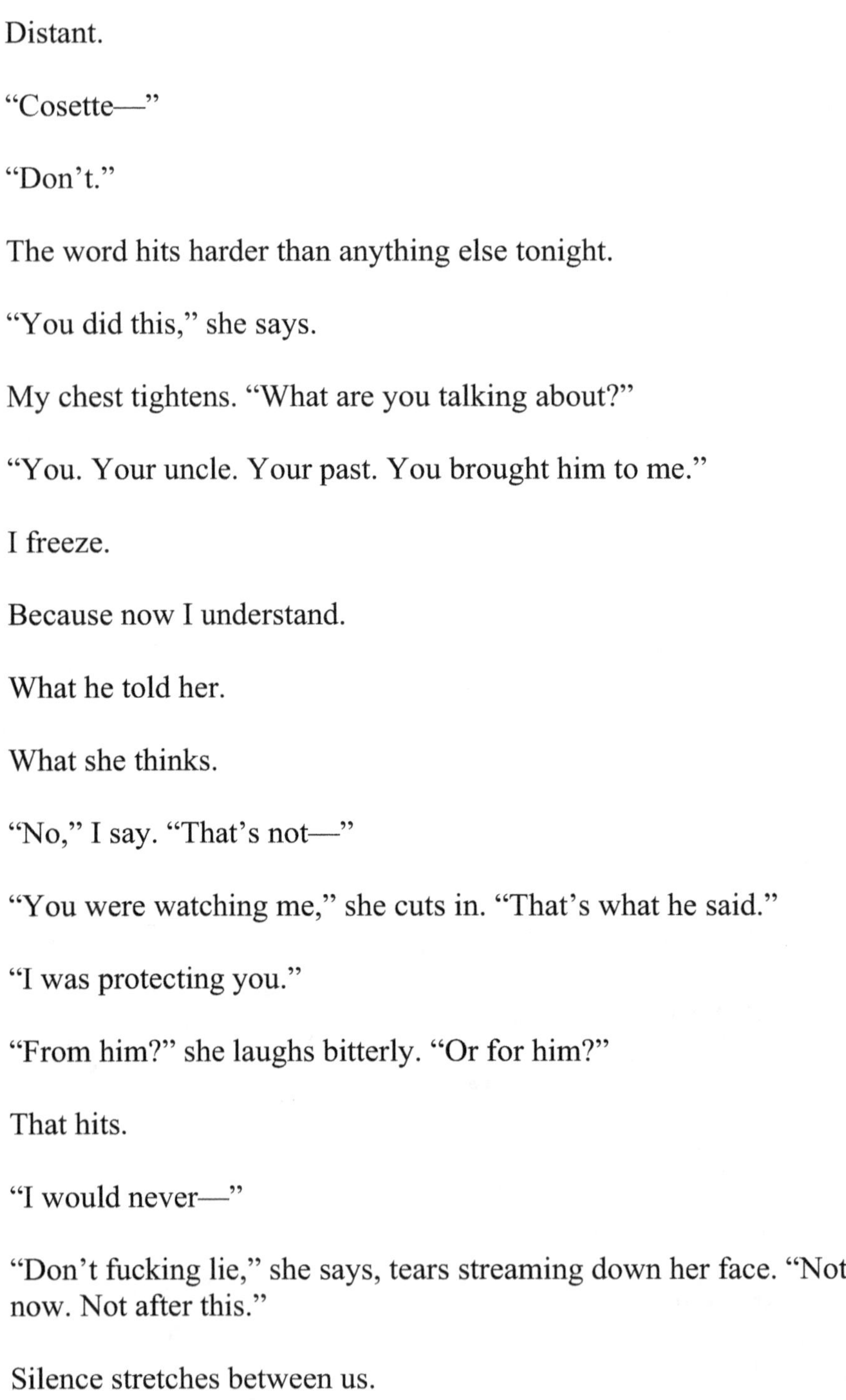

Distant.

“Cosette—”

“Don’t.”

The word hits harder than anything else tonight.

“You did this,” she says.

My chest tightens. “What are you talking about?”

“You. Your uncle. Your past. You brought him to me.”

I freeze.

Because now I understand.

What he told her.

What she thinks.

“No,” I say. “That’s not—”

“You were watching me,” she cuts in. “That’s what he said.”

“I was protecting you.”

“From him?” she laughs bitterly. “Or for him?”

That hits.

“I would never—”

“Don’t fucking lie,” she says, tears streaming down her face. “Not now. Not after this.”

Silence stretches between us.

And for the first time since I walked into this room—

I don't know what to do.

Because I can fight men.

I can destroy anything that stands in my way.

But this?

Her looking at me like I'm the enemy?

That's something I don't know how to fix.

"I came for you," I say.

Her expression doesn't change.

"You're the reason I'm here."

That lands exactly where it hurts.

I take a step back.

Distance is the only thing I can give her right now.

"Let me get you out of here," I say.

A pause.

"Where the fuck do you think you two are going?"

I turn, not recognizing the voice.

The woman holding a gun pointed level at my chest looks just like my Cosette.

"Oh, my daughter never talked about me? How rude, Cosette."

I look back at her. Anger in her eyes. This woman is not here for Cosette. Did she work for my father or my uncle?

"You took from me since the day you were born. And now you've taken from me again. It was a hard life with Eugenio, but one filled with all the money I could get my hands on," she explained.

"I'm don't give a fuck about your money or what you want. You're no mother of mine."

"Cosette, your club can help with my loss. I know you've made a name for yourself. That comes with financial security. Give me 10 million, and we'll call it even."

I glance at Cosette. She laughs, blood coating her teeth. "If you're going to kill me, do it now. You won't have a crumb of what I've built without your motherly guidance, bitch."

The woman shrugs. "Okay. That's fair." She raises the gun again at me, but before she can pull the trigger, I hear a pop, and I see blood coming from the woman's chest. The pop came from behind me. I turn to see the little boy holding my uncle's gun in his hand.

Cosette's mother drops to the floor.

I hobble over to him. "It's okay, son. Hand me the gun." His little arms were shaking so badly.

"Can I go home to my mommy now?"

"Yes. I'm going to get you out of here."

Then he nods.

I look at Cosette. She nods.

Barely.

But it’s enough.

For now.

Because this isn’t over.

I grab my phone out of my pocket. Surprised it was still intact.

“Gordo.”

“All enemies are down. Do you need any assistance?

“Yes. For 3 people. One is a child.”

“That’s what I wanted to talk to you about before you hung up on me earlier. Your uncle was into some dark shit. We found 3 underground bunkers full of children. Some malnourished. Full of scars and bruises.”

“Get them out. We’ll sort things out later.”

“Already done. Medical is on their way to your house, and your car is running out front.”

“Thank you.”

“My debt is repaid.”

“Agreed. Call me if you need anything.”

“I got your number.”

The line goes dead.

For now, I’m just relieved Cosette is safe. There’s so much that needs to be said. But that can wait until later.

I untie her and help her up. I give the little body my bloodied shirt so that he's covered up.

When Cosette stands, she quickly looks dizzy. All at once, she collapses in my arms.

"Cosette?"

Chapter Twenty-One

Cosette

I don't remember the drive.

Not clearly.

Just fragments.

The sound of the engine. The way the city lights blurred past the window. The way my body felt like it didn't belong to me anymore—like I was present, but not fully there.

Shock does that.

It pulls you just far enough away to survive the moment.

Antonio doesn't speak much. Neither do I.

For once, silence isn't tension.

It's necessary.

By the time we arrive at his house, I'm exhausted in a way sleep won't fix.

His home is exactly how I remembered it.

Secure.

Controlled.

Minimal with a touch of Italian art and his guitars.

Every detail intentional.

Every entry point covered.

It doesn't feel like a house.

It feels like a fortress.

"Come on," he says quietly.

Not commanding.

Not forceful.

Just… there.

I allow him to carry me inside. He must not give a damn about his own injuries.

I put up no resistance or asked any questions.

Because right now, I don't have the energy to fight him.

Or myself.

Or the truth.

A doctor is already there.

Of course. This man thinks of everything.

Antonio doesn't do anything halfway.

"She needs to be checked," he says.

The doctor nods and approaches me gently. "Let's take a look at you, alright?"

I nod once.

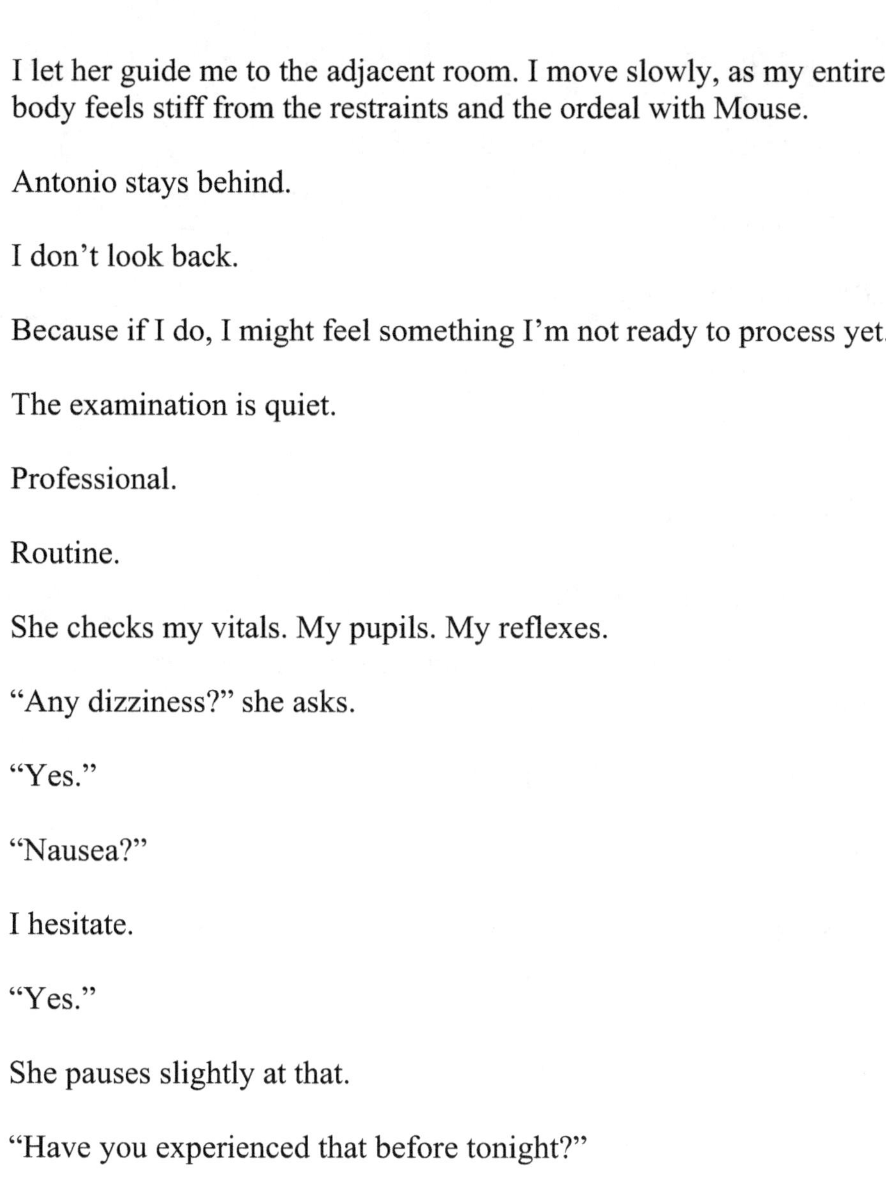

I let her guide me to the adjacent room. I move slowly, as my entire body feels stiff from the restraints and the ordeal with Mouse.

Antonio stays behind.

I don't look back.

Because if I do, I might feel something I'm not ready to process yet.

The examination is quiet.

Professional.

Routine.

She checks my vitals. My pupils. My reflexes.

"Any dizziness?" she asks.

"Yes."

"Nausea?"

I hesitate.

"Yes."

She pauses slightly at that.

"Have you experienced that before tonight?"

I think about it. The night had many moments when I wanted to vomit.

The last few weeks.

The subtle shifts I ignored.

The exhaustion.

The moments of nausea I brushed off as stress.

"…yes," I admit.

She studies me more carefully now.

Then she asks the question.

"When was your last cycle?"

My stomach drops.

I don't answer right away.

I didn't have time to think of anything else except the club and my safety…and Antonio.

"…I don't remember," I say quietly.

That's enough for her.

She continues the exam, more focused now.

A few minutes pass.

Then she steps back slightly.

Her expression softens.

"Cosette," she says gently, "it's possible you're pregnant. I'm going to do a urine test to confirm."

The words don't register immediately.

"Pregnant. No," I say automatically.

But even as I say it—

I know it's a possibility. It's what I was afraid of.

I blindly go to pee in the cup in the adjacent bathroom. Once I'm finished, I hand her the cup to run the test.

Why did I ignore the signs? I notice everything. I can't believe I ignored my own body.

"You're early," she continues. "But it's clear."

She shows me the test.

My chest tightens.

Pregnant.

The word echoes in my mind.

Louder.

Heavier.

More real with every second.

I press my hand lightly against my stomach without thinking.

Fear hits first.

Then something else follows behind it.

Something quieter.

Something I don't fully understand yet.

"Does he suspect?" the doctor asks gently.

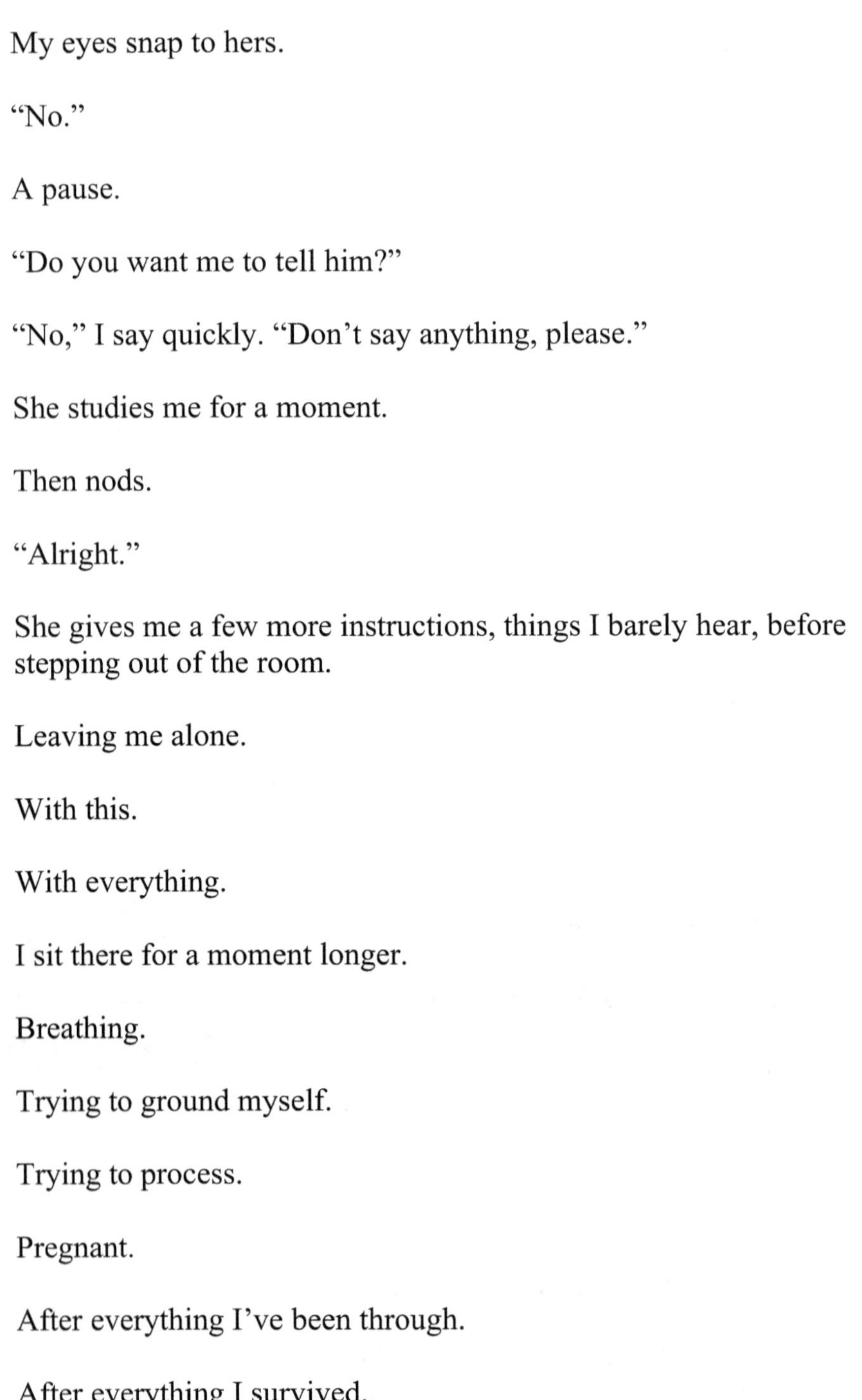

My eyes snap to hers.

"No."

A pause.

"Do you want me to tell him?"

"No," I say quickly. "Don't say anything, please."

She studies me for a moment.

Then nods.

"Alright."

She gives me a few more instructions, things I barely hear, before stepping out of the room.

Leaving me alone.

With this.

With everything.

I sit there for a moment longer.

Breathing.

Trying to ground myself.

Trying to process.

Pregnant.

After everything I've been through.

After everything I survived.

After everything that was taken from me—

Now this?

I don't know if it's a blessing or something else entirely.

I don't know what to feel. My mother sold me off. I don't even know what being a mother should look like. This wasn't in the cards for me. Shit!

I know one thing, I'm not ready to tell him.

Not yet.

Not until I understand him.

Fully.

Completely.

No more shadows.

No more unanswered questions.

I step out of the room with the doctor's assistance.

She automatically starts attending to Antonio once I'm settled on the couch.

I watch as the doctor pulls out bullets and patches him up. Once he's done with the doctor, I can tell he was anxious to discuss my welfare.

He's waiting for answers.

Of course he is.

His eyes immediately scan me.

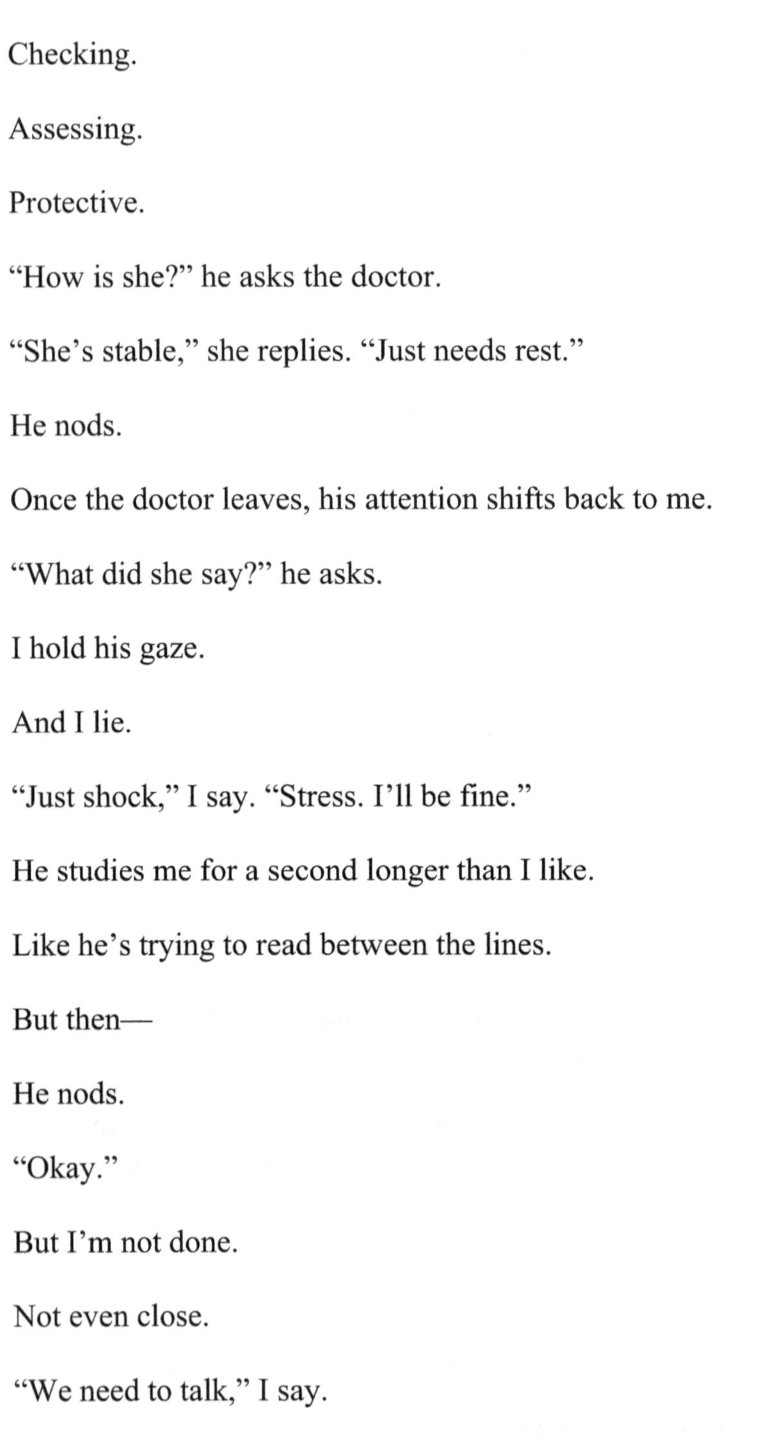

Checking.

Assessing.

Protective.

“How is she?” he asks the doctor.

“She’s stable,” she replies. “Just needs rest.”

He nods.

Once the doctor leaves, his attention shifts back to me.

“What did she say?” he asks.

I hold his gaze.

And I lie.

“Just shock,” I say. “Stress. I’ll be fine.”

He studies me for a second longer than I like.

Like he’s trying to read between the lines.

But then—

He nods.

“Okay.”

But I’m not done.

Not even close.

“We need to talk,” I say.

His expression shifts slightly.

"Yeah," he says. "We do."

I cross my arms slightly.

"Who are you?" I ask.

The question hangs between us.

He exhales slowly.

Like he's been expecting this.

"My name is Antonio Palomari," he says.

The last name hits differently now that I know who it's associated with.

"You knew," I say.

A pause.

"I knew who he was," he replies. "I didn't know you were the girl who escaped. I had a feeling. But nothing was confirmed until my uncle said it."

His uncle?

I search his face.

Looking for hesitation.

For deception.

For anything.

"And before that?" I press. "You didn't orchestrate any of this?"

"No," he says firmly.

"Swear it."

"I swear."

Silence.

Then—

"I was supposed to be watching the club. It was supposed to be my last official job," he admits. "Keeping an eye on operations. Not you. Some of your members work with my uncle. Not smuggling children, but drugs. Yes, your club is a breeding ground for our drug operation. Simple."

My chest tightens.

"But then I saw you," he continues. "And everything changed."

I don't respond.

Because I need more.

"Why didn't you tell me?" I ask.

"Because once you knew who I was, what I did, you wouldn't trust me," he says. "And I needed you to trust me."

"That's not how trust works," I reply.

"I know."

A pause.

"I do now."

Something in his voice shifts.

Honesty.

And that? That's new.

"I left that life," he continues. "Everything he built. Everything he wanted me to be."

"Why?"

His eyes hold mine.

"Because I didn't want to become him."

Silence.

Then—

"I love you," he says.

The words land softly but deeply.

No hesitation.

Just truth.

And I feel it.

My chest tightens.

Because now it's my turn.

"I need you to hear me," I say.

He nods.

"I read every letter my mother wrote me," I continue. "Every apology. Every excuse. I thought she loved me, until one of the letters revealed what she did to me. I didn't know that she was that deep in with Eugenio."

My voice tightens slightly.

"I was wrong to think she could ever love me."

His expression darkens.

"She sold me," I say. "And when I escaped… she blamed me for ruining her life."

Silence.

"She's dead now, along with him," I add. "She chose that for herself, and I have no regrets."

His jaw tightens.

"Why were your pants down around your thighs?"

"Eugenio had Mouse rape me."

I see his jaw clench.

"It's over now. Please stop looking like you want to do something crazy. By the way, whatever happened to him? Is he still running around free?"

"His corpse is rotting without his eyes, along with my uncle and your mother."

"That must be a calling card for you. Why do people call you 'Angel'?"

"I am known as the Angel of Death. The name was given to me based on how I dispose of enemies."

I sigh, nodding. It should scare the shit out of me but it doesn't. He could be a lot worse things.

"I went through hell, Antonio," I say quietly. "But I built something out of it. Something safe. Something controlled."

My eyes lock onto his.

"And you brought that world back to me."

The truth of that sits between us.

Unavoidable.

"I know," he says.

A pause.

"I'm sorry."

Not defensive.

Not dismissive.

Real.

I take a breath.

Then—

"No more secrets," I say.

His eyes don't leave mine.

"No more lies. No more half-truths. If we're doing this—if we're choosing this—it's all or nothing."

"I agree," he says.

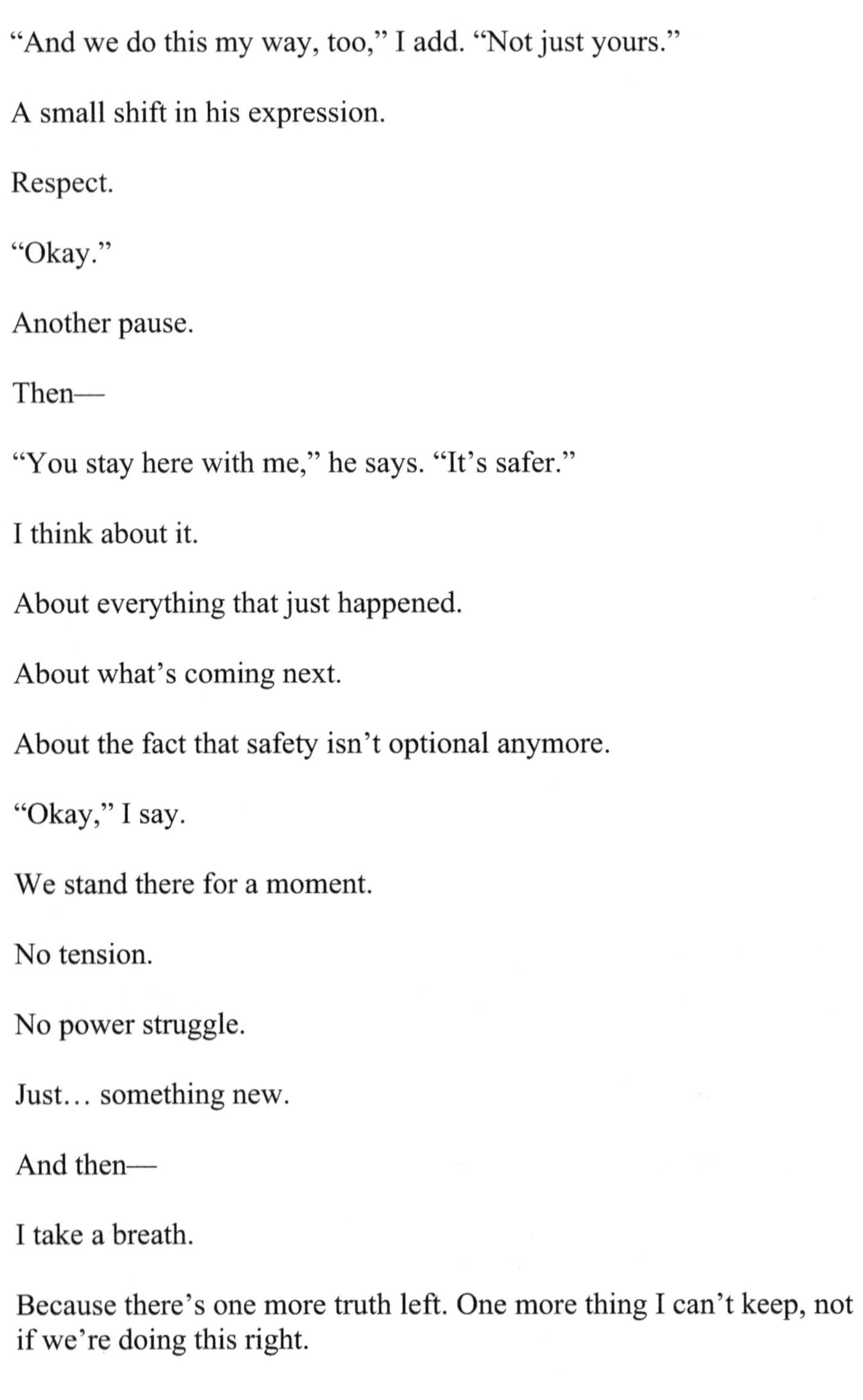

"And we do this my way, too," I add. "Not just yours."

A small shift in his expression.

Respect.

"Okay."

Another pause.

Then—

"You stay here with me," he says. "It's safer."

I think about it.

About everything that just happened.

About what's coming next.

About the fact that safety isn't optional anymore.

"Okay," I say.

We stand there for a moment.

No tension.

No power struggle.

Just… something new.

And then—

I take a breath.

Because there's one more truth left. One more thing I can't keep, not if we're doing this right.

"Antonio," I say.

His attention sharpens instantly.

"What is it?"

My hand moves to my stomach without thinking.

I meet his eyes.

And I finally say it.

"I'm pregnant."

Silence fills the room.

And everything changes.

Epilogue – Part I

Antonio

3 Months Later

I've built my entire life on power, precision, and survival. Every move calculated. Every risk measured. That's how I stayed alive in my uncle's world. That's how I walked away from it.

But none of that prepared me for this.

For her.

For what she's carrying.

For what we're building.

I stand on the deck of the yacht, the ocean stretching endlessly around us. This used to be his—Eugenio's. Another symbol of everything he thought he owned. Now it's mine, and I don't want it for the same reasons he did. I want it because it's quiet here. Because she can breathe here. Because for once, no one is watching.

My eyes find her instantly. They always do.

Cosette stands near the railing, the wind catching in her curls, her hand resting lightly over her growing belly like it belongs there. Like she's already protecting them, our precious twins. Protecting us.

My chest tightens, not with fear, but with something deeper. Responsibility. Not forced. Chosen.

I walk toward her slowly. She doesn't turn, but I know she feels me.

"You've been staring for a while," she says softly.

A small smirk pulls at my mouth. “You noticed.”

“I always notice,” she replies.

Yeah. She does.

I step behind her, pulling her close. Close enough to feel her warmth.

“How are you feeling?”

She glances at me, one brow lifting. “You ask me that at least three times a day.”

“And I’m going to keep asking.”

A hint of a smile touches her lips. “I’m fine. Still adjusting.”

She pauses, then adds, “But I’m not scared anymore.”

That matters more than anything else.

Silence settles between us, full and steady. There was a time I didn’t think I deserved this. Didn’t think I could have anything that didn’t come with blood attached to it. Now, I’d burn the world down before I let anything touch this. Touch her. Touch them.

She turns to face me fully. “You’re doing that thing again.”

“What thing?”

“Going somewhere dark in your head.”

I exhale quietly. “Occupational hazard.”

“You’re not there anymore,” she says. “You walked away.”

“For me first,” I admit. “But staying away… that’s for you.”

Something softens in her expression.

"I meant what I said," I continue. "No more secrets."

"I know."

"I meant all of it."

"I know."

I study her for a moment, then reach into my pocket. I guess now is a good enough time to do what I've been meaning to do for a while.

Her eyes flicker down, curious.

I pull out the ring. Simple. Elegant. Powerful. Just like her.

She stills.

I step closer. "Cosette."

Shit. Here goes nothing…

"You survived something that should've broken you," I say. "And instead of letting it define you, you built something stronger. You created a place where people feel safe. Where they can be who they are without fear. Seeing the strength in you and allowing me to see the vulnerable side of you has brought out emotions within me that I thought were dead."

Her breath catches.

"You changed me. For the better. I am better because of you. I will continue to be better because of you."

That's the truth I never expected to say.

"I don't want a life without you in it. I'm not going to pretend I do."

I drop to one knee without hesitation. "Marry me."

Her eyes search mine, not for weakness, but for truth.

"You're asking for forever," she says.

"Yes, baby."

A tear slips down her cheek.

"Yes," she whispers.

Relief hits me instantly. I slide the ring onto her finger. Perfect fit. Antoinette came through in a clutch. That woman knows almost everything about my girl.

I stand and pull her into me, careful but firm. She exhales against me, and for the first time in my life, I don't feel like I'm fighting something.

I feel like I'm building something. The proper way.

Something worth everything.

I kiss her deeply. Promising her more with my dick pressed firmly against her.

She giggles as she takes my hand and leads me below deck.

Epilogue – Part II

Cosette

I never thought I'd want this. Not like this. Not after everything.

Love wasn't something I trusted. Safety wasn't something I believed in. And family? That word meant something painful. Broken.

But standing here now, with the ocean stretching endlessly around me, I realize something.

I was wrong.

Not about the world. Not about what I went through.

But about what I deserved after it.

My hand rests gently over my stomach. It still feels surreal. Still new. Still, something I'm learning how to accept. Because for the first time in my life, things feel complete. Something I chose. Something we created.

Antonio moves behind me, his presence wrapping around me before his arms do. I don't flinch. I don't pull away. I lean into him.

That alone says everything. I trust him completely.

"You're quiet," he murmurs.

"I'm thinking."

"Unless you want another round, I suggest you stop thinking so much. That's dangerous."

I smile slightly. "I've survived worse."

He lets out a quiet laugh. Yeah, I'll never stop being a smart ass.

"I started the foundation," I tell him. "For trafficking survivors. Resources, housing, protection."

"Good," he says. "You're going to help a lot of people, baby."

"I hope so."

"I know so."

"I'm letting Antoinette run the club for now. That way I can focus on the foundation."

I turn in his arms, facing him. My eyes drop briefly to the ring on my finger.

"You didn't hesitate," I say.

"I never do when it comes to you."

That should scare me.

But it doesn't.

"You're still a little unhinged," I say, smiling.

"Only for you."

I shake my head, then look at him fully.

"I know about your past," I say. "The mafia. Everything."

He nods.

"And I'm still here."

That part matters.

"I'm not running," I continue. "Not from you."

"You shouldn't have to."

"I don't," I say. "I choose you."

The words feel strong. Real.

His hand moves gently to my stomach.

"We're going to do this right," he says.

"We are."

"No fear. No secrets."

"No past controlling our future."

He nods.

I take a breath, looking out at the ocean, then back at him.

"I'm going to be the mother I knew I wanted. Needed," I say quietly.

His hand tightens over mine. "I know you will."

And for the first time, I believe that too.

Not because I have to.

But because I want to.

Because this is mine now.

My future.

My family.

My life.

And this time, no one is taking it from me.

Acknowledgments

To my readers, thank you.

Thank you for taking a chance on this story, for stepping into this world, and for allowing my words to find a place with you. Your support means more than I could ever fully express.

To my family and friends, thank you for believing in me, even in the moments when this dream felt far away. Your encouragement, patience, and unwavering support carried me through every stage of this journey.

This book has been a three-year labor of love. It has challenged me, stretched me, and pushed me to grow—not just as a writer, but as a person. Every late night, every revision, every moment of doubt led me here.

To everyone who has supported me along the way—whether through kind words, encouragement, or simply believing in my vision—this is for you.

I am beyond grateful.

And this is only the beginning.

I'm so excited for what's to come, and I can't wait to share more stories with you. Stay tuned—there's so much more on the way.

With love,
B.C. Jones

One Last Thing…

If this story stayed with you… if it made you feel something… if you found yourself lost in Cosette and Antonio's world…

Please consider leaving a review on Amazon.

Your words help bring this story to more readers, and your support means everything to me.

To stay connected and get exclusive updates, behind-the-scenes content, and upcoming releases, follow me:

Facebook: B.C. Jones Writes
Instagram: @b.c.joneswrites
TikTok: @b.c.jones

Thank you for being part of this journey.

With love,
B.C. Jones

www.ingramcontent.com/pod-product-compliance
Lightning Source LLC
LaVergne TN
LVHW010644110826
845149LV00014B/2942

* 9 7 9 8 9 9 5 4 0 8 2 1 5 *